Nantucket Revenge

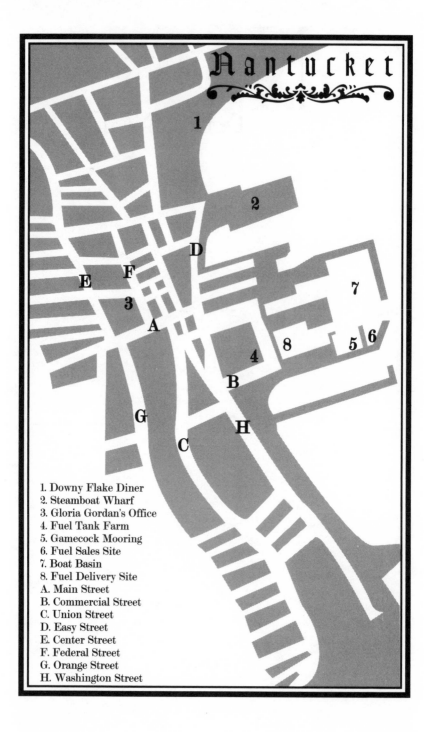

Nantucket

1. Downy Flake Diner
2. Steamboat Wharf
3. Gloria Gordan's Office
4. Fuel Tank Farm
5. Gamecock Mooring
6. Fuel Sales Site
7. Boat Basin
8. Fuel Delivery Site
A. Main Street
B. Commercial Street
C. Union Street
D. Easy Street
E. Center Street
F. Federal Street
G. Orange Street
H. Washington Street

NANTUCKET REVENGE

A Jake Eaton Mystery

LARRY MANESS

Larry Maness

LYFORD
Books

LYFORD Books
Published by Presidio Press
505 B San Marin Dr., Suite 300
Novato, CA 94945-1340

Library of Congress Cataloging-in-Publication Data

Maness, Larry
    Nantucket revenge : a Jake Eaton mystery / Larry Maness.
        p.   cm.
    ISBN 0-89141-566-1
    1. Nantucket Island (Mass.)—Fiction. I. Title.
PS3563.A4655N36 1995
813' . 54—dc20   95-9351
                                                            CIP

Typography by ProImage
Printed in the United States of America

For Tyra and Dan

Nantucket Revenge

Chapter

—1—

The fireworks started on Sunday, July 1, in a wind so strong the giant chrysanthemum shells lasted only seconds before their brilliance turned to smoke and drifted over the channel just off Jetties Beach. Fireworks weren't made for twenty-five-knot winds, but wind was better than drenching rain and far better than Nantucket's notorious blinding fog. For two years running, a heavy, wet fog had postponed the island's celebration of the nation's birth from the first weekend in July to the first clear weekday. It was a concession to the summer people and day-tripper alike and another sorrowful reminder to the year-rounder how far Nantucket bends to scoop up the tourist's dollar. So on this windy Sunday, at a little after 8:30 P.M., "Light Up the Sky" began; it whistled and banged for thirty-five minutes, building to the grand finale of red, white, and blue titanium shell salutes.

Horn blasts from the boats tugging against their moorings grew louder and stronger and mixed with the shouts and applause from those watching on shore. It was as if the fireworks signaled the unofficial beginning of an island summer—one that was about to show itself in a sickening and frightful way.

Gloria Gorham, thirty-four years old and blessed with the beguiling beauty of a fashion model, cared little about fireworks. Something troubled her far more than the wind and the staying power of a burst of colored lights in the night sky. Ironically, she was sitting alone in the gas dock office, the spot many considered to have the island's best view of the show. The single-story building covered in weathered gray shingles was nondescript except that it rose on pilings fifteen feet above the dock, providing a view of everything that happened in the harbor and on the Island Basin docks below.

The first weekend in July used to mean a party for the IB employees—a few beers, the best view of the fireworks. But not anymore. Gloria Gorham had changed that. There would be no party, no visitors stopping by the gas dock office, where she sat with her eyes closed, oblivious to the whistles and bangs exploding above her.

Six months ago, F. Gordon Gorham had flown down from Boston in The Gorham Corporation's company jet to look over what he'd just agreed to purchase. From his plane, he looked down on an H-shaped series of wharves, docks, and finger piers, empty except for the scallop fleet and a few pleasure craft that wintered over. But in spring and summer, the Island Basin filled like a resort hotel. In fact it was run like a resort hotel, the primary difference being that the guests—by either motoring or sailing from the mainland—brought their own accommodations and paid the Island Basin a nightly fee to tie up in one of its three hundred-plus dockside slips.

Considering that the minimum charge was $100 a night, plus fees for a cable television hookup, telephone, electricity, fuel, ice, and showers, F. Gordon never blinked at the $75 million asking price. Even without the assured income, he'd have paid $100 million to finally best the other deeply rooted island families, including the Coffins and the Starbucks, who had driven F. Gordon's ancestor Libbeus Fitch Gorham off Nantucket.

It was a stigma F. Gordon wanted removed. And he removed it with a single transaction—the purchase of the Island Basin, the jewel of the waterfront—announcing that the Gorhams were back on Nantucket and back in a big way. His daughter, Gloria, the person F. Gordon trusted most, was put in charge of running it, and she had done so dutifully and with precision. But tonight, leaning back against a chair made of aluminum tubes and plastic webbing, she had a hard time controlling the fear that threatened to overtake her.

This is foolishness, she thought, trying to draw from some hidden well of courage. No one pushes my family around, especially not some sour-minded half-wit too afraid to show himself. It's all just a mean-spirited joke.

Outside, dozens of tiny rockets were launched into the cool, windy night. The first titanium shell roared into the sky, followed closely by a second, then a third. Set to explode at different heights, the shells lit up the night in a canopy of red, white, and blue. Poom-poom-poom! The noise from the crowd, as if pulled along by the rockets, reached new heights of roaring approval. Somewhere out in the harbor, over the din, could be heard a faint yet lovely voice singing "America the Beautiful." At first it was hardly noticed. But slowly, as the lights in the sky went out and the smoke drifted away, the song's captivating and heartbreaking simplicity found ears enough to silence the crowd. Gloria wasn't immune to such a pure voice either. She rose from her chair and stood by the window, listening.

"A-mer-i-ca, A-mer-i-ca, God shed His Grace on thee, and crown thy good with brotherhood from sea to shining—"

The enchantment was suddenly broken by a woman's horrified scream. Gloria scanned the crowded waterfront as the muscles along her back knotted like a rope. What could have happened? she wondered as a white titanium shell exploded, illuminating the harbor like daylight. It was then that Gloria saw a woman standing in the cockpit of a small sailboat in the first row of rental moorings, one hand covering her mouth and pointing with the other toward a man in the water.

In the bright light, Gloria saw a man against a moss-slickened piling. His face looked stricken, his eyes open to the saltwater. The movement of his yellow slicker, as his arm folded and extended in rhythm with the harbor swells, made him appear as though he was waving or gesturing for assistance. But he was beyond help, beyond hearing the scream that replaced the song, beyond caring that a frightened woman was screaming at him, at death itself.

When the titanium shell burned out, Gloria shuddered like a child in the surrounding darkness. She could hear a tremendous hubbub outside as people ran up and down Whales Way and collected on the IB docks. Exactly what was happening she couldn't tell, but she knew for certain that the man who was threatening her, toying with her life, was responsible.

As calmly as possible, she picked up the phone and punched in the Boston number of Lewis Metcalf, The Gorham Corporation's attorney. "He's made his next move, Lewis," she said in a strong but edgy voice. "Just now."

"Are you all right?" There was a small silence as Gloria stared at the confused crowd below. "Gloria? Are you all right?"

"I'm fine, Lewis. I'm only glad daddy's out of the country. You haven't mentioned a word of this to him, have you?"

Mild disappointment filtered through Lewis Metcalf's voice. He'd been counsel and friend to the Gorhams for more than twenty-five years. "You know me better than that, for God's sake. Now, tell me what happened."

"I'm not sure. During the fireworks someone screamed like I've never heard before. She sounded terrified, Lewis."

"Terrified of what?"

"A man in the water." Gloria bit her bottom lip. "I think he's dead." She glanced out the window at the hordes ambling all over the waterfront. "I can feel it, Lewis. It's William, I know it. He's behind this."

Lewis took a steadying breath. He let it out, then said, "We've got to get you away from there."

"Out of the question."

"Gloria—"

"We've gone over this, Lewis. I belong here. I'm staying." Her voice was determined.

"You're just like your father. Stubborn." Lewis paused. "Has William sent you any other messages?" he finally asked.

"Not that I've seen."

"Then maybe it isn't the same," Lewis said, trying to sound encouraging. "Maybe what happened isn't related at all."

Blue police lights flashed down Commercial Street as the cruisers skidded onto Whales Way and came to a stop. "I think you'd better call your man," said Gloria. "You know how I feel about that, Lewis, but I think you'd better call him."

"Of course."

"Maybe he'll have better luck this time," she said, irritated at the thought of having to deal with Jake Eaton, the private detective Lewis had so highly recommended. "I'll call you back to find out when he's coming."

"Eaton's a good man, Gloria."

"So you've said."

"The last time wasn't exactly a fair accounting. Less than a needle in a haystack, you know. You didn't really expect him to find anything in Florida, did you?"

"He's a detective, Lewis. That's his job, detection. I'll call you back."

"Give me an hour. I think I'd better talk to him face to face."

"Fine." She hung up and stepped back to the window. Her eyes reflected the erratic dance of ambulance lights as they bounced to a stop on the cobblestones a few feet from her office.

Chapter

2

At ten o'clock that night Lewis Metcalf parked his green Mercedes in front of Jake Eaton's combination office/apartment in a four-story red brick building on Martin Street in Cambridge. Lewis rang the buzzer, then slipped through the door and started up the four flights of white octagonal tile stairs. He climbed quickly, setting a pace for himself.

Lewis was a trim and fit sixty. His natural bulk was kept down by playing squash at the University Club three times a week and jogging in between. The squash games he never missed, but a hectic schedule often kept his jogging shoes in the locker.

He had begun his legal career with Gorham Investments when it was founded by F. Gordon. Over the years as the company grew into corporate finance, real estate development, and an arm called Resorts Management, Lewis's role expanded to corporate attorney, trusted adviser, and friend. It was as a family friend that he came to see Jake Eaton.

Jake was waiting at the top of the stairs, hands in his pants pockets, his wide shoulders hunched slightly forward. He was a lean and muscular man of forty with thick dark brown hair and sparkling brown eyes. A well-trimmed mustache made his thin, angular face look fuller. He wore a button-down–collared blue shirt, unpressed chinos, no socks, no shoes. At his side was Watson, a black, flop-eared cross between a Labrador retriever and a collie.

Jake extended his hand and Lewis took it warmly. "In as good a shape as ever," Jake said. "Most clients puff and wheeze for twenty minutes before they can get a word out."

"Someday, someone won't make it to the top." Lewis smiled and bent down to roughhouse with the dog, who had rolled over on the floor and was waving his powerful legs in the air. "Hey, Watson? How's the best dog in the world?"

"Mean as ever."

Lewis stood up. "I can see that. Lucky to come away with my arms."

"He's on a diet," Jake said and motioned Lewis inside. Watson led the way and curled up under a cherry drop-leaf table in the hall.

"Thank you for seeing me, Jake." Lewis's voice was lower, more serious. "Holiday weekend and all."

"No need to apologize. You know where the best seats in the house are."

"I do."

"Take one. I'll get us something to drink," Jake said, stepping into the kitchen. At the sound of the refrigerator opening, Watson got up and followed his nose.

"I thought you said he was on a diet?" Lewis teased. He went into the living room and sat on the greenish gray brocade sofa. The opposite wall was lined with glass-fronted mahogany bookcases. Outside the windows, chestnut trees caught and held the light of the street lamps in the humid, still night air.

Carrying two brandies over ice, Jake entered the room and sat in the wing chair opposite Lewis. Watson sat quietly between them, as if sensing the shift from pleasure to business.

"So," Jake said, handing Lewis his snifter, "how's Gloria?"

"You're awfully sure of yourself, Jake." Lewis raised his glass in salute. "Cheers."

Jake returned the gesture. "Not really. Priority number one—you said so yourself. Besides, daddy's out of the country. Somebody's got to watch out for her."

"Don't let her hear you say that," Lewis warned pensively. "She wouldn't like it."

Jake sipped his brandy. "Another dislike added to the list. I suppose I'm still at the top."

"Well—"

"You don't need to answer that. Although it isn't often I take on a client who hates my guts," Jake said matter-of-factly.

Lewis shook his head. "It isn't hate. It's just that she's . . . How best to put it?" After a brief pause, Lewis—as usual—found his way to the heart of it. "Let's just say she likes her independence."

"She's a pain, Lewis. A classic pain in the ass, which, I might add, often comes with having the same last name as the founder and owner of the exceedingly wealthy corporation she works for," Jake offered with a mischievous grin.

Lewis's brows arched. "A bit unprofessional, isn't it? Talking about a client like that?"

"Just being honest."

"Or a little testy."

"About?"

It was Lewis's turn to get in a jab. "The trip to Florida," he said with a knowing smile. "You're still not over that little jaunt."

"Two weeks in Florida on a wild goose chase is a bit more than a *jaunt,*" Jake said, patting Watson's shiny coat. "Besides, my partner here nearly died of heat stroke. You don't find a dog like Watson every day, you know. Cunning. Smart. Loyal." Watson's tail thumped and his eyes sparkled like water holes in the desert.

Lewis drank half his brandy. "You'll get no disagreement from me, but that trip did get you out of Boston in the brutal early spring."

"And I was grateful. But it's not Florida I objected to—you know that," Jake reminded him. "It's the way Gloria wants the job done. She wants to handle things herself, so I'm here talking to you instead of on Nantucket where I should be."

"That's about to change," Lewis said uneasily. "Something's happened down there."

"What?" Jake asked, the playfulness gone from his voice.

"Apparently, a man was found dead on the Island Basin's premises."

"Who?"

"I don't have all the details. All I know is that Gloria called frightened. I could hear it in her voice."

"When did this happen?"

"Just before I came over here."

"She's all right?"

"Yes, yes. For the time being."

Jake sipped his brandy, thinking. He could remember clearly the meeting with Gloria Gorham in The Gorham Corporation's headquarters in Boston's downtown financial district. Jake had been in Lewis's office on the top floor of the pink granite monolith many times before, first when Jake's brother Max ran the Eaton Agency, later on his own when Max was gone. Jake recalled looking at Gloria over Lewis's polished mahogany desk and telling her not to set foot on Nantucket—not until "William," the man who had sent her a threatening letter, was tracked down.

Jake had known that, given time, he would find the man and stop him. He also had known that as soon as the meeting was over, Gloria would board the company plane and fly to Nantucket.

"What are you thinking?" Lewis asked.

"I'm thinking that the man calling himself William must be on the island."

"I'm afraid so," Lewis answered and downed the rest of his brandy. Absently, he ran his finger around the empty glass. "Why is some madman going after Gloria, Jake? I don't understand it."

"You're a lawyer," Jake told him. "Lawyers look for order and expect to find it. Sometimes there isn't any."

"'And in this world, goodness is destined for defeat.'"

"You quoting my brother to me, Lewis?"

"That's what he used to say, isn't it?"

"He did." Jake finished his drink, but the painful memories of Max wouldn't wash away.

A silence fell across the room. "I didn't mean to bring him up," Lewis said, his eyes wrinkling with memories of his own. "You'd think all these years—how many has it been?"

"Ten. May eleventh." Jake rattled the cubes in his glass and quickly changed the subject. "How about one for the road?" he asked, standing up and heading for the kitchen. He brought back the bottle and freshened both snifters.

"Thank you. I've got you booked on the six-thirty flight tomorrow morning," Lewis added.

"I'll be on it," Jake told him.

Lewis tried to smile. "She's like a daughter to me, Jake. I always wanted one, but my wife said three boys was enough. You've got to help her through this. I wouldn't want anything to happen to her."

"I'll do my best."

"That's always been good enough for me."

"Don't think I'm looking forward to it. I'm not."

"Thank you, Jake." Lewis held up his glass. "To friends."

"To friends," Jake said, his thoughts already on the island twenty miles off the coast.

Chapter

3

At 6:15 the next morning, Jake Eaton waited while airport security cleared him to board the 6:30 flight. He'd shown the scraggly-faced guard his detective's license and his permits, one for the Smith and Wesson .38 caliber he religiously carried in a shoulder holster and the other for the Smith and Wesson .44 Magnum he carried separately and used for special occasions.

Jake repacked the Magnum between an extra pair of chinos and a green turtleneck and zipped his overnight bag. He'd noticed that the security was tighter than normal. "You expecting trouble?" he asked.

The guard looked amused. "Never been checked before?" he replied, still studying Jake's license.

Jake motioned in the direction of a second guard going through a woman's luggage. The woman grimaced and stared unblinkingly at the guard. "She's not a happy camper," Jake said.

The guard handed back Jake's papers. "Our job's to see that you get there, not to make you happy." His eyes shifted to Watson. "Nice dog," he said. "One of those drug sniffers, is he?"

"All the drugs Watson sniffs are floating in the air in Harvard Square."

"Yeah, sure," the guard said with a wink. "You guys never admit to nothin'. What breed is he?"

"Mixed." Jake checked his watch.

"Best kind," the guard said knowingly. "Purebreds are neurotic as hell. This one here looks pretty normal."

"Normal as they come."

The guard looked genuinely disappointed. "You mean he really don't do nothin'?"

"He's psychic," Jake told him and headed for the plane, a fifteen-passenger turboprop on which dogs and extra baggage fought for space in the aisle.

By 7:20 A.M. the plane was circling Nantucket, a roughly C-shaped patch of sand and scrub pine surrounded by white-capped waves blowing in from the Atlantic. Famous for its whaling history, Nantucket was now more of a summer sandbox for the wealthy. The island population swells from ten thousand to forty thousand during the peak season of July and August, when old and new money with full pockets fly, ferry, or sail over in their private yachts to play hard and long on the fifty miles of sandy beaches.

At 7:30 Jake walked out of Nantucket's airport, past a pair of young police officers standing at the busy ticket counter. He went through the opened glass doors and out into the parking lot. A bearish looking man with greasy curly hair half hiding his ears waved from the driver's side of a station wagon with Island Basin painted across the doors.

"Over here," he shouted as Jake stepped closer. "You're Eaton, right?"

"And you are . . . ?" Jake asked.

"I'm Sam Kingsbury, gas dock manager. I'd shake, but you don't want this all over you." Sam held up a huge hand that had been wiped clean but still showed traces of oily grime. "Been checkin' the tank valves. Do it the first of every month. Never used to, but since Miss Gorham took over, lots of things have changed down here. Get in."

Jake tossed his bag into the rear of the wagon and snapped his fingers at Watson. The dog jumped nimbly into the back. Jake took the shotgun seat for himself.

"Yes, sir. Miss Gorham said you'd be easy to spot. Look for the guy with the big black dog. I'll tell ya, that's about all I'm good for right now. Anything smaller than a big black dog, I'd miss. Must be somethin' like shock, you know? Got no sleep. Doubt if anybody did after what happened," he said as he drove toward town.

"I take it you were there?"

"Sure. Like I said, I'm the gas dock manager. Every year for the ten or so I've been workin' here, I stay on the dock when the fireworks go off. Those pyrotechnics, or whatever they call themselves, don't really know where those things are gonna land. They say they do, but I don't believe 'em. Not with my dock." Kingsbury paused and looked over at Jake. "You ever seen fiberglass burn?"

"Never have," Jake answered.

"You would if some of them fireworks landed on a boat and then went off. Three hundred boats, some nearly two hundred feet long, would go up like that." Sam snapped his fingers. "Then there's the storage tanks. The town and the Island Basin share twelve gas and diesel tanks. Twelve of 'em—eighty thousand gallons each. Since Miss Gorham came, one of my new jobs is to repack the intake and outflow valves on one of those tanks each month." Sam held up his greasy hand. "Messy job, but she don't want no leaks. She wants those valves to shut tight. She says folks come here for the scenery—the cobblestones, the shingled houses, the clean water. All Resorts Management needs is an oil slick on the water to ruin it. So, we don't take no chances. Whether they need it or not, I redo those valves. You'd think after last night I could skip a day," Kingsbury said and shook his head. "I shoulda known better." He cut Jake a quick glance to read how far he could go. "You friends with Miss Gorham?"

"I know her."

"She's damn tough. I wouldn't want that repeated, you understand."

"Not a word," Jake said. "What happened last night?"

"She didn't tell ya?"

"I haven't spoken to Miss Gorham in some time," Jake said. They passed a line of youthful bicyclers peddling toward the beach.

Kingsbury pointed a blunt finger at the riders. "Kids. They never think they're gonna die, you know? They think they're gonna live forever. Not to say Nate Cooper had any idea what was gonna happen to him."

"What did happen?" Jake asked again.

"Somebody killed him."

"Cooper?"

"Yeah."

Jake rolled up the window so the driver's words wouldn't get lost. "Go on," he said.

Kingsbury put both hands on the wheel as if to steady himself. "Well, I was on the dock, like I said. I started off on the gas dock, then moved farther down when I heard a lady screamin'. It was sorta spooky, ya know? Fireworks goin' off, somebody singin', more fireworks, then this god-awful scream. I think that's why I didn't sleep. Every time I closed my eyes I heard that scream and saw Nate Cooper's eyes starin' back at me. Somebody killed him, like I said." Sam shuddered as he steered through the rotary and took a right turn toward town.

"You knew him?"

"You couldn't live on Nantucket and not know Nathan Cooper. That wide grin of his—always beamin', snappy little gait, a wave of the hat. But he wasn't grinnin' last night, no sir. He was scared, you know? I could see it in his eyes. He musta seen it comin', but what the hell you gonna do when somebody nails you to a piling with a harpoon?"

Jake glanced quizzically at the driver.

"You didn't know that either?"

Jake shook his head.

"You new at this line of work or somethin'?" Sam asked. "I mean, Jesus . . ."

Jake ignored the question. "Who recovered the body?"

"God, she hasn't told you zip. She think you might not come or somethin'?"

"The body," Jake repeated. "Who recovered it?"

"*Recovered* ain't the word for it. More like taken down from public display. How would you like to be hangin' there like some soggy coat with six feet of harpoon stickin' out of your belly?" Kingsbury asked as they entered downtown Nantucket. "It makes you wonder what Nathan did to deserve it, don't it?"

He pulled up in front of a two-story freshly painted dark gray colonial on Federal Street, three blocks from the waterfront and the Island Basin docks. The brass plate on the door read The Gorham Corporation/Island Basin Branch. "Second floor," Sam said. "She's waitin', although it ain't one of her strengths, if you know what I mean. I'd get up there if I was you."

"Thanks for the advice," Jake said.

"Anytime."

Chapter

4

Sam Kingsbury had told only part of the story. It was true that Gloria Gorham did not like to wait, but she was impatient about most things in life. She wanted things done quickly and done well. She had completed her B.A. at Harvard in three years and her M.B.A. in one. When she joined her father's firm, F. Gordon had put her in charge of the corporation's newest division, Resorts Management; in five years, RM was the leading profit maker. The backroom snipes about F. Gordon's nepotism were stamped out with year after year of record bottom lines. The present unpleasant situation represented the first snag in Gloria Gorham's otherwise perfect life.

Jake climbed the plush carpeted stairs to the second-floor office and stood before a pair of mahogany doors. The one on the left was marked Private; the one on the right had Resorts Management engraved on a polished bronze plaque. Watson heeled at his side as Jake walked into a small and empty reception area. It's early, probably not in, he thought and picked up the appointment book on the neatly kept desk. He glanced at it, then stepped around the desk and through the open door into Miss Gorham's posh office.

She was on the phone, seated behind a solid cherry captain's desk. A wall of leaded-glass fan-top windows overlooked a courtyard garden. A double student's lamp with dark green shades cast a warm glow on her tanned, solid-looking arms. At thirty-four Gloria Gorham could easily have passed for under thirty. She had a small, graceful body and a bold, compelling face with striking greenish eyes set off by high cheekbones. The only flaw—if it could be called that—was a slightly bent nose. Jake wondered how it got broken.

Tomboy, he thought. Probably the first girl in the neighborhood to play Little League and hit home runs.

Gloria brushed back her shoulder-length light brown hair with one hand and put down the phone with the other.

"It's surprising how fast word of something like murder travels," she said. "That was a man on the Cape. He has a seventy-foot motor yacht and Basin reservations for two weeks starting tomorrow. He wants to know what the hell's going on down here."

"What'd you tell him?"

"I told him I was about to find out," she said and stepped around to the front of her desk. She was wearing a sleeveless coral top with scooped-out arms and matching slacks. "Sit down," she said. Jake chose a leather-covered chair. Watson curled up beside him. "I can't honestly say I'm glad to see you again, Mr. Eaton. I was hoping that by now this would all be over."

Jake didn't comment, although he'd hoped for the very same thing.

"But," she continued, "Lewis Metcalf has the utmost confidence in you, and I have the utmost confidence in Lewis. He's even gone so far as to suggest in board meetings that it would be in the corporation's best interest to stop contracting you for these background checks and the occasional . . . What was it you were hired to do before this?"

"Find an embezzler."

"And you did, as I recall."

Jake deflected the backhanded compliment with a half smile. His ex-wife had often started an inquisition with the same superior tone, but she had never managed to intimidate Jake either.

"I found him," Jake finally said. "Hand still in the till."

"Yes. Well, Lewis wants to stop working on a contract basis and bring you on full-time. I assume you're aware of this."

"He's mentioned it."

"And you've turned him down."

"Yes."

"Why?"

"I'm not the tall-building type," Jake said, looking straight at her. "Top-floor corner offices don't do anything for me."

"And what's the real reason?" she asked, as if the game had gone on too long already.

Jake shifted forward in his chair. "You never met my brother, did you?" he asked.

"No."

"Too bad. Max was a hell of a detective but a very unhappy man. He couldn't slow down. He couldn't take time to stop and smell the roses. He would've worked himself to death if someone hadn't shot him."

"You don't sound sorry that somebody did."

"Oh, but I was." Jake leaned back and looked Gloria straight in the eyes. "Do you believe we learn from our mistakes?"

"Sometimes."

"In my business that's not good enough. You've got to learn from everything. D'you know what I learned from Max's death? I learned that there's not a hell of a lot of difference between losing your life and having somebody ruin it. Accepting Lewis's offer to join your firm would ruin my life, Miss Gorham. I think deep down, Lewis knows that, but he makes the offer anyway."

"A little game between men." Her voice was full of disapproval.

"Something like that. Besides, nothing's certain. Someday I might surprise him and say yes. But that's not why we're here, is it?"

"No," she said coolly, then paused. "Can you do the job this time, Mr. Eaton?"

"Lewis could have saved you a bundle on that one," Jake said matter-of-factly. "Somebody using the first name of William—probably not his real name—and a Florida postmark on an envelope are not exactly a lot to go on."

"And you told Lewis that?"

"I did."

"And he didn't tell you it was my idea to send you to Florida?"

Since Lewis never told Jake how to run an investigation, he didn't have to be told that it was Gloria's idea. But he shook his head anyway. Best not to fight with the client even if it would make him feel better. But what was he to do? He'd started the case at Lewis's request and he was going to finish it.

In March, just after it was announced that The Gorham Corporation had purchased the Island Basin and that Gloria was moving to Nantucket to personally run it, a letter had come to her Boston office. It was composed of words and letters cut out of a newspaper and pasted together on lined stationery. It began "Dearest GG" (no one called her GG).

We go back so far, I'm sorry I can't deliver this in person, but I'll be there for the fireworks. Might even make a few when this ends on the Fourth of July. Sort of a celebration for some of the wrongs about to be corrected. Of course we can't correct them all, but a payment with interest will make me feel better about those that aren't. Be prepared. I'll let you know.

Until July,
William.

Jake's advice was to wait. If it was a crank letter—and most were—nothing would happen. If it wasn't, the best thing to do was wait for the next move and maybe the first mistake. Gloria, however, wanted action, and action meant two weeks in Florida chasing phantoms.

"Well, it *was* my idea," Gloria said and leaned against the desk on her outstretched arms. "I was hoping you'd get lucky and find him. Or, if you didn't, maybe word would get around that a private detective—all the way from Boston, for God's sake—was down there looking for him."

"And what did you expect?"

"I expected you to catch him or at least to scare him off," she snapped. "Besides, we had nothing to lose."

"Afraid we'd have to ask Nate Cooper about that," Jake said and watched the anger rise in her eyes.

"That," she said, her voice unsteady, "was a cruel thing to say."

"And maybe true," Jake offered. "Why don't you fill me in?"

Gloria told him essentially what Kingsbury had, adding only that Nathan Cooper had been a friend of hers.

"A friend who might still be alive if you'd listened to me," Jake said. He received an icy stare. "That's twice, Miss Gorham, and it's something we've got to come to grips with. Florida was a waste, and not taking my advice when I suggested coming down here last week to keep an eye on things may have cost a man his life. I run the investigation. Understood?"

Gloria Gorham bristled. "I didn't want you here last week. I read over that letter a thousand times and 'a little payment with interest' made sense only one way: money. I was more than willing to pay off this person and be done with it."

"Meaning he's already asked for money?"

"I mean no such thing."

Jake didn't believe her.

"I simply mean I thought I could handle it without your interference." She paused and swept the hair from her face. "Before I go on, let me make one thing clear. My father is a very wealthy man, but he did not buy the Island Basin to make more money. He bought it because of pride. The

Gorhams were one of the earliest families to settle here, and when my great-great-great-grandfather lost his foothold and left for the mainland, my family lost that connection. When the Island Basin went on the market, my father saw a way to buy back that heritage. This purchase, this *reconnection* with what he thought had been lost forever, made my father a happy man. I didn't want to spoil that happiness by letting him know that someone was blackmailing the family. Nor did I see any reason to complicate matters by bringing you or the police into this. The fact is, as I said before, I thought I could handle it myself."

"What changed your mind?"

Her head dropped forward and her voice softened. "I knew something horrible had happened when I heard that woman scream, and I . . . I guess I lost my nerve. That's a hard thing for a Gorham to admit, Mr. Eaton. We pride ourselves on not losing at anything."

For the first time since he'd known her, Jake felt that Gloria Gorham had let down her guard. Human after all.

"How well did you know Nathan Cooper?"

"Reasonably well. He was president of the bank we do business with on the island, plus he once had an interest in buying the Island Basin."

"What happened?"

"My father outbid him," she said flatly.

"Were there any hard feelings?"

"There are always hard feelings, but business is business." She sagged as if she'd finally realized that, in light of what had happened, business was somehow no longer important. "It was such a horrible thing. So violent and ugly. Who could have done it?"

"That's what I'm here to find out. Did you tell the police about William's letter?"

"No."

Jake was ready to duck when he asked, "Waiting for my advice?"

Her calm reply startled him. "Partially," she said. "I'm willing to admit mistakes. Perhaps I haven't handled myself in this matter as well as I should have, but I am not one to sit by and do nothing. If you want an apology for sending you off to Florida and for not wanting you down here last week, I'll give it. But I want results in return. Is that clear?"

"Couldn't be clearer," Jake said and stood. "I'll need a car and a place to stay."

"Across the hall from here, behind the door marked Private, is my apartment. You're welcome to stay there, and I'll move down to the Basin on my father's yacht, or you can have the yacht. Both have everything you need—take your pick."

"No need for you to move. I'll take the yacht."

"Fine. Sam Kingsbury on the gas dock will see that you're settled and will arrange for the car. Oh, and one more thing. Today is Monday the second. The Nantucket papers come out weekly on Thursdays. I can see the lurid headline possibilities because of the way Nathan Cooper was killed. I do *not*," she said with emphasis, "want this turned into a circus."

Back to the heartless woman, thought Jake. "Thursday's the fifth, Miss Gorham. If William has his way, this'll all be over by the Fourth of July."

Chapter

—5—

Midmorning in downtown Nantucket is usually quiet. This one, the morning after a brutal murder, was unusually so. A few joggers pranced by the still-unopened shops, and a middle-aged couple sat on a wooden bench sipping coffee from Styrofoam cups and reading the morning papers brought over from the mainland on the first ferry of the day. The flatbed vegetable truck backed into its customary spot near Walnut Street, but the young lady who sold fresh flowers was nowhere to be seen. And no window-shoppers gawked into the trendy shops that sold everything from designer T-shirts to designer cookies. Too much excitement last night, Jake thought as he dodged a wobbling moped carrying riders old enough to know better.

Jake walked down Main Street and cut through the A&P parking lot. Watson nosed through some loose papers, licking his lips for tastes that might have been, and stayed by Jake's side.

They passed the tank farm on their right—little more than two large city lots with twelve metal silos painted light gray. Must be so the folks from New Jersey don't get homesick, Jake thought, and breathed in another chestful of gas and diesel fumes. He glanced at the weathered rental cottages on Commercial Street with names like Periwinkle, Meridian, and The Barnacle. They were simple wooden houses, with cedar shingles and center chimneys that gave them all a pleasant, modest look.

Commercial Street feathered into Commercial Wharf and eventually into the gas dock, where Jake found Sam Kingsbury waiting with what appeared to be a set of building plans tucked under his arm.

"Miss Gorham called," he said. "Just let me put away these blueprints and get you a set of car keys. Come on up."

Jake followed Sam up a flight of stairs. Out in the harbor a gusty wind raced through as vacationing boaters sat under their dodgers to escape the chill. Three wharves over, a cluster of men stood near the yellow plastic police barrier marking the crime scene. Jake had seen it all before: the inevitable inquisitiveness of neighbors and friends—the curious wanting to get close, but not too close, to death. They would shift their feet and stand back and consider themselves for one more day luckier than the deceased. Jake called it one of life's little victories: someone died unexpectedly and that someone wasn't you.

At the top of the stairs, a man of medium height with a build that would one day turn flabby stood pounding on the door. When he saw Kingsbury, he pounded harder and pointed at the sign taped inside the window requiring all vessels to remain in the Basin. "What is the meaning of this?" he demanded. "You can't keep me here. My wife and I won't stand for it!"

"I'm not keepin' you anywhere, Mr . . . ?"

"Ashley. Peter Ashley. Slip four-oh-two."

Sam nodded understandingly. "The *Bertram*."

"That's right, and we're taking her out of here this noon."

"You best check with the police, Mr. Ashley," Sam said with the voice of a diplomat. "Chief Sinclair's the one who posted the sign. No boats leave the Basin until he gives the word."

Ashley puffed his chest as his face reddened. "But we didn't see anything. What questions can we answer?"

"I'm not the police," Kingsbury said. "You have to ask them that."

The man seemed about to explode. "You're ruining a perfectly fine holiday, the whole damn lot of you! See if we ever come back here again!" He stormed down the steps.

Undaunted, Kingsbury took out his keys and opened the office door. "I hope to hell he doesn't come back," he said and showed Watson and Jake where the daily operations of the Island Basin were handled. Everything from slip reservations to buying fuel and ice was done in two small businesslike offices. The outer office was divided in half by a customer counter and looked like any other service space except for the bank of marine radios bolted to the wall. Channel 69, the commercial channel the Island Basin monitored, was eerily quiet.

Kingsbury stepped into his office and put the blueprints in the bottom drawer of his wooden desk. "Construction schematics for the docks," he said. "You wouldn't believe how much repair goes on here. The water moves, the boats move, the dock moves. Always somethin' workin' loose and needin' to be fixed. I try to get a crew on it before it goes all to hell." He picked up a set of keys from the top of his desk and tossed them to Jake. "You mind a station wagon?"

"The one you picked us up in?"

Kingsbury nodded. "She's out front," he said. "A real tank, but what I'm about to show you will make up for it." Sam led the way down the dock to a finger pier that reached fifty feet or so out into the protected waters of the Island Basin. There, tugging gently against her spring lines, was a forty-eight-foot custom Rhodes sailing sloop. "A beauty, eh?"

"Lovely," Jake answered with genuine admiration.

She had a dark blue hull with red waterline and matching cove stripes, freshly painted tan canvas decks, highly varnished spruce spars, four bronze opening ports on both starboard and port, bronze winches, and six brass Perko cowl vents, set off with a teak afterdeck enclosed with beveled glass windows on all sides. She was one of a kind and called *Gamecock*.

"You bet she's lovely," Sam said and stepped aboard. "Lookin' after her is the one extra job I don't mind."

Jake and Watson followed Sam down the companionway, where the study in contrasts began. *Gamecock*'s exterior was the picture of period perfection; below was a tasteful, modern wonder complete with microwave and refrigeration in the galley, a dining area for six, a hot water shower, a satellite navigation station, Loran, radar, marine and land telephones, a stereo, and a VCR. To keep the main cabin looking and feeling like an old English club, all appliances were hidden behind satin-finished teak louvered doors.

"Very lovely, indeed," Jake said and set his bag on the galley counter. "Daddy's?"

"Daddy's. He's out of the country on vacation. When he's off the island, they let friends stay here. If I could afford it, this is where I'd be, let me tell ya—on the water in a one-of-a-kind head turner. But you know the old sayin': if you got to ask the price, you can't afford to own it. She was built in '38 for one of the mansion owners over in Newport. F. Gordon found her damn near sunk up in Maine and spent more than five hundred thousand on the refit."

"Sounds like F. Gordon likes to spend money," Jake said.

"You look around the harbor and on the docks at some of the big boats that come in, and you'll see that spendin' money is what Nantucket summers are all about. That's why the people come. They want to see and be seen, and they don't give a damn what it costs. They just don't want to be inconvenienced."

"Like that fellow Ashley," Jake said knowingly.

"What a jerk. Can you believe it? Although Miss Gorham wasn't much better. The cops were around here all night askin' questions," Kingsbury said. "She was madder'n hell. Afraid her customers were gettin' upset."

"Murder has a way of doing that," Jake said, then thinking ahead. "I'll need to talk to this Chief Sinclair. What'd you say his first name was?"

"Don't know that I did. Russell's his name."

Jake jiggled the car keys. "Where can I find him?"

"Police station's three blocks over. Might try there."

Chapter

—6—

Nantucket's police station was a one-story modern brick building on the corner of South Water Street. It was built for the off-season five-man police force and had ample room for the dispatcher's communications post, desks for the duty officers, a two-cell lockup, and the chief's office. During the summer, however, the station was crowded. When the island's population swelled from ten thousand to forty thousand, fifteen special resort police were hired to direct traffic, quiet the rowdy theater lines when a good movie came to town, and answer tourists' questions. The special police were mostly college students—criminal justice majors from the mainland who came to the island for a little professional experience and a good time.

After Nathan Cooper had been pulled from the water, placed in a body bag, and taken to Cottage Hospital for an autopsy, four of the special police turned in their nightsticks and resigned.

"Deserters," Chief Russell Sinclair mumbled to himself as he sat in his office, the police radio blaring in the background. "Man, do I hate deserters."

Russell Sinclair was retired army and looked it. He was fifty-eight, well over six feet tall, wide and thick chested, and had slightly grayish red hair. The sun and wind had etched deep furrows into his freckled face. He was born on Nantucket, left at eighteen to join the army and see the world, and spent most of his time in the service as an MP transporting payroll and prisoners. Most prisoners were deserters—guys always looking for a way out when there wasn't one. They made his blood boil.

When the intercom buzzer sounded, Sinclair braced himself for another round of resignations.

"A detective to see you, chief," the dispatcher said.

"A what?"

"A private detective. Fella named Eaton."

"And what does this fella named Eaton want?" Sinclair spit out. To him, private cops were just a step above deserters. A small step.

"He wants to talk to you about Nathan Cooper. Shall I send him in?"

Sinclair's entire body perked up. What the hell would Nathan Cooper be doing with a private cop? he wondered.

"Sure. Send him in," he said warily and went to the door. When Jake entered—Watson had stayed outside in a shady patch on the front lawn—Sinclair fired away. "I didn't know Nate had any use for a detective," he said.

"Sounds like you don't have any use for me either, chief." Jake put out his hand. "I'm Jake—"

"I heard and I don't." Sinclair walked back to his desk without shaking Jake's outstretched hand. "I'm a very busy man, Eaton."

"I can imagine."

"Was Nate Cooper a client of yours?"

"No."

"Didn't think so," Sinclair said and sat heavily in his chair. "Have a seat." Jake took one. "What is it you want?"

"Talk."

Sinclair studied Jake, then said, "Let me guess. You're down here on vacation and this Cooper business caught your eye."

A trace of amusement crossed Jake's face. "Want to try again?" he asked.

The chief frowned. "No, the truth be known. What are you doing here?"

"Working with a client."

"Who?"

"Gloria Gorham."

Sinclair's eyes narrowed and he made no attempt to hide his displeasure. "I should've guessed. Little Gloria, our own Miss Gorham of Nantucket Island. How'd we get along all these years without her?" he asked sarcastically.

"I see you've met," Jake said.

"We have."

"She grows on you."

"Not if I can help it."

"Look," Jake said, "why don't I go out and come in again? We can shake hands, sit down, and have a good man-to-man about what the hell's going on down here. If I can help you, I will. If I can't, I'll tell you so. You want to try that, chief, or do you want to keep jogging down this road?"

Sinclair glared across his desk without saying a word.

"All right," Jake said, breaking the silence. He stood. "Working alone's fine with me."

When he turned to leave, Sinclair slammed both fists on his desk. "Sit down!" he barked. "I've had enough of this 'working alone,' as you call it, from Missy Gorham. She may do what she damn well pleases off the island, but here on Nantucket, when a murder's involved, she's just another trust fund baby with fancy hired help—like you—trying to save her bacon. I've had it up to here, Eaton." He drew a slow line across his brow with his open hand. "Working alone got us in this damn mess."

Jake lowered himself back into his chair. "You sound like you knew something was about to happen."

Sinclair shook his head disappointedly. "Knock it off, will you? You're Missy Gorham's lap boy, you must know what the hell's been going on. Just because I'm a cop on an island doesn't mean I'm dense. Two and two still make four even twenty miles offshore. Of course, Missy Gorham didn't think I could figure that out, even after the hit on her old man's boat."

Jake felt anger inching up his spine as he realized her betrayal.

Sinclair saw it settle in Jake's eyes. "You didn't know about *Gamecock?*" he asked, a sense of satisfaction enveloping him as he recognized the look on Jake's face. "I'll be goddamn, she's made a fool out of you too, ain't she?"

"Once or twice," Jake said flatly, a knot simmering in the pit of his stomach. He wondered what the hell else Gloria hadn't told him. "What about her father's boat?" he asked.

"Somebody broke in and tore it apart. Nothing taken that we could tell. Someone just trashed it."

"A prank?"

Sinclair shrugged. "I thought so. We get a lot of that around here. Families come down for the summer and in two weeks the kids are bored all to hell so they go out and look for a little excitement. Breaking the law is right up there at the top, so we find dinghies untied and floating free, an occasional break-in and a run on the liquor cabinet, missing sailboards— that sort of thing. They steal the stuff and hide it. They don't want any of it . . . except the liquor. It's just part of being down here for the summer. But the hit on that boat was different. Hateful, almost like whoever did it had a real mean streak. It didn't seem like kids. A shame too. You ought to see *Gamecock*. A real beauty."

"I'm staying onboard," Jake told him.

"Then you know. It's got everything and then some. So why not take something? I don't know. It just didn't ring true for kids—but none of this does," he said, looking down at the open folder. "Two days later, someone went aboard the passenger ferry *Eagle* while she was tied up on the ferry dock and dumped water in her fuel tanks. The next morning she left, loaded with passengers, and her engines seized a few miles out. The Coast Guard got her before she ran aground and towed her back."

"Definitely not a kid's stunt," Jake said.

"Neither is . . ." Sinclair's voice trailed off. "I'm a little uncomfortable with this, Eaton. I don't know what I ought to say to you." He closed the folder and thought a moment. "You said you might be able to help me. How did you mean that?"

"Miss Gorham's been threatened," Jake answered.

"By?"

"I don't know."

"Big jump from threatening a trust fund baby—a woman at that—to breaking a man's neck."

"I thought Cooper was harpooned," Jake said.

"That's right, but the medical examiner reported the cause of death to be a broken neck. Someone lashed him to a piling below the waterline before driving in the harpoon for effect."

Definitely not a kid's stunt either, Jake thought. "Miss Gorham said Cooper was president of a local bank."

"Nantucket's First National."

"Anything out of the ordinary there? Unusual transfers? Large transactions? Money missing?"

"No. Nathan Cooper was a kind, sixty-three-year-old man looking forward to retirement."

"Doesn't sound like the sort who'd want to own the Island Basin," Jake said.

"Who told you he did?"

"Miss Gorham. She said it came down to a bidding war and Nathan Cooper lost."

"Or the island lost," Russell Sinclair said with a hint of sadness. "Nate was bidding for the Nantucket Preservation Society, not for himself." He rose from his chair and crossed the room to a wall map of the waterfront where three distinct areas were clearly visible. He pointed to the single, most northerly pier.

"They call this big, ugly cement monstrosity Steamboat Wharf. It's where the ferry comes in from the mainland. The state owns it and the Steamship Authority over on the Cape takes care of it. This area here," he said, pointing to the cluster of North, Straight, Old South, and Commercial Wharves, "is referred to as the Island Basin . . . a pleasure boaters' paradise. Privately owned and kept clean and pretty for the I-B guests. The Hy-Line ferry lands there when they're not on strike like they are now.

"And over here," he said, pointing to a small dock forty yards past the Basin, "is the dock the town owns and maintains." His finger rapped against the map. "Right there, Mr. Eaton, is where what remains of the famous Nantucket fishing fleet ties up. All three or four of 'em," he said and sat back down. "Nathan Cooper thought—and I and a hell of a lot of other Nantucketers agreed with him—that it is a crime for this island, which was the whaling capital of the world for more than one hundred years, to treat the working fishermen the way we do. The Island Basin has more than three hundred slips for pleasure boaters but not one—*not one*—reserved for a fishing boat. It's like a fishing boat isn't welcome in its own waters, and Nathan was trying to change that."

"By buying the Island Basin?"

"That's right. Welcome the fishermen back home, help the industry grow again," Sinclair said as he folded his arms across his chest. "Hell, man, every state with water has fish farms. No reason we can't do it right here on the island. You anchor some nets to the bottom and you're in business. The Nantucket Preservation Society was looking into all those options and preparing a bid for the Basin, but then The Gorham Corporation came in with an open checkbook. Price didn't matter. Old man Gorham wanted to own it, and he swooped down and paid up. How you gonna beat that?"

"You're not," Jake said.

"Damn right you're not, and a lot of folks resented it. The waterfront is a natural resource to this island, and some corporation that specializes in managing resort hotels moves in and takes it over, then has the gall to put some woman in charge. Well . . ." Sinclair stopped himself in full scowl. "Like I said, it caused a lot of resentment."

From his pocket Jake pulled a copy of the letter William had sent Gloria. "Enough for somebody on the island to play little games like this?" He handed the letter to Sinclair.

The chief took it and read it over, his eyes racing down the page, then locking back on Jake. "Where'd you get this?" he asked as the color drained from his face.

"It came to her office early this spring."

"Mailed from Nantucket?"

Jake shook his head. "Florida, but it could've been pasted up anywhere."

Sinclair was hunting for his voice when Patrolman Richard Shean, in his crisp Nantucket blues, burst in the door. "Sorry, chief, but . . . chief?"

"I don't want to hear about it!" Sinclair said and waved him away. The last thing he wanted to hear about was another rental cop's resignation.

"It's the mayor, sir. He's on the phone. Says it's urgent. He wants you in his office in ten minutes."

Sinclair turned his attention to Jake. "You wanna take a little walk?" he asked.

Jake nodded.

"Tell the mayor I'll be there in five . . . with company," Sinclair said and got up from his desk.

"Yes, sir." Shean bolted out the door.

When Sinclair and Jake stepped outside, Watson snapped to attention and broke for Jake.

"Yours?" Sinclair asked.

"Mine," Jake said and playfully rubbed Watson's head until his eyes kindled.

Sinclair didn't know what to make of it. As an MP he was used to hefty, snarling, and snapping shepherds and pinschers, but this big black dog was the happiest, brightest-eyed creature he'd ever seen. "What's his name?"

"Watson."

"You're kidding."

"Used to be Watty, at least that's what it said on the box I found him in. Happens around Cambridge all the time. Somebody gets a puppy, a neighbor complains that he's ruining the apartment building, the puppy gets booted."

"So much for trust and loyalty," Sinclair commented facetiously.

"Yeah," Jake said. "So I took him in. Best partner I've ever had."

"You know, you're hard to figure, Eaton. You work for a bunch like the Gorhams and you've got a black dog for a partner." Sinclair led the way to the town offices, one building over. "How come?"

Jake shrugged. "He followed me home," he said as Watson pranced ahead.

"That how you got hooked up with the Gorhams? Missy followed you home too?"

"I'm not sleeping with her, Sinclair," Jake said blandly. "I'm working for her."

"That's what I mean. I don't see the fit."

"You would've had to know my brother."

Sinclair motioned up the cement walk toward a sprawling red brick building. "He on the island, too?" he asked.

"He's dead." Jake didn't wait for a response. "He started the agency, and the first major client he landed was F. Gordon Gorham himself. You might say that Max and F. Gordon started at the same time. Out of respect for my brother, I did a few jobs for them when I took over. That was ten years ago." Jake stopped at the front door. "Like picking up Watson, it seemed the right thing to do."

"Trust and loyalty ain't dead after all."

"Not in my book. How about yours?" Jake asked.

"There's only one thing I'm loyal to and that's this island. I hated it as a kid. I thought it was too damn small and kept me closed in. You know how it is when you're eighteen."

Sinclair opened the door and went in. Jake and Watson were right behind.

"After a few years in the army, I saw it for the special place it is. My old man used to tell me there was no other place like Nantucket, but who listens, right? Not me."

"Was your father a cop?" Jake asked.

Sinclair laughed and shook his head. "Naw. He was a commercial fisherman. On the water every day of his life right up to the time he died."

"So that's why," Jake said, surprised, "you hate the Gorhams."

The chief stopped in his tracks. "Hate?" He was going to deny it, then changed his mind. "All right. I don't like the Gorhams. I don't like what they stand for. Nathan Cooper used to say that someday Nantucket would sink to the bottom of the ocean under the weight of all these tourists. I think money's gonna sink her—the wrong kind of money. The Gorhams buying up our waterfront and running it like a resort hotel is the wrong kind of money. To be honest, I wish to hell they'd never heard of this island."

Sinclair seemed momentarily uncomfortable with what he'd just revealed. He leaned back against the railing at the bottom of the stairs and thought for a second or two. "Fact is, Eaton, when somebody tore hell out of the

Gorham's boat, I was kinda glad. Couldn't have happened to a nicer fella, you know?" He lowered his voice to a throaty wheeze. "But when the ferry went aground with all those innocent people, that's when I changed my mind." His shook his head in disbelief. "I don't want one innocent soul hurt. Not one."

"You're likely to get more than that if you've got a lunatic loose on the island."

"That's why I want you to meet Andy." Sinclair was climbing the steps. "Maybe you can talk some sense into him."

Chapter

7

The door was cracked open. Chief Sinclair knocked and stepped through. "Andy, there's somebody outside—"

Andy Tillis jerked to life. "*You,* Russell," he said. "It's you I called and you I want to see. What the hell do you mean shutting down the Island Basin?" he roared.

"I didn't."

"It amounts to the same thing," Tillis said. He roamed about like a restless, caged animal. "Jesus Christ, man. Use your head. You and your men taking statements from all those boat people and leaving orders that no one was to leave until you followed up. What is that if it isn't shutting the damn place down?"

"Police work, Andy. If you paid attention to what was really happening on the island, you might have heard of it. Talking to those folks now is a hell of a lot easier than tracking 'em down later."

Mayor Andrew Paul Tillis was a small, energetic, forty-seven-year-old man with an unmistakable stubbornness about his own view of the world and how Nantucket fit into it. For Andy, the world was the goose, Nantucket was the golden egg, and his job as mayor was to polish it. He owned a small engine repair shop in Madaket but preferred the mayor's office and the sense of power it gave him.

Mayor Tillis placed his plump hands on Sinclair's shoulders and rocked him very gently back and forth as if trying to shake a bit of sense into him. "You can't hold those people, Russell, you know that."

Sinclair stepped out of Tillis's grasp. "Twenty-four hours. Thirty tops. That's all we need. It's not much to ask, Andy. Somebody might have seen something."

"It's one hell of an inconvenience, Russell. People do not come to Nantucket to be inconvenienced," Tillis said sternly.

"Tell that to Nathan Cooper."

"Nathan Cooper's dead. If you want the island economy to follow him to the grave, anger those people with their big yachts and their open checkbooks. Look," Tillis said, "I don't want to tell you how to run your investigation, but—"

"But Miss Gorham does, right?" Sinclair quipped. "I figured she'd call you when her paying guests started complaining."

The mayor's hands shot into the air like some television preacher. "And it's not like they've got anything to complain about, is there, Russell? Oh, no," he said sarcastically. "I mean, for God's sake, a man was found dead down there last night, that's all!"

"Which is why we've got to go public, Andy. We can't keep quiet about William's threats any longer."

Tillis stiffened as if cold water had been splashed in his face. "I told you I would handle that," he said. "Besides, you said yourself it might be some crank."

"Not after the ferry went aground, I didn't." Sinclair's voice carried a warning. "Look, Andy, we don't see eye to eye on a lot of things, but on this we've got to work together. I'm willing to release every vessel at the Basin if you'll order Miss Gorham to shut down until this mess is over."

Tillis's eyes widened. "Order her to shut down? This is July, Russell. Do you understand what you're asking?"

"I'm asking you to get people off the island while we still have the chance. That's what I'm asking." Sinclair's expression grew hard as he waited for an answer. "You're not going to do a damn thing, are you, Andy?" Sinclair went to the door. "Well, maybe this will change your mind."

Jake stepped in, Watson at his side. As he shook hands with Tillis, Jake's internal barometer told him the man was not to be trusted. He reminded Jake of a salesman about to close a deal. Would you buy a used car from this man? No way, Jake thought. He told Watson to sit.

"Mr. Eaton has something I want you to see," Sinclair told the mayor. "Show him the letter," Sinclair said to Jake. Jake handed it over.

The mayor read it and knitted his brows. "Where'd you get this?" he asked in disbelief.

"It came to Miss Gorham a few months ago in Boston," Jake told him.

"A few months ago?"

"That's right."

"Then it can't possibly be the same man," Tillis said.

"The same man who sabotaged the ferry? And, unless I miss my guess, threatened your airport?" Jake said as amazed looks crossed the faces of Tillis and Sinclair. "I don't know how or what happened, but I knew something was up when I got on the plane this morning. The security's never been more than token before. This morning they nearly took the collar off Watson. Then when I landed, there were more cops at this airport. Doesn't take a genius to figure out that William's monkeying around with the two primary means of getting to and from the island."

Russell Sinclair glanced at Tillis, and when the mayor chose to silently look away, Sinclair answered. "That's what I didn't tell you back at the office. Andy got a call one day after the ferry incident. A man who identified himself as William said that when he was ready, he would keep any plane leaving the island from making it to the mainland."

"When he was ready?" Jake repeated.

"That's right," Andy Tillis said. "And he proved that he could do it that very afternoon. A man taking private flying lessons made an emergency landing after a remote-controlled incendiary device went off, destroying all instrumentation. The poor bastard nearly had a heart attack."

"A firebomb?"

"Perfectly engineered to do the job and burn out in seconds," Sinclair added.

"What did the feds say?" Jake looked at both men. "You did call it in?"

Tillis went to the window and fiddled with the blinds. Looking out onto the busy street with happy, carefree vacationing families strolling by, he finally said, "The federal aviation boys filed a report on it. They said the cause was an electrical short. Since no crime was reported, there was no need to alert the FBI or anyone else."

"No crime?" Jake's eyes showed his impatience. "How about bringing down an airplane?"

Tillis turned away from the window and looked solemnly at Jake. "I don't think you catch our drift, Mr. Eaton. We don't want any intrusions. Not the Coast Guard, not the FBI. No one needs to know we've got ourselves a little problem."

"How'd you hide it? Tamper with evidence?"

"Russ did a little cleaning up before the authorities examined that aircraft. A few items did get removed, and I was most grateful."

Sinclair lowered his head, fearing that his shameful regret might be visible in his face. Jake shook his head slowly, disgusted with the two men before him.

"Don't be so quick to judge," Tillis said, as if speaking to a child. "We

were only doing what we thought best. Under the circumstances you might
have done the same."

"You don't know me very well," Jake told him.

"Ah, well, that's where you're wrong." Tillis smiled as he began a clumsy
attempt at flattery. "Your reputation has preceded you," he said, handing
Jake back the letter written to Miss Gorham. "Gloria's spoken of you often."
He said her name as if they were old friends.

"Has she?" Jake wondered in what terms.

"Ummm." Tillis thought a moment. He knew this was a sensitive topic.
"I have coffee with her most mornings. Wonderful woman. Smart. Clear-
headed. She told me about your eagerness to track down this William fellow
in Florida."

Jake's interest was up. "Did she now?"

"She did."

"Couldn't wait to get after him, could I?"

"Apparently not," the mayor said. "One of your problems, as I understand it. Rushing around, stirring up everything but not always getting your
man. We wouldn't want that here. The island's too small. Word would
get out in no time that you were chasing this manaic around." Tillis stopped,
momentarily embarrassed for the detective. "Gloria says you have the best
intentions, but somehow you come up short, that's all."

"So, to keep me off the island, she said nothing to me or Lewis Metcalf,"
Jake mused. "That gave her and you time to hatch your little plan."

Tillis couldn't hide his pride. "I wouldn't say 'hatch' is the best way
of putting it, but yes, Gloria and I thought through how we ought to
handle this."

"But you didn't count on a man being murdered."

"No, of course not." His tone emphatic. "No one ever mentioned any
violence. We looked at the whole situation as a disruption."

"An *inconvenience* . . ."

"That's right."

Jake was appalled at the man's stupidity. "And now that a man's been
killed, you still think you can ignore it?"

"We're not ignoring anything."

"Just a gun pointed at your head."

"Now see here." Tillis's voice was edgy. "You've got to look at this
from our point of view. We're in the service business, and you can't pro-
vide services if no one's on the island to serve. It's common sense. Some
people harvest wheat; we harvest summer people. We cultivate them. We

put up with their traffic, their noisy parties, their clogging up the aisles in the supermarket with their fat little kids, and whatever else they want to do so that we can take their money. Crass but true. We harvest them like any other perennial."

"And if they knew there was a madman loose on the island?" Jake asked, knowing the answer.

"They'd leave in droves," Andy Tillis said.

"Or try to. If the airport's shut down and the ferry line's closed, they'd be stuck out here like sitting ducks while you take their money and risk their lives. You make me sick," Jake blurted. "You and Gloria both."

"If! If! If!" Tillis stammered as the blood rushed to his face. "If what? If exactly what? If this William fellow makes some specific demand, I'm certain Miss Gorham and I can find a way to meet it. But until then, what am I supposed to do? Throw up my hands? Tell people to run for their lives when we don't—I repeat—*do not* have all the facts? Tell them there's a rattlesnake loose in Disneyland? No way. The voters would have a ghost town and I'd get run out of office. Forget it."

Jake took a step toward him. "Anybody ever tell you you're a bastard?"

"Many times." The mayor seemed almost happy about that fact—taking it as a sign of strength. "I know you don't believe this, Eaton, but I'm doing what's best for Nantucket."

"Sure you are," Jake said bitterly.

"Gloria feels the same way. She's misunderstood is all. She's doing what's best for the island. You don't spend millions of dollars to start a business down here, then turn right around and try to ruin it."

Jake had stopped listening. He turned to leave, and Watson followed.

"Where are you going?" Tillis asked.

"Out."

"You mean home? Running out on us? You're not going to lift a finger, are you? It's just like Miss Gorham said. You couldn't do the job even if we wanted you to."

Jake stopped, turned, and walked slowly toward the mayor, who was backing up with each step Jake took toward him. When Tillis could go no farther, Jake reached out and clutched the knot of his tie in a solid, angry fist.

Jake glared down at the unpleasant little man and said through clenched teeth, "I don't give a damn what 'Missy Gorham' said. I don't give a damn what you say, or your chief of police, who ought to know better than to tamper with evidence. We need to get one thing very clear: stay the hell out of my way. Understood?" Jake jerked on the tie for emphasis.

Tillis's eyes were bulging. "Do something, Russell. I am in physical danger. Goddamnit, Russell . . ."

Sinclair's attention was on Watson, who was crouched low in front of him, ears back, ready to move on Jake's command. Jake cut Sinclair a look inviting him to step in. "Yeah, Russell, do something. It might be right for a change."

Sinclair stayed frozen. Jake gave one more jerk on the mayor's tie and turned back toward the door. "Come on, Watson," he said, and they went out.

Sinclair attempted to follow, but Tillis—puffing deeply for breath—grabbed his arm. "You watch him, Russell. He threatened the mayor of your city, and if he so much as spits on the street, I want his ass in jail!"

Sinclair furiously pulled away his arm and stormed out the door. At the foot of the stairs he caught up with Jake. "He can be a real sonofabitch," Sinclair said. Jake opened the door and stepped into the sunlight, Sinclair right behind him. His car was a block away and Jake headed for it in silence.

"Some day," the chief said, "I'll punch him in the nose."

Jake quickened his pace.

Sinclair broke into a trot and got ahead of Jake. Walking backward, nearly stumbling, he pleaded with Jake, "Look, I feel like an ass, all right? Say something, for Christ's sake."

The veins bulged in Jake's neck as his anger steamed inside him. "You wouldn't want to hear it."

"Try me."

"Try you?" Jake pressed on, his eyes narrowing in a rage. What the hell had he gotten himself into? he wondered as he strode along. He felt all the frustration of a man weighing feathers in a windstorm, and suddenly he had a mental picture of Gloria Gorham with her finger on the fan's switch. He wanted to reach out and grab her, reach out and slap some sense into her. Or reach out and slap her for the hell of it, her and Andy Tillis both.

Jake swept past Sinclair and on to his car. He jerked open the driver's side door and held it while Watson jumped in and slid across the seat. Jake got in and started the engine. The rear wheels spun, blocking out the last of Sinclair's plea for some understanding.

Jake brought the wagon to a clumsy halt in front of The Gorham Corporation's office on Federal Street and jumped out, leaving Watson inside. He climbed the stairs in twos and opened the door on the Island Basin offices so abruptly that he startled the receptionist.

"Where is she?" Jake demanded, his eyes boring through the young woman sitting behind the desk. She was looking up at him with wide, uncertain eyes. "Miss Gorham? Where is she?"

The woman pulled nervously at her blond hair, unable to speak and equally unable to take her eyes off the angry man standing before her.

Jake knew what he looked like to her. When he felt trapped or betrayed, he became a brawler, a fighter with an internal measure of danger so keen he could sense the unsettling calamity about to befall him. His whole body prepared to meet the threat. He realized that he was frightening a very pretty young girl.

Jake took a step back and a deep pull of fresh air. He exhaled and leaned forward slowly with his hands outstretched on the desk. The receptionist didn't take her eyes off him.

"I didn't mean to scare you," Jake said softly, forcing a smile. "I'm working for Miss Gorham. Eaton's the name. Jake Eaton. I'm a private investigator. Is she in her office?"

The woman shook her head. "No." It was a distant, quiet reply.

"Do you know where she is?" Jake tried.

This time a nod. "Yes."

"Where?"

"She went to comfort Lydia Cooper, Nathan's wife. It wouldn't do if you were to barge in there."

No, it wouldn't, Jake thought, and he stood up straight. "By the way," he said, "could you tell me the name of the medical examiner?"

She did and provided Jake with his home address, looking relieved when he headed back out the door.

Chapter

—8—

Dr. Lucas Hendricks, Nantucket's medical examiner, retreated to his garden as an antidote for the death and pain he dealt with every day. It always amazed him that something as frail as a flower could fight back against his foul moods and win. He wondered if his garden was big enough to counteract the shock and anguish of his friend Nathan Cooper's death.

He and his wife, Elizabeth, had just gotten home from an all-night vigil with Lydia Cooper, who was waiting for her daughter to arrive from the mainland. Lucas had given his wife a sedative and sent her to bed, and he changed into his work clothes and stepped into his backyard flower garden. He was down on his knees weeding when Watson came bounding around the side of the house.

"What the hell?" Hendricks gasped, glaring at the black dog wagging his tail and trying to lick his face above his neatly trimmed gray beard. "What in the bloody hell!"

"Watson!" Jake came around the corner.

"Can a man find no peace?" Hendricks was brushing the soil from his hands. His glare shifted from Watson to Jake, who was standing before him.

"I knocked but—"

"I don't want an explanation," Hendricks snapped. "I want to be left alone. If I wanted company, I wouldn't be out here in the backyard, now would I?" Hendricks, a slightly built man in his fifties, sat back on his heels. "Who are you?"

"My name's Jake Eaton. I'm a private detective."

"Your dog?" It was an accusation.

"My dog."

"Scared the hell out of me sneaking up like that," Hendricks grumped, but he softened slightly as Watson nuzzled him once again. Watson liked Lucas Hendricks, in spite of the good doctor's gruffness. "What do you want?" he asked Jake.

"Some information."

"Only one thing you'd want information on, and I would prefer not to talk about Nate Cooper's death," he said, sinking a spade deep into the soft dirt. "Run through like a whale."

"But not the cause of death," Jake said, joining Hendricks on the lush green grass.

The doctor eyed him cautiously. "How would you know a thing like that?" he asked.

"Chief Sinclair told me."

"Russell? He told me to keep the cause of death quiet. Just like him to say one thing and do another." Hendricks turned his attention back to the spade and the sandy dirt.

Jake picked at a blade of grass and pulled it up by the shallow roots. "I take it you've done an autopsy?" he asked.

"Preliminary. Russell wanted the cause of death right away. Andy Tillis was leaning on him, if you want my opinion. You wouldn't by any chance be working for the mayor, would you?"

"No."

"Good."

Jake pulled another blade of grass. "You sound like you don't have much use for Mayor Tillis."

"I don't. When the Gorhams first got interested in buying the Island Basin, Andy did an about-face. One minute he was publicly supporting the Preservation Society's efforts to take control of the Basin, the next he was spouting something about Nantucket's best interests lie ahead of her, not back there in the past. He did all he could to make sure The Gorham Corporation beat us out."

"Us?"

"The Preservation Society. I'm a board member."

"I didn't know," Jake said.

"Yes, well, I don't suppose it makes much difference now, what with Nathan gone. He was the driving force, really. I don't know what will happen," he said, as if resigned to some unknown fate. "I suppose like other organizations it will die out. Killed like Nathan." A sadness rolled through him. "How could somebody do such a horrible thing to such a fine man?"

"I was hoping you could help figure that out. Any idea how his neck was broken?"

"I do. It was twisted . . . snapped to one side." The image was unnerving, but he continued, his voice filtered through fatigue and distress. "There were bruises, in my opinion caused by a strong hand grabbing him under the throat. I fixed the time of death at somewhere between two and three in the afternoon."

"How can you be so sure?"

"Nathan, Steven Treadle, and I had lunch together at Steven's house out at Polpis. We were discussing whether or not to approach Miss Gorham about donating some dock space—not much—and perhaps some money to the Preservation Society. She's a very wealthy woman, you know, and we rather hoped she'd see the virtue of revitalizing Nantucket's fishing heritage. Nathan dreamed of that all his life. So did Steven."

Jake asked automatically about Steven Treadle.

"Ah, a wonderful man," Hendricks offered. "He's director of Nantucket's Historical Society and the third board member of the Preservation Society. Nathan and I were the other two. We finished lunch at just before two yesterday, and high tide was just after three. Nathan was tied to the piling sometime after high tide," Hendricks said.

"How do you figure that?"

"I can see you don't know much about Nantucket tides," the doctor answered. "The island's got about a three-foot tidal difference between high and low. Nathan's head and part of his chest were out of the water when that poor woman saw him and screamed. Whoever put him there must have calculated that he would be visible around the time the fireworks were ending."

"So he was tied underwater?"

"That's right. The tide changes roughly every six hours. Sometime just after three, Nathan Cooper was tied to a slippery piling and harpooned with sufficient force to drive the tip five inches into the wood. It's something the devil would do," Hendricks said and gently turned the soil at the base of a white-flowered nicotiana with rhubarblike leaves. The flower's beauty wasn't enough to keep his mind off his old friend Nate.

"Some psychopath must have done it," he said softly. "I still can't believe it. Being a doctor in such a small place brings me face to face with much I don't care to believe. You look across the desk at someone you've known all your life and tell them—calmly, professionally, so the shock stays out of your voice—that they're going to die. Or, worse, that someone they love is. When I do that, I can't go on with the rest of my day. I can't do it." The doctor looked searchingly at Jake, his hand gently stroking Watson's fine coat. "I never could. I've had to come out here and be among live things . . . even if they are only plants." He paused as a car door shut in the drive, followed immediately by pounding on the front door.

With great effort, Hendricks pushed himself to his feet and started for the noise with tender, unsteady steps. Jake and Watson followed and found Sam Kingsbury on the porch ready to pound the door once again.

"What is it, man? My God, trying to wake the dead?" Hendricks hollered.

Kingsbury ignored him. "The receptionist told me I'd find you here," he said to Jake. "There's been another message."

Chapter

9

William Rice eased up on his portside oar, stroked harder to starboard, and slid his tender gently beside the thirty-five-foot wooden cutter that was his home. The *Dolfin* she was called, and for the past twenty years he'd sailed the old tub from Florida to Maine and back again, working in boatyards when the mood struck him or stealing when it didn't, for cash for repairs and for supplies.

Last spring he'd been working at the Southern Marine Center in Florida when he'd met that private cop. He'd had his six-foot, one-hundred-eighty-pound frame squeezed into the engine room of a blown Detroit diesel when this guy had hopped aboard and begun asking a thousand questions. Will, with that deadpan calm of the lawless, those icy blue eyes devoid of humanity, had looked right through Jake Eaton and said he'd never in his whole life heard of the Gordons . . . the Gorhams . . . what was that name again? Never heard of them, he told Jake and went right back to work.

It had been a lie, of course. But Will Rice was a damn good liar. He'd practiced the blank, expressionless stare and the deceptively pleasant smile, using both when needed like any tool in his red metal toolbox.

He'd hoped not to see Jake or his black dog again, but he'd observed them cruising through town in the Island Basin station wagon just an hour ago. It was a disappointment, but William Rice was used to that. Disappointment was part of his world, his very being, like some green and rotten primeval sea trying to seep up and drown him.

Only he wasn't ready to go under, not yet. When the time was right, he'd dig his own grave big enough to take the whole world with him if need be, but the time was not right. First he had a mission, a mission spurred on by the absolute certainty that the Gorhams were the cause of all his problems.

He'd been off the Florida coast sitting in his damp boat, surrounded by everything he owned in the world, cooking another tasteless dinner on his alcohol stove, when Gloria Gorham's cold, businesslike smile seemed to belittle him even from the grainy newsprint. The *Wall Street Journal* article said the Gorhams were coming back to Nantucket! After all those years, F. Gordon had fought his way back and put his daughter, Gloria, in charge. She was education, money, and power. Will Rice was nothing, had nothing. Here he was, floating, bobbing up and down in an endless sea.

It was then that he'd pasted together a collection of words to match the collection of horrors he felt within, and mailed it. He hadn't been sure what to do next; then Eaton had showed up asking a lot of questions.

The truthful answer was yes, Will had heard of the Gorhams. When Oliver Rice, Will's father, had too much to drink, the name Gorham would come up like some clump of bile. His father was dead now, but William could remember him sitting on the porch in a white wooden rocker expounding, a can of beer in his hand.

"A man's reputation," Oliver used to say between sips. "A man's reputation is brought down, ruined, by a poisonous few. You know who I'm talkin' about, don'tcha boy? Damn right y'do. If I was ta die right now, don't put me in no grave if there's a Gorham buried near. Promise me that."

William always did. Then he sat back and listened as his father, a sprig of a man in his late years, rambled on. "It's envy, boy," he'd say. "Can you imagine that? The Gorhams being envious of us? Well, they were. Envy ate some of 'em alive. You couldn't have nothin' better than the Gorhams—it drove 'em crazy. Least that's the way I was told it. I was told it by my own daddy that some of them Gorhams wouldn't take a happy breath unless they knew you was miserable. And we are, Will. The name of Rice means nothin' no more. Nothin'."

"Maybe we ought to change that," William had said once, but his father was either too drunk or too trapped in his own thoughts to answer. Oliver had come to accept the injustice as fate—a fate he hated, but fate all the same. When sober, Oliver would say, "The human mind can put up with only so much pain. Forget the Gorhams. We don't stand a chance against them."

But William couldn't forget them, although he was scant on the details. All he knew was that Randall Rice, his great-great-grandfather, had gone from being a respected Nantucket merchant to someone fighting to win back his reputation. When the money ran out, the good name of Rice vanished as quickly as Randall had when he took his family off the island and died in disgrace.

William had wondered when he looked into Gloria Gorham's newspaper eyes if she were looking past him, nonentity that he was. If she was, that would change. He was on Nantucket to make certain it did. He would prove that he was a man to be reckoned with.

Sitting in his cockpit, he opened a cold beer from his cooler and looked out across the harbor toward the lighthouse on Brant Point. Squawking gulls rose and dove as day-trippers fed them from the docking ferry. A small gaff-rigger tacked effortlessly through the anchorage as the bright sun sparkled on the water. It didn't seem an appropriate setting to decide life or death, but William was doing it. Jake Eaton could recognize him, so he would have to die, just as Nathan Cooper had.

It had rained the day William had his appointment with Cooper. William had cleaned up onboard, shaving with warmed water left over from coffee. He pulled on a clean shirt and slipped into a foul-weather top. The hood kept the driving rain from running down the nape of his neck as he rowed into the dinghy dock near the town pier, tied up his tender, and walked to the bank at the top of Main Street.

Will had climbed the granite steps and entered the classic portico behind a trio of elderly women wanting to cash traveler's checks. He strode confidently to the receptionist's area and announced he was here for his appointment. When asked his name, Will replied, "Robert Henry. Robert W. Henry."

He'd been shown right in, and had taken a seat across from the spotless oak captain's desk in Nathan's equally spotless office. Will had to suppress the urge to tell Nathan that he was going to kill him. One of those reach-over, touch-the-arm, man-to-man, low-voice chats that often ends in an intimate, low laugh. Don't take offense, Nate, but before tomorrow afternoon, before the tide turns, I'm going to kill you. Zap! Just like that. Rack the fuckin' balls, 'cause the game's over.

But the actual conversation hadn't been like that at all. Will was humble and shy, calculating and prepared, knowing that nothing could save the banker before him. And Nate was equally charming. He began with a warm handshake and a cheery, sparkling-eyed smile. He had a ruddy complexion from his sixty-plus Nantucket summers, a balding head covered in freckles, and a rim of silver hair trimmed neatly around his ears. Most of all, Will liked his eyes. They were honest and commanded attention.

A painting of whaleboats out on the hunt caught Will's attention. The banker nodded his approval and said, "It was a common sight a hundred years ago. Wooden boats filled with island men out chasing whales. Like most things past, a bit romanticized now but all the same quite a sight."

"I imagine it was," Will said. Then he went for Nathan's weak spot. He wanted a boat loan. A few thousand was all. Not pleasure, hell no. He wanted to fix up an old wooden fishing boat, a scalloper, so he could stay the winter and fish these grand Nantucket waters. Lot of history around here, you understand, and ol' Will just happened to have an interest in local history. He'd been studying it for days in the library.

"There are other banks, I know," Will Rice had said, "but I like to deal with a man who has a personal interest in what I propose. And I'm not talking about just lending money. I'm talking about how I plan to use it on a fishing boat."

Cooper blushed with pride. "Then you've heard about our efforts with the Preservation Society?"

"Read about it in the paper," Will said most sincerely.

"Be a wonderful thing if it ever happens. And I have hopes it will if we keep working at it."

"How can you miss?" Will Rice asked.

Cooper hadn't wanted to explain the problems of competing with the Gorhams and said solemnly, "There are ways."

Will nodded. "You mean the Island Basin?"

"Yes, that," Cooper said, mildly surprised at what this off-islander knew. "You have done your homework," he said.

"Wouldn't want to make a mistake." Will smiled at his prey. He was having the time of his life sitting there stalking. He wanted to reach out and pat Cooper on the cheek, tell him everything was going to be all right. Everything was under control. But maybe it wasn't. For a split second, Will thought the man sitting across from him, staring at him, was reading his mind.

Will smiled, reached across the desk, and picked up a pen. He handed it to Nate Cooper. "Shall we get started?"

"Yes, yes. Most certainly . . ." Nathan Cooper glanced at the loan application. "Mr. Henry. Let's see now. Shall we take a gander at your current need?"

"Seven thousand."

"Is that all?"

"I plan to do most of the work myself. And the *Dolfin*, which I'll put up as collateral, is documented."

"Bring the papers with you?" Cooper asked, writing.

"Left them onboard. I thought you'd want to inspect her anyway. She's anchored out in the harbor over near Monomoy. Be happy to give you the nickel tour."

Cooper loved boats and brightened. "And I'd love to take it," he said. "It's not a bank regulation, you understand, but I inspect as many of the wooden boats as I can. Own a leaky old catboat myself. Like my wife, wouldn't give her up for the world."

"How about tomorrow around noon?"

Cooper waved that off. "Having lunch. After two?"

"Two it is," Will said and, like gentlemen, they shook on it.

The following day at just after two, Nathan Cooper had pulled into the small parking strip near the Monomoy public beach and walked the fifty yards to the water on the shifting sandy road. The brisk, cool wind had chased away the sunbathers. William Rice was alone, waiting.

"How far out's your cutter?" Nathan Cooper had asked.

Rice pointed in the general direction and said, "Blue waterline. Not far."

"Going to be a hard row in this wind. Shall we plan for another day?"

William Rice answered by pushing his dinghy into the water. He held it steady while Nathan Cooper removed his shoes and socks and rolled up his pant cuffs to keep the small breakers from getting him wet. With Nate in the stern, Rice pushed out into deeper water and got in. He set the seven-foot spruce oars into their locks and pulled hard and even strokes toward the *Dolfin,* two hundred yards out. The twenty-knot westerly had built up a nasty one-foot chop, but the dinghy—evenly balanced by both men—powered through with only an occasional splash over the gunwale.

"Going to be a terrible night for fireworks, if this keeps up," Cooper said. "They'll pop and blow right out to sea. You much for fireworks, Mr. Henry?"

"Not much," Rice answered, his attention focused on the oars' stroke and on the little man facing him.

Rice realized he was staring, and tried to shift his gaze, but it was too late. An uneasiness had already settled into the boat that even the harsh wind couldn't blow away. It was the kind of uneasiness that cannot find itself in words but is found in the quickening hearts of animals and men when danger is sensed.

"What is it?" Nathan Cooper was on full alert.

"Nothing."

"Something," Cooper said, and looked around as if he'd suddenly discovered he didn't know where he was.

"Just a little rough weather, Mr. Cooper," Will Rice said. "Nothing more."

"Row me back."

"Scared?" Rice teased.

"Row me back! Now!"

"Not possible."

Cooper had begun to tremble. "What do you want?"

The wind made the dinghy hard to pull around, but Rice maneuvered her to the *Dolfin*'s lee side. He shipped oars and held onto the toe rail. "Climb aboard," he ordered.

"I asked you what you wanted." Cooper's voice had lost its pace.

"I want you to see my home, Mr. Cooper. Now, get aboard." Cooper hesitated. Will grabbed his arm and stood him up. "Do it!" William said and followed him on deck.

"Mr. Henry, please—"

"It's Rice."

"So?"

It was the worst thing Nathan Cooper could have said.

"So?" William repeated, and in a move as bleak as heavy fog, he had reached across and snapped the banker's neck.

Chapter

—— 10 ——

Sunlight streamed through the windows of the gas dock offices. Any other day the bright sun would have made Jake feel warm and relaxed, but not today. Not with Gloria Gorham gnawing at him from across Sam Kingsbury's small office where she'd found the shoe box with "GG Dearest" scrawled across it in red crayon. The box lay crumpled and broken on the floor.

"Nice," Jake said, picking it up. "Dropkick? Or your basic tantrum?"

Gloria's insides were still churning. "I got mad." She was pacing, arms folded across her chest. "The audacity of . . . of . . . him breaking in here and leaving that damn box. It's outrageous!"

"Right up there with kicking hell out of a box," Jake commented. He put the box on the desk and glared at Gloria. "Have you ever heard of evidence, Miss Gorham?"

She glared right back and said in a low, seething voice. "Yes. And don't mock me. I told you I got mad."

Jake leaned toward her, across the desk. "You don't understand what mad is, Miss Gorham, but you will if you ever lie to me again." He let the thought hang in the air and pulled back from the desk. "I met with Andy Tillis about an hour ago. He told me about the *Gamecock* break-in, the attack on the ferry, and the incident at the airport. Makes my job a lot easier when I'm out there running around in the dark. What else haven't you told me?"

"Nothing."

"And I'm supposed to believe you? I don't think so."

"Look, Mr. Eaton—"

"No, *you* look," Jake said, pointing his index finger at her.

Gloria's arms dropped to her side. She was struggling with herself as well as with Jake, trying hard to regain control. "Don't point your finger at me!" she blurted.

"Sit down."

"I will not."

Jake didn't hesitate. He put both hands firmly on her shoulders and moved her like a petulant child to the sofa. He pushed her into the seat with one solid shove. "And stay there," he snapped.

Gloria paid no attention. She was nearly on her feet when Jake motioned to Watson. Watson placed his sixty pounds right in front of her and stood his ground.

"What's he doing?" Gloria asked, shrinking back from Watson. With a silent show of white teeth, the dog had transformed himself from pet to policeman.

"He's making you mind for once in your life. Too bad he can't make you tell the truth."

Gloria's eyes left Watson and settled on Jake. Slowly, she sat back down. She took in a deep breath, then crossed one leg over the other and swung it nervously.

"Want to tell me about it?" Jake asked.

"Not particularly," she said, but the fight was gone from her voice. "He called me," she said finally.

"William?"

"Yes."

"When?"

Her shoulders shrugged slightly. "The first time, ten days ago. Somewhere around there."

"What did he want?"

"Nothing. At least he didn't say anything at first. It seemed like he just wanted to talk, to hear my voice over the phone. I wouldn't go along, of course. He started laughing at me. It was a mean, snarly little laugh, so I hung up on him," she defended.

"How long did it take for him to call back?" Jake asked.

She looked surprised that he knew. "Not long. A few days. He said he wanted to meet me. Alone."

"Where?"

"On a boat. He said he'd never been on a boat before. How did he put it? Yes, I remember. He said he wanted to meet on a boat with a 'picture of privilege.' His words."

"Did he ask for anything?"

The question made Gloria uneasy. "In an odd sort of way. He said he wanted me to sit across from him, to look at him, to make sure he was really there." She glanced nervously at Jake. "He said I owed him that much."

"Anything else?"

She hesitated, debating whether to lie. Not this time, she thought. "He wanted a hundred thousand dollars. Cash."

"And you agreed," Jake said, wishing she had called him then and there.

"Yes. At first." Her leg was swinging a little harder now. "I said I'd meet him on *Gamecock*. He could pick the time and I gave him my word I'd be alone."

"And he trusted you?"

"I don't know. I didn't go," she answered. "I put the money in a package with his name on it and left it for him on the chart table."

"And when you didn't show up, he tore the boat apart."

"It was horrible," she said, as if she still couldn't believe it had happened. "Sam Kingsbury spent days putting her back together."

"And the money?"

"I guess he took it. It was gone," she said and looked at Jake. "That's the truth. I swear it."

Jake believed her. "Why didn't you tell the police what really happened?" he asked thoughtfully.

"If you knew Russell Sinclair, you wouldn't have to ask."

"I've met him."

"Then you know," she said. "I don't think he likes women. Or maybe it's just me he doesn't like." She motioned with her eyes toward the docks. "He's down there right now making the lives of my guests miserable. How many questions does he have to ask?"

"Enough to get answers," Jake said and stepped around the desk. He picked up the broken box and studied it from every angle. It could have come from any store on the island that sold shoes. "Did you tell Sinclair that William had made another contact?"

"No."

Jake put the box down. "When did you find the box?" he asked.

"This afternoon. A few guests left word at my office that they were leaving the Basin no matter what the chief of police said. I came down to ask for their patience and found the package on Sam's desk. I knew who it was from before I opened it," she said deliberately, without passion.

"Was the office locked?"

Gloria nodded. "Yes. It had been all day. Sinclair requested it."

Jake stepped into the hall and opened the outside door. The lock was a solid dead bolt. Jake examined the faceplate, closed the door, and came back into the room. "It's been picked," he said, admiring the man's work. "Only one small scratch. What was in the box?"

"Look in the top drawer," Gloria said. Jake opened it and took out a bottle of Southern Comfort. Floating in the neck was a clear plastic sleeve. "Cute, isn't it?" Gloria added. "A message in a bottle. Open it up. You'll see why that box isn't in one piece."

So much for fingerprints, Jake thought as he removed the sleeve. Inside was a neatly folded section of brown paper bag, cut into a perfect six inch square. Written in block print with the same red crayon used on the box lid was a message:

Stood up. Not nice, GG. I might start to feeling
beneath you. Maybe the banker will cheer me up. First
the banker, second the accuser, then you, GG.
All dead. Keep the bottle, it'll be all you have on the
Fourth after each of the wrongs has been corrected.

Like the first message, William had signed it.

"Sadistic bastard, isn't he?" Jake said, rereading the note. "Does any of this make sense to you?"

"No, none."

"At least he hasn't moved up the date. We've still got two days."

Gloria looked directly at Jake. "Can you stop him?" She glanced down at her hands, then back up at Jake. She could feel the trouble surround her. Before, she'd felt immune; now she felt the inevitable weight that comes with having your life threatened.

"I can stop him," Jake told her. "Once I find him, I will." Gloria didn't seem reassured. "Don't judge me by my trip to Florida. I can stop him."

"Of course," she murmured, then asked, "Care to take a little walk—you and your guard dog?"

Chapter

——11——

Near the end of Eel Point Road was a gravel turnoff that led to a stretch of gently rising dunes ribboned with thin lines of scentless dune grass. A short walk beyond was Dionis, a flat, hard plain of narrow sand separating the crumbling dunes from the wash of Nantucket Sound. It was Gloria Gorham's favorite beach. She and Jake were walking there, with Watson running lazily up ahead.

The still calm of the morning had turned into the usual stiff southwesterly by midafternoon, and the Sound was dotted with trim white sails. A golden retriever dove in and out of the surf, playing a game of toss and fetch with his master. Watson watched, then joined in, taking his first salty ocean swim after a sandy yellow tennis ball. Somehow it was delicious. Watson seemed to love every plunge and stopped only after Jake and Gloria had moved too far ahead for his sense of duty.

Jake's shoes and socks dangled from two fingers of his right hand. He dug his toes in the sand with each slow step. "Very nice," he said.

"Not the esplanade along the Charles River," Gloria answered. "When I was at Harvard, I used to do some of my best thinking while I walked along there at night."

"Thinking about?"

"About what I was going to do when I got out of school. About whether or not I wanted to join my father's firm. About being on my own for a few years. About life mostly," she said, acutely aware that all of a sudden it might come to an end.

"Never digging out from under a crisis?" Jake asked, stretching his shoulders forward, rolling them left, then right. It was relaxing, like the sand and the wind and the sound of the never-ending ocean washing against the beach.

"Never had any crises," she said, feeling more at ease as they strolled along. "I was a happy kid except when my mother died."

Jake knew the story but wanted to hear it from her. "An accident, I think Lewis said."

"That's right. A plane crash near Paris. I was four. Daddy and I were going to meet her there. He'd stayed behind to finish up some work. I was in preschool, and it was unthinkable to take me out to go along with mom." The attempt at sarcasm led nowhere. "The family joke is that father re-married the corporation."

Jake looked at her quizzically. "I didn't think you had other family," he said.

"I meant Lewis. He's a second father. An uncle. Sometimes the brother I never had. Lewis watches over all of us."

Jake turned to face her. "He's certainly fond of you," he said.

She returned the look. "Meaning you're not?"

"I didn't say that."

"You didn't have to." She was looking down the beach again. Watson was twenty yards ahead, rolling playfully on his back on a mound of wet seaweed. "I know how I come across. I see it in Sam Kingsbury's eyes, in Chief Sinclair's, yours. It's the price of doing business," she said matter-of-factly.

Jake finished the sentiment. "In a man's world."

"That's right. In a man's world."

"And now a man is threatening to kill you. A man who says you two go back a ways. That must mean something to you."

Gloria shook her head. "As if I haven't spent hours thinking about it. What did I ever do?" She sounded annoyed. "Who did I hurt so badly? I come up blank. Completely."

Jake thought a moment. "Maybe you're not thinking back far enough," he said. "How about Harvard and some dashed love affairs? A pile of broken hearts?"

"Is William pining away because we were star-crossed lovers? Dinner at the Harvest restaurant, an hour of reading Blake aloud, wine, snowball fights, then tender passions in my bed? Sorry, Mr. Eaton," Gloria said. "I read *Love Story* too and it didn't happen that way for me. And what did, didn't include any Will, William, or Willie."

"Who does it include?" Jake asked.

"Who am I sleeping with? That's a little personal, isn't it?" she asked. "The fact is, I'm not seeing anyone at the moment."

Jake half expected the deception. It went along with having an affair.

"I already know about Richard Graham," he said. "Beacon Hill, a surgeon, well off, and married."

"Damn you," she murmured under her breath.

"Part of the job." His voice was without judgment. "You can't have any secrets and expect to survive. The one thing you hold back might be the key to keeping you alive."

Suddenly, she stopped. "All right. If that's the way it has to be, we'll start with you. Who are you sleeping with, Eaton? Or are you married? Married and sleeping around like Richard Graham? Call him. He'll tell you it's not so bad."

"You're wasting time."

"Meaning you don't want to talk about it."

"That's right." Jake walked ahead. Gloria caught up to him.

"Well, I do," she said as Watson raced by, quartering the beach like a bird dog. "I would never enter into a business deal without all the relevant facts, yet here I am trusting my life to someone I know nothing about. I don't like that and what I don't like, I do something about."

"That you do," Jake said and brushed back wind-whipped hair from his face. "All right," he said, "but then we get back to business. Agreed?"

"Agreed."

"What do you want to know?"

"Everything."

"A little far reaching, isn't it?"

"I'm not a trained professional like you," she said, teasing. They walked along in silence before she asked, "After your brother's death, why'd you stay in this business? That would've been a good time to close up shop."

"I thought about it."

"And?"

"I couldn't think of anything better. Besides, there were some loose ends that had to be taken care of. The cases didn't stop just because Max got killed. Somebody had to handle them and that somebody was me. One thing led to another, and here we are."

"Yes, here we are." They exchanged a deeply curious look.

"Something on your mind?" he asked.

"As a matter of fact there is." She tried to smile but it turned sour. "You know I'm not very good at saying I'm sorry, but for those lies I told Mayor Tillis about you, I am very sorry."

"What brought that on?"

"A touch of honesty remembering all the times Lewis sang your praises. He says you're the best there is, and I made you look like a fool."

"Lewis is a softie," Jake said.

"Like you, maybe?"

"I eat my Wheaties."

Gloria shook her head. "I don't mean that way. I'm sure you're strong enough to handle yourself. I mean in other ways. Like how you look after Watson. Most men wouldn't have taken him in." She smiled at Jake as if she'd finally gotten the upper hand. "Lewis told me how you found him in a box."

"I thought you knew nothing about me," Jake teased.

"Bits and pieces. Why'd you keep him?" she asked.

Jake shrugged. "I needed a reminder of how vulnerable we all are. Dogs are good for things like that—Watson in particular. Packed up in a box and tossed out. Not a good way to start life."

"You felt sorry for him."

"He needed help, a little kindness, love maybe." He shrugged again. "I was walking by. Turns out we were a match. Sometimes that works, sometimes it doesn't," Jake said, thinking of Jane, his former wife. She was the only woman Jake had loved completely, and when she left, he put up walls to keep out the pain. Jake wasn't sure if anyone would ever be able to climb them and get back in. He wasn't even sure he wanted them to. "I was married for seven years," he told Gloria. "It took that long to figure out we weren't a match."

She looked carefully at him. "What happened?"

"She fell in love with another man. I'll give her credit," Jake added. "She didn't try to hide it. She told me what had happened, that she loved somebody else, and that was it. She wanted out."

"I'm sorry," Gloria said solemnly. "Really."

"So am I," Jake said, thinking of the lesson his marriage taught: love is a hostile camp—in some cases, more so than tracking a man bent on murder. "Now, let's go back to work. Did anything unusual happen in prep school?"

With new seriousness, Gloria started answering all his questions, as if their relationship had moved to a different level. "At Trinity? No," she said. "I remember it as wonderful. I was involved in everything. Drama club, sailing club, school newspaper; and I got straight As. I was very happy there. It's out of fashion, I suppose, but I've been pretty happy everywhere. It's one of the perks of wealth—the opportunity to be happy. I've taken advantage of it. That is until I started running the Island Basin. I wouldn't exactly say these have been pleasant days."

They walked along quietly, listening to the sea, Gloria filling in the lapses with talk of her past—her days at Harvard, her decision to join her father's corporation. Jake took it all in but found nothing that led him any closer to the identity of a man called William.

Watson ran circles around them, then plunged ahead, snorting and sniffing after some vaguely kelpy scent. Gulls soared overhead, calling to one another in a throaty gag as they scanned for food. Somewhere down the beach a radio played and children dared the shallows with delighted shrieks.

"You said you'd been happy until coming here to Nantucket?" Jake said.

"That's right."

"But this isn't the first resort you personally have taken over and run for your father."

"It's the fifth," she said. "I usually research the property for its investment value, then make my recommendation. If we buy the operation, I go to the site and put our management style into place. Poor management is usually why the resort was put on the market in the first place. Once the glitter and glitz of owning it wears off, or the reality of living in a place like Las Vegas takes hold, owners usually lose interest. They can't wait to get back to Indiana. We don't let that happen," she said with confidence. "Resorts Management means management. We go in with our eyes wide open."

Jake kicked an empty can whose label had been worn away by the sand and sea. "While I was waiting to come down here, I ran the personnel records of the other four resorts you've taken over. I did a routine check on all the employees who were fired or who quit."

"And?"

"You're not a very popular lady in some circles, but nothing to connect anyone to this. And that's the trouble," Jake admitted uneasily, "there's nothing to connect to anything. We've got to dig a little deeper."

A four-wheel-drive Land Rover crested the dunes to their left and slid wildly down to the water's edge, narrowly missing Watson.

"Jerk," Jake muttered.

"That's one of the problems of being out here on this small, overcrowded island. Half the people—the good guys—want quiet walks along the beach. The other half—jerks like that—want to use the beach as a racetrack. What you get is endless bickering. All the PR in the world, even the heavy doses laid on by Andy Tillis, doesn't help. It's a mess, pure and simple," she said and kicked at the can, missing.

"You sound like you want no part of it," Jake said.

"I didn't. I recommended we not buy the Island Basin," she said and read the surprise on Jake's face. "Nantucket has some major decisions to make regarding what it wants to be. It can become more of a museum, like the Preservation Society wants, or it can be a model waterfront resort. I didn't see that it was in the best interest of Resorts Management or The Gorham Corporation to buy in before that decision was made. But daddy wanted to, and now we're perceived as the major force that came in and flattened the local Preservation Society," she said.

The Rover accelerated in their general direction, lunging and jerking its way through the sand. At first, Jake was unsure if the driver was merely careless or an outright danger, but when, fifty yards ahead of them, the Rover turned and came straight at them, he knew. Instinctively, he whistled for Watson, but the dog had already sensed the danger and was running toward them, barking at the Rover.

Jake gripped Gloria's arm and surveyed the surroundings. They were thirty yards from the water and twenty from the sloping dunes.

"Do exactly as I say," Jake told her over the noise of the laboring Rover engine. "You've got to make the dunes. No matter what happens, don't stop running. Climb up as high as you can. Now go!"

He pushed her forward as the Rover cut around a cluster of beachgoers with such reckless speed that it sent parents running hurriedly for their children. Gloria ran and stumbled as the sand gave way under her feet. She fell, scrambling ahead on all fours before regaining her footing.

Jake was between her and the Rover, his .38 in hand aimed at the bouncing and bucking windshield. With each lunge, the sun reflected from the glass, making it impossible for him to see who was behind the wheel. Jake aimed. The beach was not crowded, but people were now running wildly in all directions. Jake didn't want to chance a ricochet hitting a child, so he fired two warning shots over the cab.

The driver changed course and barreled straight toward an exhausted Gloria, who was struggling through the sand like a drowning swimmer. In seconds, a few tons of steel would roll over her. Watson was racing toward her as she grabbed for handholds in the sifting sand. She was ten feet from the protection of the dunes, twenty from being hit by the raging Rover.

"Watson!" Jake shouted, pointing, and in an instant the black dog flung himself against Gloria's back and knocked her into the protective fold of the dunes. The driver—without changing course—had the dog in his sights. The Rover raced toward him. Watson darted right, away from the dunes and Gloria.

Quickly, Jake dropped to one knee and raised the revolver. The Rover—its engine growling like an animal—pitched with terrifying speed and made a run straight at him. There was no turn, no slowing down, no chance for a safe shot with all the people still on the beach.

Throwing sand everywhere, the Rover closed in. Jake faked to his left, then jumped right as far as he could, confident that the four-wheeler couldn't easily change direction. But even at that, he cleared only by inches.

Then the Rover circled with fine precision and bore down on him again, gaining speed as it came, cutting off any hope Jake had of jumping free this time. In the loose sand, he certainly couldn't outrun the vehicle.

He would have to take the chance and fire.

When the Rover was nearly on him, Jake raised his Smith and Wesson and fired two blind shots into the front windshield. The Rover swerved; the engine howled, gaining speed as the rocking right fender spun Jake around and sent him flying.

Chapter

—— 12 ——

Rice fought the tightness in his jaw as he drove. At the Eel Point intersection, he turned the Rover right on Madaket Road and drove the speed limit toward the parking area at Smith Point some four miles away. He was furious at himself for what he'd failed to accomplish. He'd had Eaton down, rolling in pain, and he failed to finish him off.

Failure was an ugly idea for William Rice. He'd seen enough of it in his life. It made him doubt for the briefest of moments that he could finish what he'd started. In frustration, he slammed his clenched fists against the padded dash, sending bits of broken glass skittering around the cab. Eaton's shots had hit the windshield, just inches from where Rice sat.

Next time, he thought to himself, he wouldn't play with GG or the damn dog. Next time he would concentrate on Eaton and finish the job. Life on Nantucket would be so much better with Jake Eaton dead, he thought, and drove on in an angry silence, a silence that made the veins stand out on his neck.

Rice glanced at his watch and increased his speed. He wanted to leave plenty of time to ditch the Rover and catch up with Gibby Bennett before Gibby's tarnished-dime eyes glazed over from too much booze. If that happened, Rice would have to make the short boat trip on his own, and he didn't want to do that—not now. He wanted Gibby sober, at least for the time being.

Smith Point was a sandy spit on the western tip of the island, separating the Atlantic Ocean from Madaket Harbor. It was a popular area because of the pounding surf and good fishing when the blues were running.

When the blacktop ended, Rice drove the shot-up Rover as far back into the sandy parking area as he could and left it. He then walked the mile or so back to North Cambridge Street and crossed the bridge that provided the only land access to the boatyard at the mouth of Hither Creek. He looked like a casual tourist in his boat shoes, khaki shorts, and faded blue cotton sweater. He was careful to act the part—strolling along, taking his time. He arrived at the boatyard just after 6:30 P.M.

As expected, the yard office and outbuildings were locked, including the small outboard shop owned by Mayor Tillis. Rice slipped a signed greeting—"Having a wonderful time"—under the mayor's locked door and walked toward the dock where Gibby Bennett, red and puffy like the heavy drinker he was, sat on the flybridge of his forty-two-foot prewar Elco power cruiser. The old white boat begged for attention, but Gibby—the town drunk— was rarely in the mood to give it, so the vintage cruiser remained patched and randomly painted.

"Plans still onboard, Gibby?" William Rice asked. The boat dipped slightly under his weight as he stepped aboard.

Gibby held up Sam Kingsbury's copy of the Island Basin blueprints and said through a toothless grin, "Right where ya put 'em. Don't know why you want the damn things. I tol' you I'd show you around. Us'ta work there, ya know. Over thirty years, ya know? Thirty years at the Island Basin only ta git fired by some damn woman. A woman should never fire a man, Will, and that's the damn truth," Gibby blurted.

Will had heard the story over a few beers late one night on the town dock. Gibby had been out fishing. He'd caught a few and drunk a few more. Will found him stretched out on the dinghy float looking up at the heavens, talking to the stars with an uncertain look plastered across his face. Will had seen the look before. It was the look of a man who'd lost his map to reality.

"So?" Gibby asked. "We goin' on a cruise like you promised?"

"I never break my promise," Will Rice answered.

Gibby's head bobbed like a baby's. "A man's man," he said, patting Rice on the back. "So? We goin'?" he asked again.

"You bet," said Will.

"You bet's right. Gonna back ol' *Betsy* outa here an' take us a little cruise. Best time ta go, if y'ask me. Early evenin' . . . wind dies down. This ol' boat don't go fast but she goes. Runs on alcohol just like me. You wanna get the forward lines? I'll crank her up and take care of the stern." Gibby fired the engine, which came to life with coughs and sputters.

In minutes, Gibby Bennett had backed from his slip and was headed out the narrow and shallow Hither Creek channel, notorious for catching unsuspecting boaters on its shifting sandy bottom. But running aground on Nantucket was usually not life threatening unless it was during the heavy seas of a nor'easter. There were no heavy seas now. There was barely any wind as the old boat moved out on the tide.

"You ever hearda Tuckernuck Island?" Gibby asked as he steered through the familiar channel.

"Never have," Will Rice said absently, his mind working on something else.

Gibby pointed to a patch of ocean. About a mile away rose a clump of sand and grass. "Ain't much there now," he said. "A few houses. Gotta have a boat if you wanna go out there. Used ta be a fella could walk from Smith Point all the way out to Tuckernuck an' have a few beers. It's a shoal now. Rip the bottom right outa your boat if you ain't careful," he said over the engine's low rumble.

"And I'd imagine you're careful," Will Rice said.

"Damn right. This ol' tub's the only home I got. She goes down, I'm sunk." Gibby checked the instrument panel to his right in front of the wheel. The rpm, oil, and water pressure gauges were encased behind glass. Gibby snapped a stubby finger against the oil gauge. The needle jumped up from zero. "Gotta fix that," he mumbled to himself and stood back from the steering station. With a sweep of his arm, he said, "She's all yours."

Will stepped to the wheel and took over.

"Just head for the red nun off to starboard. When you get to 'er, come off on the black and white channel marker just beyond the breakwater. Take us 'bout half an hour to get to it, so I'll just fix us a little drink while we wait. Might even have a farewell toast or whatnot to ol' Nate Cooper. You heard 'bout that, I imagine?"

Will nodded. "I heard."

Gibby ducked below and popped back up with two glasses, one partially full. "Helped myself while I waited for ya," he said and poured two drinks, neat. "Didn't get any ice."

"This is fine," Will said and took his glass.

"Damn stuff melts before I can get it out to the boat, then it waters down what you're drinkin'. Who needs it?" he asked and drank heartily. "That's to you, Nathan Cooper," he said, looking up at the now hazy evening sky. Over on the mainland the billowy cumulus clouds were catching the streaky pinkish light. "So, you never said. What d'ya think?"

Rice sipped his Southern Comfort. "About what?"

"The banker gettin' killed."

Rice thought it was terrible. Terrible he couldn't explain to Gibby—a man who would really appreciate it—how he killed the old man, stuffed him in a sail bag along with a harpoon, and rowed him to the Basin for his final tuck-up. I did it, Rice wanted to say. In broad daylight, no less. I did it. But all he said was, "Terrible. Got to watch yourself every minute."

Gibby poured himself a refresher and said with a nod, "Ain't that the truth. I guess Nate never thought of that."

"I guess not."

"'Course, he prob'ly never figured somebody was goin' ta kill 'm. He prob'ly figured it was just another day ta get through, ya know? Then, out of nowhere, somebody got 'm. Sure as hell wasn't no accident. And I'll tell ya somethin' else. If I know Nathan Cooper, it prob'ly took three or four guys ta get him down."

Rice looked at Gibby in mock surprise. "That strong, was he?"

"Wiry."

Will nodded and steered out away from the land. Ironically, he was just off Dionis, which was empty except for a few fishermen and a police four-wheel drive parked near one of the dunes, blue lights flashing silently.

"Wonder what's goin' on over there?" Gibby mused.

"You haven't heard?"

"Heard what? I haven't heard nothin'." Gibby was clearly disappointed.

"This afternoon. Some guy nearly got run over by a Land Rover."

Gibby strained his eyes for a look along the beach. "You're kiddin'."

"Nope."

"Who?"

"Not sure, but I heard it was a private cop," Will Rice said, enjoying his little game with Gibby, who was getting more wound up by the second. "If I was you, I'd be getting worried about your little island. I mean, what's going on out here? Some banker gets killed, a private cop comes in, somebody goes after him with a Land Rover. I'd say Nantucket was going to hell in a handbasket," Will said. "Straight down, no stops. Do not pass go."

"Bullshit."

"Just what it sounds like to me," Will said and held out his empty glass, which Gibby Bennett gladly refilled.

"It ain't *goin'* ta hell, Will. This island's done went. And I oughtta know. I come over thirty years ago, back when a workin' man could live here and call the place home. But, hell no, not now," he said. He drank freely and kept on talking. "Now ya can't even afford the rent 'cause some little rich kid'll pay five times what it's worth just ta lay around on the damn beach. It's sorta like them Indians, ya know? The Indian was too fuckin' stupid ta know he's livin' in America . . . livin' in a paradise, but he was. He had fresh water, fresh air, and land ta burn. Then comes the white man and builds Manhattan—the first shoppin' mall, you might say. The dumb Indian walks away with a bunch of beads, thinkin' he's happy. That's the way it is on Nantucket. Only difference is, I ain't got it as good as the Indian. The guys with the money already bought ever'thing up and is sellin' the island away to the rich bitches from Texas or anybody else with the bucks—like Gloria Gorham. She fired me, ya know. Terrible. If ya ask me, a hurricane'd be the best thing could ever happen. Wipe the slate clean and let us start over."

Twenty yards from the marker he'd been steering on, Will eased the *Betsy* into the channel entrance of Nantucket Harbor. He backed off on the throttle and sighted in the red markers he'd keep to his right on the way in.

"Trouble is," Will said, "you can't start over. You either live with what's dealt or you go after the dealer. Those are the options. Play the hand or make somebody pay. You shut up or you do."

"Shut up or you do." Gibby swirled the liquor in his glass and said it over again to himself, "You shut up or you do." Had a nice little ring to it, he thought, and drank his glass dry.

Between the breakwater and Brant Point where the channel was the narrowest, the current against them picked up to two knots. Gently, Will moved the throttle forward to hold speed. He aimed for the white buoy that marked the deep water off the shoals of First Point. The *Betsy* glided past, throwing no wake as she turned left around the point and into the water leading to Wauwinet.

"You know my trouble, Will?" Gibby finally said. "No real . . . you know. No real guts." Gibby pursed his lips. "That's my problem. No guts at all."

Will took the bottle and poured his own drink. "At least you're not lying to yourself," he said. "Most guys think they could've been heavyweight champ, or president of the United States, or a millionaire. Most guys go on about that crap until they find somebody or something to blame the failure on. I've heard it a thousand times. If only."

"If only what?"

"Who the hell knows?" Will didn't try to hide the bitterness in his voice. "If only they hadn't gone to Nam, if only they hadn't gotten married, if only they hadn't had breakfast. It's a way out, a dodge." Will eased the throttle back again. The current was with them once they rounded the point and was pushing them along. "My old man used every excuse in the book. Always had an excuse for being a nobody." Will looked evenly at Gibby. "You know what being a nobody's like?" he said.

"Damn right." Gibby drank and thought about it. "Damn right I do. I hate it, Will."

"Everybody hates it," Will said as he angled toward Second Point. Behind him the bright orange sun slid between the two church steeples near the center of town. Nantucket glowed in the cool evening air.

Gibby felt a chill and shuddered as if ice had been cracked against the base of his spine. He tipped the bottle for another drink, but it was empty. Without thinking, he went below and brought up a full one. The *Betsy* powered effortlessly ahead.

"I've no use for a man who makes excuses," Will said, his voice cynical and hard. "It's a waste of time, it's a waste of your life. You've got to be thinking about what you've come to do, then do it."

You shut up or you do, thought Gibby Bennett, and he held up the bottle so Will could see it in the fading light. Will declined as Gibby helped himself.

"Take this afternoon," Will Rice said.

"Umm?"

"This afternoon. Dionis. The detective."

"Right. Right . . . sure." Gibby was dimming faster than the sun. He bent at the waist and sat unsteadily on the starboard side locker. He took another swallow. "Run over or some damn thing," he said, his words slurry. "Island's goin' ta hell in a handbasket an' the only thing that'll stop it is a hurricane."

"Even a hurricane won't stop me," Will Rice said, and like the twilight his mood seemed to darken. In his mind he was back in the Rover chasing down the only man on the entire island who could recognize him. He saw Jake raise the revolver, he saw the flash and the windshield shatter. He saw Jake get away and felt his stomach twist into a knot. "Ever know when you've made a mistake, Gibby?" Will asked dryly.

"Sure . . . lotsa times."

"Can't make any more, can we?"

Gibby's head wobbled. "Nope."

"Because we don't want to die until we're ready, do we?"

"Oh, hell," Gibby sputtered. "Hell, no," he said with curiously distant eyes. "We'll do better next time."

"Next time." Gibby was clearly lost. "What next time?"

"Are you drunk?" Will asked.

"Sorta."

"Good, because I'm going to kill you," Will Rice said. He stuck his finger between Gibby Bennett's unfocused eyes and grinned. "Bang! You're dead."

Gibby heard the words and saw the hand directed at him like some big fleshy gun. Bang? He felt something very cold settle on his heart. Bang? He must be mistaken, he thought. This is Will. This is my friend Will Rice.

"Bang," he mumbled to himself. A tiny drop of spittle rolled from the corner of his mouth and settled on his chin. "Bang!" He said it louder this time. Will was smiling, so it must be a joke. Before he knew it, he was all baby smiles, then laughter and crocodile tears, gasping for breath. Bang? A dead man? Oh, sonofabitch . . . his stomach was cramping it was so funny. Dead? Whew! This guy Will is some card.

While Gibby laughed, Will monitored the depth sounder and followed the chart closely until he was next to shore in ten feet of water. Then, he headed into the wind and dropped the thirty-pound CQR. He payed out fifty feet of rope and backed the *Betsy* down until the anchor held firm. When he cut the engine they were surrounded by darkness and desolate quiet. What moon there was looked like it was being pulled backward through the clouds.

Will went back to the cockpit and stared at Gibby so strangely that the smile fell from his drunken face.

"What is it, Will? What'sa matter?" Gibby could hear his heart beating, the blood rushing through his veins like something inside him was breaking up and floating away. He wanted to speak but his tongue was like cold lead in his mouth. "Will . . . ? Wha . . . wh . . . wzzzzzzzz."

Gibby was paralyzed.

Will Rice moved quickly. In seconds, the old man lay dead with a snapped neck.

Rice picked up Gibby's body and laid him on the portside bunk. He then closed all the window curtains and switched on the inside lights. The *Betsy* could now be spotted from a passing boat or even from shore, but no one could see in.

Working quickly, Rice snapped open the latches on the engine compartment hatchway and swung open the two massive doors, exposing a rusting engine block on the floor below. He was too big to comfortably get inside the cramped space, but by lying on the cockpit floor and leaning down headfirst, he could easily reach four of the six through-hull fittings. The other two he had to reach by working his way into the cramped space, stretching around hoses and hot engine parts.

He closed each sea cock to keep out the water, then cut through the heavy rubber tubing with his knife. He did the same with the sea cock in the galley and the two forward in the head.

Back up on deck, Rice lowered the rubber dinghy that Gibby Bennett carried on the transom-mounted davits. When the dinghy was halfway to the water, he climbed over and stood on the aft swim platform. From there he removed the two-horsepower engine that was secured to a cockpit stanchion and clamped it on the dinghy. After checking the fuel level in the gas tank, he lowered the dinghy the rest of the way into the water and got in. On the second pull, the engine fired. He shut it off and climbed back aboard to wait.

It was too early to move in.

Chapter

—— 13 ——

Watson's round liquid eyes were full of sympathy as Jake limped across the floor of The Gorham Corporation's outer office and opened the door. Chief Sinclair stood there stiffly, almost at attention. He removed his hat, tucked it under his right arm, and stepped inside, unable to overcome the feeling that he was intruding.

"How's the leg?" he asked.

Jake limped back to the sofa and sat. "Sore," he said. "But I'll be all right."

"You're damn lucky," Sinclair said and noticed Gloria standing framed in her inner office doorway. The dark green cotton sweater draped over her shoulders matched her green shorts. Her features looked slack, slightly weary, as if she'd aged years in a few hours. "You're damn lucky yourself," the chief told her. "I could have two more murders on my hands."

Gloria joined the two men. She offered Sinclair a seat with the motion of her hand.

"No thanks. I won't be here that long."

Gloria kneeled near Watson, who was curled in a tight ball, eyes watching Sinclair. She petted him lovingly.

"One more murder maybe," Jake said. "The attack on the beach was meant for me, not Miss Gorham."

Sinclair arched his brows. "You were the target? But the threat was directed at her, not you."

"That's right," Jake agreed. He shifted his position, trying to get comfortable. From the hip down on his right side, he was one long, tender bruise. "First the banker, Nate Cooper. Second the accuser, whoever that is. Third, Miss Gorham."

"I think we can do without the 'Miss Gorham' from here on out. Almost being killed tends to break the ice," Gloria said and stood. "I have a full bar in my apartment. Would anyone but me care for something to drink?" Jake opted for a vodka gimlet on the rocks. Sinclair had nothing but thanked her for the offer. When she left to make the drinks, the chief sat down.

"I don't like this, Eaton," he said nervously twirling his hat in his hands. "I don't have any answers yet, but I have a theory in mind. This William fruitcake is a tease. He dangles a message here, a note there, to rattle our cage and get us all worked up. He lays it right out for us. He wants a banker, then wham! he gets a banker. He wants to show us he can bring down a plane, he brings down a plane. He—"

"He wants to stop the ferry from running, he stops the ferry," Jake added. "There's a pattern here, Sinclair, and the pattern is success. Whatever William has wanted to do, he's done, because he's taken the time to plan every move. My guess is he sees what he's doing as a kind of torture, a ritual he wants to put Gloria through. That's why he didn't run her down today. He wasn't ready."

"So you think he was after you?"

"I do."

Sinclair leaned back in his chair, thinking. "Why?" he asked. "Why lay out such a plan, then possibly screw it up by going after you?"

"I've been wondering that myself, and right at the top of the list is that I can recognize him." Jake paused, then said, "I must know him. From somewhere, I know who William is, and he can't afford to take the chance that I might bump into him."

"And ruin all his fun," Sinclair said bitterly as Gloria came in carrying drinks.

"Whose fun?" she asked as she handed Jake his gimlet.

"The man nobody knows," Sinclair said politely. He had promised himself to be nice. "But there is somebody we do know. Gibby Bennett."

"Who's Gibby Bennett?" Jake asked.

Gloria made herself comfortable, sipped her scotch, and said, "A former employee. I fired him for drinking on the job. Or more to the point, for being drunk on the job. He was told to never set foot on the I-B docks again."

Sinclair said to Jake, "Only Gibby has a mind of his own. He does what he wants, when he wants, if he's got the money in his pockets to pay for it."

Jake sipped his drink. The vodka burned slow and cold going down. "What's any of that got to do with William's threats?" he asked.

Sinclair shrugged. "Don't know for sure, except half a dozen I-B customers swear they saw Gibby Bennett the night of the fireworks right here on the docks. One couple places him at the end of the pier where Nate was found."

"And you think Bennett's somehow involved in all of this?" The doubt was clear in Gloria's voice.

"Don't know," the chief answered. "It's worth looking into. He did threaten to go down fighting when you fired him," he reminded her.

"I understand," Gloria admitted. "And I had some of your officers remove him once from the docks—but murder?" She shook her head. "I don't know. Gibby's too petty to think seriously about something like murder."

"Best thing to do is bring him in and ask him," Jake said.

Sinclair nodded. "We're trying. He lives on an old cruiser out near Madaket. I sent one of my men out there a few hours ago. Gibby and the boat were both gone. Nobody knows where he went."

Gloria rattled the ice in her drink. "You don't really think Bennett is behind all of this, do you?" she asked.

"Behind? No," Sinclair answered. "Involved? Maybe. You couldn't exactly chalk him up, or any of the other men you let go, as friends." What he'd meant as a simple statement came out more like an accusation, and Gloria pounced on it.

"I'm not one to make idle threats, Mr. Sinclair," she said, eyeing him. "I made it known when I first came that I would reward effort and dismiss anyone who didn't do his job. Further, I was very clear that any man who couldn't comfortably work for a woman should resign."

"Any takers?" Jake asked.

"No. But there should have been. Some men can't take orders from a woman. It affronts their masculinity and leads to an attitude that is unacceptable in a Resorts Management enterprise."

"Which is?" Jake pressed.

"Negativity, Mr. Eaton. They bitch and they whine." She cut Sinclair a chilly glare.

The chief could feel his ability to be nice slipping away. "So you fired them," he said. "Kicked some good men right out the door."

"With proper notice," Gloria said indignantly. "Except for Mr. Bennett, who I fired on the spot. Some of those yachts weigh more than a hundred tons, and helping dock them is no job for someone who can't think clearly, let alone stand up straight."

"It's a double standard, isn't it, Miss Gorham? I'd venture to say that half your guests sail over here drunk."

"I'm surprised you haven't asked them, chief," Gloria bit back. "You and your men have been on the docks with them all last night and all of today."

"And it paid off when Bennett was identified, didn't it? Maybe you'd like to call the mayor again and give him the good news," the chief said sarcastically.

Jake had about had it with their sparring. "Enough, all right? We've got two days to stop a maniac, then you two can slug it out wherever you want. I might even buy a ticket. Fair?"

Sinclair didn't answer. His stomach had soured just being around Missy Gorham. He'd really tried to not let her bother him, but she reminded him of all those cocky, self-assured officers he'd had to salute in the army. Just once before he left the service, Sinclair had wanted to knock one in the nose. He wished he'd done it.

Gloria's gaze was lost in her drink.

"One thing bothers me about that message in the bottle," Jake offered, hoping to get the conversation back on track. "It was overdone. A real attention getter."

"It got hers," Sinclair said, thinking of the smashed and broken box, the fingerprints Gloria had smudged when she opened the contents. He wondered if he was capable of hitting a woman in the nose. No, he thought. I couldn't hit a woman, not even Gloria Gorham. But, God, she is irritating.

"But why deliver the box to Kingsbury's office?" asked Jake.

"Why not?" Sinclair replied.

"That office was locked per your order, chief. This office was open. Why risk breaking in when the package could have been delivered here?"

Gloria was looking at Jake with an inquisitive expression. "Why would he risk it?" she asked.

"Maybe there was something in Sam's office he wanted. We need to have Sam go through it and see if anything's been stolen. And right away," Jake added as the phone rang.

Gloria picked it up. "It's for you," she said coolly and handed it to Sinclair.

He tried a smile but gave a curt nod instead. "Thanks. Hello?" He listened intently. "Be right down," he said and hung up. "We may have something," he told them both. "Not sure yet, but one of the I-B guests thinks he caught something on videotape."

Chapter

—— 14 ——

"Come aboard, come aboard," Morton Colder said as he stood proudly beside his wife on the deck of their sixty-four-foot power yacht. They were both in their early fifties, overfed and underexercised, dressed in matching lime green polo shirts. "Always glad to help the police," Morton continued, his paunch swinging like jelly under his shirt.

"Not that we ever have," Janice chimed in with an embarrassed smile. "We wouldn't want to give these people the wrong impression, would we, Morton?" She was laughing now. Laughter as pose. It fitted her like a glove.

"No, no, no. Never before had the opportunity, but if we had . . ."

Janice took over. "If we had, we'd have been glad to. Now come aboard, please." Janice helped Gloria step over the gunwale and warmly shook her hand. "And Miss Gorham, Morton and I were hoping to have you come onboard this trip, under different circumstances, of course—you and a few of our business associates. This sort of thing can't be very good for property values, can it? I mean, a murder. Terrible, just terrible. That's what I said to Morton. Terrible."

Morton and Janice Colder knew something about property values. They were in real estate, the kind where they'd buy up a hundred or so acres of tall pine and granite, bring in the bulldozers, lay out the roads and utilities, throw up a few models, and announce in the Sunday papers that Hickory Run or Willow Bend was now available for living pleasure for a mere $300,000 a pop. Their custom yacht was just a little show-off proof that they had a running start up the hill of big money.

"Morton Colder," Morton said, shaking Jake's hand. "My wife, Janice."

Russell Sinclair followed them on deck and did the other introductions.

Watson, however, found himself a spot on the dock. Jake didn't tell him
to stay; Watson made the decision on his own after sizing up the Colders
as baby-talkers. Watson hated to be talked to like a baby. He was a dog
and damn proud of it.

"The tape, Mr. Colder," Sinclair said. "You've had a chance to look it
over and find the section?"

"Indeed I have," he said proudly. "Like I said, always glad to help."

Sinclair forced a smile. "Of course," he said. "Can we see what you've
got?"

"Certainly. Like I told the officer before, I'm a gadget nut. Something
comes on the market that runs on batteries and I've got to have one."

"Maybe two," Janice added with a giggle and motioned for all to sit.

The VCR was in the middle of an afterdeck the size of a small apartment. Jake took the only chair; the others made their way to the curved
sofa, covered in a blue- and orange-flowered print. A vase of cut flowers
sat on the glass coffee table.

"A cold drink before we get started?" Mrs. Colder asked. She looked
disappointed when Jake and Russell Sinclair declined.

"I might take something," Gloria said and followed Janice Colder through
the sliding glass doors and inside the massive yacht. Must be "management style," Jake thought. Anything to make a client happy, and Janice
Colder was clearly happiest showing off her possessions.

"At any rate," Morton continued, "I just got this new Sony VN-900 Cam-
corder with 420,000 pixels—you know, a real honey—and I was on the docks
playing around with it. Just sort of getting the feel of it, panning along
the docks . . . just playing, you know. We came down here to play, you
understand. Pure vacation . . . might drum up a little business but—"

"I understand," Sinclair broke in.

"Never expected anything like this. A murder, you know. Police
everywhere . . . real exciting. I got some of your men in action if you'd
like to see how they handled themselves in the line of duty," Morton said.
"It's on another tape. Real professional the way they asked all those questions, took down all the answers, you know, although Janice thought they
were quite the inconvenience. As a matter of fact, that's why she wanted
Miss Gorham inside. She wants to complain, you understand. Everybody
on the dock's up in arms about it except me."

"Could we get back to the man under the dock?" Jake queried, decid-
ing on the direct approach.

"Sorry. Carried away. You sure you wouldn't like something to drink?"
Morton asked.

Jake waved him off. "How'd you come to get him on tape?"

"By accident the first time," Morton said.

"You got him more than once?" Sinclair asked.

"That's right. The first time was pure accident. The second time—yesterday —I taped him as soon as I saw him under the docks. I thought he might have something to do with the fireworks, you know. You always hear of these crazy stunts and gimmicks and how they go wrong sometimes. Big resort plans something fancy and everything burns to the ground!" He looked to see that the women were out of earshot. "I wouldn't want Miss Gorham to know, but this tape was my insurance policy if something did go wrong. If I had that big gorilla on tape crawling around down there under those docks, she couldn't deny anything and would have to pay. God knows she can afford it."

Sinclair was getting anxious. "Can we take a look?" he asked.

"Sure." Mr. Colder flicked the remote control. "I wasn't trying to be an artist or anything, remember that. Just practicing, getting used to the new equipment."

With that disclaimer, the screen showed a few seconds of people walking the docks looking into gallery windows, boaters polishing brightwork, and sunbathers reading on deck. Mayor Andy Tillis even made a brief appearance. When he saw the camera pointing at him as he walked jauntily past, he stopped and looked into the lens.

"Morton," Andy Tillis said in greeting. "Having a good time this summer?"

Morton's voice came back, the picture still on the beaming mayor, "We always do."

"As it should be," Tillis said. "My best to Janice. And thank her for that lovely donation to the auction. Enjoy the fireworks." Tillis waved good-bye and walked on.

Colder beamed at Jake and Russell Sinclair. "A fine man," he said. "Does what he can to make ours a nice visit." Colder turned his attention to the tape. "It's coming up here. It'll be a little dark, but I was just checking to see how she'd do in poor light, you know. All the shadows and those blacky-green pilings are more like *no* light than poor light when you get way up in those support braces. Black as hell under there," he said. Then on the screen came a surprise. Instead of shooting at the end of Old South Wharf where Nathan Cooper was found harpooned to the piling, the camera picked up the docks one hundred yards away along Swains Wharf, right across from Whales Way.

"What's he doing down there?" Jake asked Sinclair, who couldn't understand it either.

"There," Morton Colder said and froze the frame on the grainy image of a man under the docks hanging from support braces. The figure was so hidden by wooden struts and shadows, it was impossible to see his face.

"That it?" Sinclair asked, clearly disappointed.

"Play it back and let it run," Jake said. As before, the vague image of a man could be seen for no more than a second or two as the camera moved past him.

Sinclair murmured, "What in the hell?"

"Like I said, I got that by accident." Morton fast-forwarded the tape as he spoke.

"When?" Jake asked.

"Day before yesterday. Same day I got Andy on tape. At any rate, yesterday, July first, the day of the fireworks when I saw the same thing—a man moving around in those pilings—I went right for my camera."

"About what time was that?"

"Around four o'clock. Ready? Here we go." Colder hit the play button. The camera zoomed forward toward Old South Wharf.

"That's the piling where we found Cooper," Sinclair said and leaned forward for a closer look. The picture was clearer this time, still dark because of the huge shadows cast by the bulkhead and the planking along the docks, but definitely clearer.

From the waterline to the dock, the pilings rose twelve or more feet, with the support braces forming what looked like the trestle for a railroad bridge. Inside the crisscrossed frames a man was carefully working his way through the timbers. He was large and agile, moving slowly in a crouch, pulling himself along timber by timber with his strong arms. The picture Morton captured was of his back. Slowly, as the man muscled his way for a better hold, his face began coming into view out of the shadows.

"Hold it right there," Jake said, but just as he said it, the camera jerked swiftly to the right, missing a clear shot of the man's face.

Sinclair winced. "Damn it!"

Morton felt the despair. "Sorry," he said.

The camera had cut to a small wooden dinghy tucked in behind some corner bracing that formed a right angle for one of the finger piers coming off the dock. The little boat was mostly blocked by the huge pilings and was veiled in shadows, but when it swung out a foot on its painter, it was in clear view.

"What's that?" Jake asked.

"His dinghy," Morton answered.

"Not the boat," Jake told him, pointing to a large nylon bag sitting in the bottom of the little boat. He turned to Sinclair. "It's big enough to hold a man," he said. "Nate Cooper's probably inside."

A shiver went through Morton Colder. "Dear me," he said, cringing at the thought. "I was thinking fireworks, you know. Insurance protection. Things like that. I wasn't thinking murder."

"It's all right, Mr. Colder, no one knew at that point," Sinclair said as the camera began to move left and right along the underside of the dock. "What else have you got of the man?"

"That's what I'm saying. I've got nothing more of the man. Janice wanted to do a little shopping before the fireworks, so I put the camera away, and when we got back the dinghy was gone. I didn't think any more about it until your men came around asking if we'd seen anything out of the ordinary. You're welcome to the tape," Morton Colder said as his wife and Gloria stepped back through the sliding glass doors and onto the deck.

"We just took the tour," Mrs. Colder said proudly.

"And it was lovely," Gloria responded diplomatically.

"Well . . . ," Janice tried her best to be humble.

Morton removed the tape from the machine and handed it to Russell Sinclair.

"Thank you very much," Sinclair told him. "I'll see to it you get the tape back."

"Like I said, always glad to help the police—if I was any help," Morton said as Jake and the others left.

"Some help," Sinclair grumbled when they were far enough down the dock so the Colders couldn't hear him. "Two damn passes at the guy on two different days and he comes up with nothing."

"That's about what we've got. Nothing," Jake said. "Mind if I borrow the tape?"

Sinclair handed it over. "You see something?"

"Shadows," Jake said. He winced as a sharp pain jabbed through his bruised leg.

"You don't look so good," Gloria told him.

"I'm fine."

"No, I think she's right," Sinclair said. He glanced at his watch. It was ten minutes after midnight on July 3.

"That tape," Gloria said. "Is that all you're going to get from my guests?"

Sinclair nodded. "It looks like it."

"Then I can open up tomorrow and tell them they're free to go?"

The chief hesitated, but he couldn't think of another reason to keep the Island Basin closed. "I guess you can at that," he said. "Even if things aren't normal, we'll make it look like they are for at least one more day."

"Thank you," Gloria said, a load lifted from her. "At least somebody has some good news."

Jake decided not to take the comment personally. "You should get some rest," he told her. "You look a little tired. Sinclair, would you make sure she gets home?"

"Sure. I'm going that way."

"And Gloria, worrying's a waste of energy. We've got twenty-four hours. That's a lot of time for William to make mistakes."

Chapter

——15——

Except for the occasional halyard rhythmically tapping against an unseen aluminum mast, it was quiet below decks on *Gamecock*. Jake gave Watson some fresh water and cracked a raw egg over a bowl of dry food—the dog's favorite except for cold pizza—then poured himself a Remy Martin out of the stock obviously laid in for F. Gordon. Nice, thought Jake. Being a zillionaire has its perks, like a VCR on an old wooden boat.

Jake slid back the louvered pocket door, turned on the set, and popped in Colder's tape. He forwarded it past the opening scenes and false smiles of Mayor Tillis, and started paying close attention when the underside of Swains Wharf came into view. The section of tape with the man under the dock lasted maybe two seconds before Colder had panned his electronic toy down the docks—not enough time for Jake to learn anything.

He forwarded the tape to the shots taken the next day of Old South Wharf. There were about ten seconds of the man on this segment—mostly side and back views as he carefully maneuvered his way through the timbers. The man was large—a gorilla, Morton Colder had called him—with enormous strength and agility. He was dressed in dark clothing—the shots were so poor that Jake couldn't tell exactly what he was wearing—and his movements were quick and confident.

"Can a gorilla swing through trees?" Jake asked as Watson cocked his head toward him. "There's a guy who can. Almost like he's not human."

Jake sipped his Remy and studied the tape, hunting for anything that would help him. Suddenly the camera jerked and the dinghy came into view. It was tied to a piling by a thin painter. The camera followed the piling through a maze of trestlelike timbers. Jake slowed the tape to a frame-by-frame advance. Slowly the frames crept forward until a coil of rope hanging alongside a piling became visible. Above the coil, the blade of a knife came into view. Jake stopped the tape and studied the shot.

The rope appeared attached to the base of the blade, but it was not the blade of a knife. It was part of a harpoon, and the man under the docks was reaching for it.

"Want to see our boy, Watson?" Watson stopped munching. "This is our little William swinging through the vines. Look familiar?"

Watson tilted his head to the right and concentrated on what Jake said as if he understood every word. Sometimes Jake thought he did.

"Even without the face, there's something about him. Something I know but can't put my finger on."

Watson answered with a snappy, sharp bark.

"You talk too much," Jake said and rewound the tape. He replayed it at normal speed, sipping his cognac, then played the tape through again. Watching a man prepare to harpoon Nathan Cooper made Jake feel decidedly uncomfortable.

He shut off the tape and poured himself another drink. Minutes passed as thoughts flitted to and fro like angry wasps. He wanted something to grab onto, something substantial, and all he had was grainy video.

Jake picked up the telephone and dialed Gloria's apartment. She answered on the second ring.

"One question," Jake said.

"Don't you ever sleep?" she asked.

Jake was smiling. "Been watching home movies," he told her.

"Did you find something?" He could hear the anxiety in her voice.

"Maybe. When William called you, he said he wanted to meet on a boat—is that right?"

"That's what he said, yes."

"Because he'd never been on one?"

"That's right. That's why I suggested *Gamecock*. Why?"

"I think he's made his first mistake," Jake said. "A man doesn't row a dinghy to shore with a body in it unless he knows how to handle a boat."

Gloria's voice jumped an octave. "You mean he could be on one in the Basin?"

"Or in the harbor," Jake said.

"I'll call Sam."

"You call no one." Jake let the order hang there. "D'you understand? Stay out of this until I call you back."

Gloria's line was quiet. Finally, she hung up without saying a word. Jake put down the phone, checked the load in his .38, and went out into the cockpit. He flicked the beam of his flashlight on the dock and stepped off the boat, more aware now than before of the pain in his leg.

Watson spun a three-sixty and trotted along beside his master, eyes wide, a line of hair on top of his neck bristling. He knew this was work, and all his senses were on alert. The cool night air was exhilarating, but the dog suppressed his urge to run and adjusted his pace to Jake, who was moving slower than ever. The dampness had stiffened his leg even more.

At the end of *Gamecock*'s finger pier, they turned right and walked down past the gas dock, past the storage rooms and the IB laundry. The slip-slap of water against hulls was the only sound. Straight ahead was Commercial Street. Years ago Commercial Street was extended by pilings so the fuel dock could be added. Swains Wharf paralleled Commercial Street to the inside. Small and squat shingled cottages were built on the wharf so close to the dock that more than one drunken vacationer had stepped out his front door into the protected water of the Island Basin. It was just past those cottages that Morton Colder had photographed William the first time and where Jake and Watson now stood, unnoticed by the arm-in-arm couples who passed along Whales Way.

Moving quietly so as not to disturb those asleep on their yachts, Jake walked out far enough on a finger pier so he could look back at the bracing under the main dock. From somewhere in the basin came music and soft voices mixing with the flow of water as a pump kicked in and emptied a bilge. The sounds were soft yet clear, carried along and somehow sharpened as they traveled over the water. Jake bent down and aimed the light across the moss-covered pilings and the heavily bolted framing that supported the planks on top of the dock. He could see nothing. But William had been down there for some reason and Jake wanted to know why.

He told Watson to stay, then he grabbed hold of the metal ladder that hung from the dock. Carefully, he put one foot under the other and began his gradual descent into the musty pitch black. A foot from the waterline he stopped, switched on his flashlight, and pointed it up under the planking. An electrical trunk line ran under the dock and split off into feeder lines at each topside outlet box so each boat could have shore power. The line looked new, well secured, and untampered with.

Jake followed the power line with his light back toward the street where it went under Whales Way in a four-inch metal pipe. Next to that was a larger metal conduit with several eight-inch pipes running through it under the street. One of the pipes—Jake guessed it was the feeder line for the gas dock—followed the power line farther out on the docks. Six other pipes—two painted green, two red, and two silver—curved back along a pier behind him and soon became obscured by the tied-up boats. The only thing Jake could clearly see as the pipes snaked out of sight was the bold black stenciled warning: Zone 1—No Smoking—No Open Flames.

Jake's leg was aching, but he ran the light over the struts and braces again before painfully climbing back up the steps. "Next time, I'm sending you," he said and shook Watson's head roughly back and forth. Watson whirled with delight.

"Anybody ever tell you you're an idiot?"

Watson uttered a throaty growl.

"Thought so," Jake said, and with a silent wave of his hand stopped the playfulness as quickly as it had begun. Watson turned away, looking down the dock.

Jake switched off the flashlight, and he and Watson moved slowly toward the raised office building on the Island Basin's fuel dock. A controlled tension rose through Jake, and Watson seemed to sense that they were being watched. With a low growl, the dog stalked along, staying right next to Jake. As they moved closer, Jake caught the silhouette of a man; he was frozen, hiding in the shadows. Startled at being noticed, the figure darted around the fuel pumps.

Jake touched Watson's neck. "Stay beside me," he said and tucked the flashlight inside his belt. He drew his .38 and held it comfortably in his right hand. Come on, William, he thought to himself as he slowly made his way between two dark cottages and came out on Commercial Wharf. Anytime, gorilla. Go on. Make a mistake.

Jake stood fifty feet from the corner building that housed the IB laundry. With good legs, a short dash. With the painer he had under him, it looked like a mile. He bent low and took off, his right leg throbbing with each stride. Jake tried to keep his gait steady and even, to hide his weakness from his unseen adversary.

Watson made the distance easily. When Jake caught up he leaned heavily against the laundry room door and breathed deeply, focusing his mind on a man he couldn't see in the darkness ahead, blocking out the chilling memory that competed for his attention.

It was ten years ago that Jake and his older brother, Max, were working a blackmail case in Boston's Fenway district. It was cool and dark, just like tonight. Max was to deliver the money to the middle of the footbridge nearest the basketball courts. The bills were marked, the serial numbers logged. No reason for heroes. Max took the bag as planned and walked to the center of the bridge. Then a single rifle shot knocked him over the handrail and into the shallows of Muddy Creek.

For months afterward Jake had nightmares. Hulking silhouettes taunted him as Max cried out in the slow-moving brackish water, "Jake . . . help. Help me, Jake." Howls in a dream. Fuzzy voices rolling through space and painful memory. Jake remembered two things: running toward Max, and a blow to the head so fierce he thought a bullet had struck him. He fell; then the kicking began. Two men stood over him, taunting him, kicking him until his ribs were broken and his face was bloody, while Max continued to cry for help. It was a kind of torture Jake would never forget.

When the assailants had left and Jake could finally move, he found his brother facedown in the water, dead. The cops said what cops always say when someone gets killed in Area B. Bad neighborhood. Shouldn't have been down there in the first place. People get shot down there. People get killed. We'll do our best to find out who did this, but don't hold your breath.

Jake didn't. He got out of the hospital and hunted them through the underbelly of Boston. Two guys who didn't give a shit about Max or life in general. Two guys who'd do a little time and walk, as if that were one of life's normal rhythms. Do time and walk. Do time and walk. Like it had a finger-snapping beat to it or some damn thing. Do time and walk.

Only they couldn't walk when Jake finished with them. He had to drag them to the Area B Police Station on Dudley Street, smiles all gone, cockiness all gone. Almost ready to confess but not quite. Maybe do a plea. Any offers? Looks like a busy day in court. Judge looks mighty frazzled. Say, Your Honor, how 'bout a break? Smart move. The judge sentenced them to ten years, knocked it down to two, which meant nine months real time before a new pair of untied Adidas hit the streets. All part of American justice.

It wasn't easy but Jake had to live with that. Mark his time. Go all knotted up inside when the dead voice of Max rolled through his brain, when he felt the kicks slamming again on his ribs, heard the taunts, the jeers, the fun two thugs were having, like it was Saturday night at the roller rink. Jake would never forget the taunting. Maybe someday the rest of it would fall from memory, but the pleasure those two got from killing he would never, ever forget.

One day in Area B, two men were found shot to death in an alley. The cops thought of Jake and brought him in for questioning. Nothing personal, but those two did snuff your brother. Did kick the hell out of you. True enough, but Jake had answers. He simply told them the truth: people get killed down there. The trick, he thought but didn't say, is to make sure it's the other guy who dies.

The lights that normally shone on the fuel pumps and the gas dock office were out, leaving in darkness the entire length of the 300-foot dock. Jake crouched low and scurried alongside a green-hulled cutter. He and Watson stopped and listened for some sound, strained for some glimpse of unnatural movement, but they heard and saw nothing out of the ordinary.

"Let's go get him," Jake told Watson softly as they moved steadily down the dock toward the fuel pumps and offices. He gave Watson a hand signal and the dog—ears up like tiny radar screens and his body lowered into a stalking, slinking gait—darted off to the right to circle the building. Jake—moving slowly, with the caution of a damaged man—veered left under the steps and crept up to the corner of the building.

A black dog surprising a man in the dark can startle him into giving himself away. That was what Jake hoped. Or, even better, scare the man into making a break for it—right into the barrel of Jake's .38. Jake didn't think William was the kind to run, however, so he slipped around the building's corner and silently inched his way along.

To his right he heard the slight shuffle of a shoe. Instinctively he spun toward his attacker, but his sore leg slowed him down, and a massive arm locked around his throat. Then, in seconds, a second arm smacked down on his wrist and sent the Smith and Wesson flying across the dock.

Jake reached up with his left hand—his right was momentarily useless from the blow—and tried to tear away the arm that was choking him. It was impossible, but the movement provided enough purchase for Jake to jump up and smash his feet against the ice machine, sending both men staggering backward into the guardrail. The pain shot through his right leg like fire, but the attacker caught the full force of the rail in his lower back and flinched just enough for Jake to free himself.

Jake struck the man's stomach with his right hand, then spun him and cracked down on him with both hands. The man grunted an ugly hoarse sound and dipped to one knee just as Watson came tearing around the building.

"Wait . . . wait!" The man was waving frantically in the darkness as Watson bore down on him. "The d . . . the dog . . ."

"He won't kill you," Jake said, barely able to control his anger. He'd recognized the voice of Sam Kingsbury. It was Kingsbury who'd been lurking in the shadows, playing the stupid role of spy. But none of this was a game, and Jake wanted Sam to come away with that lesson. Without warning, Jake jerked Kingsbury to his feet and nailed him with a right that slammed him hard against the building. "Watson won't kill you, but I might," he shouted.

"Je . . . Jesus, man." It was all Kingsbury could get out.

Jake hit him again for good measure. "That ain't the half of it," he snapped and shone the flashlight in Sam's blinking eyes. "What the hell are you doing?"

Kingsbury was dabbing a hand against his jaw and looking at the blood. "You have ta hit me so damn hard?" he asked.

"I ought to break your fucking neck!" Jake flicked the light on the dock and retrieved his gun. "Explain."

"Miss Gorham," he said, rubbing the side of his cut face. "She called me 'bout an hour ago. She didn't want any more surprises for her guests and said I was ta come down and watch the dock."

Jake glared through Kingsbury. He spun on his heels and furiously walked away.

"Hey!" Kingsbury's voice stuck in his throat. "Eaton, wait. Where you goin'?"

Jake was halfway up the dock. "To talk to my client," he shouted back.

Kingsbury ran after him and tugged at his arm. "You can't do that. No way. She'll have my job, Eaton. I swear it."

They stopped, facing each other. Kingsbury was taking deep, long breaths of air, trying to calm himself. Jake, still burning hot at Gloria's interference, stared at him evenly.

"I mean it, Eaton," Kingsbury said, his voice low, as if the admission shamed him. "I had orders ta stay clear of you. You weren't supposed ta know I was down here. If you go bitchin' and moanin' ta her, I'm gone." He snapped his fingers. "Like that. Gone. Cut me some slack, will ya? It may not seem like much of a job, but it's the only one I got. I never saw you and you never saw me. What d'you say?"

Kingsbury's fear of Gloria Gorham saddened Jake. "Go home," Jake finally said and turned back toward *Gamecock*.

"But I'm supposed ta—"

"Go home, Sam. I won't say a word if you go home."

Jake heard Kingsbury's footsteps moving off the dock. They were heavier than Jake remembered, as if carrying a man with weight on his back, the cage of his own limitations.

Chapter

—16—

The knocking on *Gamecock*'s cabin roof rumbled through the boat. "Anybody home?" Russell Sinclair asked as Jake appeared from belowdecks. "Saw Sam out in the parking lot," the chief said. "I told him I wanted a complete inventory of his office. He said he'd do it in the morning, that he was going home."

"Best place for him," Jake said irritably and went back below.

Sinclair climbed wearily onboard. "What was the fight about?" he asked and stepped down the companionway.

"Manhood. Sam lost his and was down here looking for it."

"Sam's okay."

"Sure, Sam's just fine. Like everything else down here on the wonderful island of Nantucket."

"What's eating you? Or are you always grumpy when you're pulling an all-nighter?" Sinclair asked and leaned against the galley counter where the bottle of Remy Martin stood open. He picked it up.

"Help yourself," Jake said.

"Little out of my league." He put the bottle back down. "You didn't answer."

"You don't need another reason to dislike Gloria," Jake told him and offered him a drink. "I don't need another reason either, but I got one."

"Sam Kingsbury?"

Jake nodded. "Sam was just following orders. Stupid, but orders all the same." He handed Sinclair his whiskey and poured himself another cognac. "Some people don't understand luck, Sinclair. They see a world controlled by reason and think if they order the right people around, they can make reasonable things happen."

Sinclair sipped his whiskey. "Your client, perhaps?"

"My client, perhaps. But you can be lucky only so many times," he said. "When it runs out, likely as not you end up dead. At least that's the way I explain why I'm alive and my brother isn't. I was lucky; he wasn't. Out there on that dock tonight, I was thinking about the night he died." Jake took a drink and sat on one of the companionway steps. He looked at Sinclair and said without emotion. "The two men who shot my brother stood over me . . . taunting, playing with my life. They enjoyed terrorizing everything around them. That's when it dawned on me, Sinclair. The method to William's madness is exactly that—taunting. He started out playing with Gloria's life, now he's widening the playing field a little at a time. He'll take whatever he's given, then go for more. It's the nature of the beast."

"How do you figure?"

"Look at where he started," Jake explained. "He sends a note to the Gorham's Boston headquarters, and what's it get him? Me in Florida. My guess is that's where I bumped into him," he said. Jake rubbed his leg. "He returned the favor and bumped into me."

Sinclair looked doubtfully at Jake. "You're saying the note worked?"

"In an odd sort of way, maybe better than he expected it would. The Gorhams reacted. He got to them, rattled their cage. One note and I drop out of the sky. It must have looked very easy to him. Then he shows up here and sees how easy it really is."

Sinclair shrank from the reproach. He could see what was coming. "The hit on the ferry," he stated.

Jake nodded. "And you did nothing. He does the same at the airport," Jake reminded him.

"I told Andy we had to do something," Sinclair defended. "I wasn't alone in this."

"I'm not blaming you, chief," he lied. "I'm simply telling you that if my theory is right, William was simply testing the water the first time around. He wanted to see how far he could go, how much he could get away with, and at the same time let you know of his capabilities, of the risks he's willing to take." Jake swirled the liquid in his glass before taking a sip. "He's fearless now, Sinclair."

"We don't know that. That's the trouble," the chief shot back. "We don't know a damn thing about him."

"Not what he looks like," Jake agreed. "Not his real name. But we know him. He's smart. He knows his way around boats and planes well enough to put them out of commission. He knows incendiary devices, which means he probably knows explosives. He's organized. He plans every move down to the details like the falling tide. And he's a killer who's promised to kill twice more."

Sinclair said nothing. Minutes went by. When he spoke, his voice was low and tremulous. "One thing that bothers me," he said, "is the people on that ferry. D'you know how many people she carries on one trip? Nearly two thousand men, women, and children when she's full, and she's always full in July and August. I lay awake some nights knowing deep inside that he's going to strike that ferry again. It shakes me right out of my sleep."

Jake stood. "I wouldn't put it past him, chief. I wouldn't put anything past him, which is why I was looking around under the docks earlier. Didn't you find it curious that William was a hundred yards away from where Cooper's body was found? What the hell was he doing down there?"

"I wondered that myself." Sinclair shifted his weight. "I figured he was looking for a place to unveil Cooper's body."

"I don't think so," Jake said. "Tucked up there in that corner, he wouldn't get much of an audience to see his work. William likes an audience. No, he was after something else in that maze of wires and pipes."

"Only thing down there's a bunch of supply conduit. Fuel lines out to the gas dock mostly."

"Zone One?" Jake asked and refreshed his drink. "I saw all that."

"Nothing pretty about it, that's for sure. That's mostly why it's under the dock. That and it's next to the tanker pier. Every drop of fuel on this island comes over on tankers from the mainland. Tugs guide 'em in and they off-load."

"Make for a big fire," Jake commented.

"Big enough to burn down the whole town. But not a drop comes off a tanker until the fire department is on the scene and gives the okay. Zone One is the Island Basin and the tank farm. If the Zone One alarm rings, everybody in town knows what to do. There's more than a million gallons of gas and diesel in that tank farm. It'd blow the town right off the map if something happened down there."

"Like a gorilla playing with matches?"

Sinclair shook his head, unfazed by the threat. "Impossible," he said. "The farm's surrounded by a chain-link fence and patrolled by I-B employees twenty-four hours a day. Missy Gorham started all that when she took over. She's afraid an oil spill would ruin her business."

"So Kingsbury told me," Jake said, remembering Sam's greasy hands on the ride into town yesterday morning. It seemed like a hundred years ago. "I'd check it out anyway, chief," Jake added. "Just to be sure."

"Will do."

"And quietly. Wouldn't want to make Gloria's guests any more nervous than they already are."

"They'll be gone in the morning," Sinclair said. "We've questioned 'em all, got as much as we're going to. That's why I stopped by. If you're done with that tape, thought I'd go over it a time or two. Sure as hell not going to get any sleep until all this blows over."

"That's for sure. You can watch it here if you like." Jake hit the rewind button. On the screen, Mayor Andy Tillis walked backward across the pier like a poorly trained Charlie Chaplin without his twirling cane.

William Rice hauled anchor and guided the *Betsy* slowly past the red nun off First Point. He set the engine at just under 800 rpms. Headway was all he wanted. Quiet, slow headway and at a low rpm so the engine didn't rumble and the boat didn't throw a wake.

Once past the nun, he headed northwest instead of north, which would have taken him back out the channel. Northwest took him through the main harbor and into the thick of the anchored and moored boats.

Slowly he picked his way, making gentle corrections at the wheel to guide the old boat in a series of small S turns through the anchorage. He gave each boat a wide berth, taking no chance of fouling his prop in somebody's line.

In the middle of the harbor, he turned *Betsy* twenty degrees to starboard and cut the engine to barely over idle at 500 rpms. He wanted to move very slowly so he didn't have to use reverse to stop. A revving engine would draw attention, and he didn't want attention—not yet anyway. So he crept along in the nearly total darkness toward the Island Basin.

The most crowded part of the harbor was closest to the Island Basin and the dinghy dock. William carefully wove his way through the moored boats until he was into the access channel that led to the IB slips. He cut back power once again and drifted ahead at little more than one knot.

The idea of circling around, gathering speed, and coming in full tilt momentarily crossed his mind. It was a nice picture: a big explosion and, like a matchstick dollhouse, everything on fire. But that wasn't the way he wanted it. William knew what he wanted to do and how he wanted to do it. Ramming the *Betsy* into the Island Basin wasn't the way. It was a nice thought, but it wasn't the way.

He checked the channel for any late-night traffic, and when he saw that it was clear, he turned off the engine and drifted forward to drop anchor just inside the IB bulkhead. He was directly in the middle of the access channel. He let out thirty feet of rope—not enough to anchor properly but enough to stop him from drifting into the docks. Secured, he went below briefly to work on the sea cocks, then he came back on deck carrying something wrapped in a worn blanket.

He climbed into the dinghy with the package, tied a stern line to *Betsy,* and held the line as he started the dinghy's engine. Just as before, the two-cycle purred to life.

It was now a simple matter of positioning. The anchor held the bow as William maneuvered *Betsy's* stern to the precise spot. When he was satisfied with the placement, he released the line and motored back out into the protection of the crowded harbor.

He looked back once, but the *Betsy* was already gone.

"You hear that?" Jake asked.

"Dinghy engine," Sinclair said. "Probably some damn fool kids making another raid on the dinghy dock. Never thought I'd look forward to something as simple as that—bored kids takin' a joyride in somebody else's dinghy."

"At this hour?"

"Best time. Everybody but us is asleep," Sinclair said. He turned off the videotape. He hadn't paid much attention to it anyway. "Guess I'd better be on my way," he said, standing. "Maybe I'll walk back along the tank farm just to take a look for myself."

"Wouldn't hurt," Jake agreed. He followed Sinclair out into the cockpit.

The night sky was brillant with a canopy of stars. Sinclair gazed at the sight and said wearily, "I feel like I'm hanging from a window ledge and my fingers are about to straighten. It's a long way down, you know?"

"I know," Jake said as Sinclair turned to look toward him.

"You've been around the block a time or two. What's your feeling on this? You gonna save your client and my island?" Before Jake could answer, Sinclair's radio squawked. He pressed the send button and spoke into it. "Sinclair here."

"We found the Rover, chief," the radio voice said.

"Where?"

"Smith Point. Way back in the parking area."

"On my way," he said and stepped off the boat. "Any interest?" he asked Jake.

"I'm always interested in the man who tries to kill me," Jake said. "But I'm headed in the other direction. Thought I'd pay a visit to Steven Treadle."

"If we don't sleep, nobody does. Right?"

"That's about it," Jake answered as he closed the hatch. Watson was waiting on the dock.

Chapter

——17——

Jake drove out of town in a wet ground fog. It was so thick that a salty taste hung in the cloudy air. Through the windshield, he could see nothing except the diffused reflection of the car's headlights. It had been a long day and he felt tired and incredibly alone.

He reached over to rub Watson's neck and thought momentarily of his former wife. The car's lights and his tired eyes played tricks on him, and he thought he saw her reflected in the windshield. She had chestnut hair, brown eyes flecked with gold, and a complexion as soft and flawless as creamy silk.

He'd met her in Harvard Square after one of those summer rainstorms that send people scurrying for cover. Jake was under a storefront awning when Jane, soaked and out of breath, ran into him, dropping a stack of art history books.

Jake seemed in love with her instantly. She was saintlike to him—inquisitive, interesting, and lovely. She was a graduate student at Harvard working on her Ph.D. and preparing a dissertation on American painters of the twenties. At first she seemed surprised that he was interested in her work, but Jake would listen for hours, intently, with reverence, as she explained its importance. His work as a detective fascinated her as well. It was an experience beyond her own, exciting and dangerous.

Eventually they were married and the complications of being in love began to surface. Jane wondered if she'd made a mistake. Jake noticed, with curious detachment, the limits of his strength as he tried to hold their marriage together. He had spent his life protecting others, only to find that in matters of his own heart, there was no protection.

He would never discover to his satisfaction what killed their love, but the thought that he had killed it was never far away. How did it happen? How did desire turn to grief, and memory of past good times strike at the heart? It was one mystery beyond his detection, and it teased and tormented him. In the beginning everything had seemed so right, so perfect. As the years ticked away, an ominous spell seemed to settle in around them and left them with nothing to hang onto. Finally, Jane moved out.

Her leaving gnawed at him, sent him picking at his food and taking long night walks along the Charles River. One night, he spotted a movement in the shadows so subtle it startled him. He listened for sounds, watched for additional movements before stepping forward. What he found was a round, furry black ball with huge pool eyes, a sturdy snout, and feet like paddles.

The puppy—Jake guessed three months or less—was in a cardboard box with food, water, and a blanket. Attached to the box was a typed message: "Landlord says one of us must go. Whoever finds him, please take care. Watty's special."

"Abandoned, huh?" Jake asked as the pup clawed his way over the top of the box and threw himself at Jake's feet. "Me too."

That was three years ago, and they'd been looking out for each other ever since.

Four miles outside of town on the Polpis Road past the Lifesaving Museum and the Field Station at Quaise, Jake slowed down and watched for the small weathered bungalow covered with roses. It was in the curve, just as Steven Treadle said it would be, as was the narrow, sandy road one hundred yards past it. Jake took the road to the left and headed for Polpis Harbor, a small, shallow anchorage used by those who could afford the house and the boat and the seclusion provided by this part of the island.

The entrance to Steven Treadle's driveway was a latticework bower shrouded in fog and large enough for a small truck to pass under. Jake drove through it and scattered a dozen grazing rabbits whose eyes flashed in the headlights as they darted off. Watson saw the kaleidoscope and perked up.

"Care to make chase?" Jake asked as he stopped the car in front of the house. "Go ahead, maybe one of us will catch something." He opened the door and Watson bolted into the darkness.

The house itself—a sprawling two-story saltbox dotted with skylights and enormous windows facing the harbor—was brightly lit. Jake was walking up the brick walk when the door opened.

"Mr. Eaton?"

"Steven Treadle?" Jake said and reached out for the obligatory hand-shake. The man was in his mid-fifties, with a thin face so wrinkled it re-minded Jake of a spider's web. He had a full head of brown hair streaked with lines of white. His pale blue eyes were wide with anticipation. Or maybe it was fright. Jake wasn't sure, but it was clear that Treadle was the picture of privilege, complete with strong, straight teeth, a well-cared-for body, and features produced by a genetic code that identified the car-rier as WASP.

"I apologize for the hour," Jake told him, glancing at his watch. It was nearly 4 A.M.

"Can't sleep anyway. Tried but . . . well . . . I see Nate. Nightmares, I guess. I was watching a movie when you called. Gene Kelly and Debbie Reynolds—Singing in the Rain. Third time today. Please, please come in," Treadle said. "At a time like this, we all need company, don't you think?"

"It helps, I guess," Jake said and entered a large, open living area exqui-sitely decorated with antiques and nautical artifacts, in shades of soft blues, grays, and browns. In the center of the room, a long staircase went up to the second floor, where a glass wall looked out over the water. Somehow, the dramatic house didn't fit Steven Treadle, the conservative man who liked to watch musicals. Jake's expression turned quizzical.

"My wife," Treadle explained. "She's a decorator. Marge? Marge, Mr. Eaton's here."

From the kitchen, Marjorie Treadle entered, carrying an inlaid wooden coffee tray. She was fiftyish, stylish, and pretty. She wore a polished-cotton chintz sundress with bare shoulders. Around her neck hung a string of small pearls. She seemed to Jake like the type who twenty years earlier would have walked around with the look of the unattainable.

"I saw the lights, dear. And a dog tracking something out front, right through the flower garden," she said, none too pleased.

"Mine," Jake said. "Good for him to be a dog sometimes. All this detective stuff drives him a little crazy."

"You're kidding," she said and set the tray down on a polished oval coffee table.

"Not kidding," Jake said. "His name's Watson. We're partners." Marjorie gave Steven a quick look that questioned Jake's sanity. "You could do worse," he said and took the offered coffee. "Thank you."

"Cream?" Marjorie asked.

"Black," Jake answered. He got right to it. "I understand that Nathan Cooper had lunch here the day he was killed."

"He did," Steven answered. "Along with Lucas Hendricks, the other board member of the Nantucket Preservation Society."

"I like to cook, Mr. Eaton, so Steven invites the others here for their meetings," Marjorie explained. "It's very informal. They sit on the patio when it isn't too breezy, looking out over the water and the dunes. That way they're surrounded by what they're trying to protect: the simple beauty of the island."

"Everyone always enjoyed it," Steven said with a sad, forced smile toward his wife, who tried gallantly to smile back. "But you don't think, do you, that what happened to poor Nathan had anything to do with the Society?"

"No, I don't," Jake answered. "Not directly."

"Good," Steven said, relieved. "The battle over who would finally purchase the Island Basin was, at times, quite heated. It crossed my mind—"

"You don't have to protect me, Steven," Marjorie said stiffly. "I'm more than willing to own up to what I said, which was that I wouldn't be at all surprised if the Gorhams were somehow behind this. I'm not the only one on the island who thinks this way. Harsh, I agree—maybe even cruel— but I wouldn't put it past them. They can be a mean lot, Mr. Eaton. And I guess you know you won't win any popularity contests on Nantucket by working for her."

"So I've gathered," Jake said. "But Gloria Gorham didn't have anything to do with this."

Marjorie straightened in her chair. "I didn't say she *did* it, Mr. Eaton. I just said I wouldn't put it past her, the way they came in here and threw their weight around. Unseemly. They didn't care one whit about the island, just grabbing up more property. And for what?"

"Marjorie . . . ," Steven cautioned, "it's not the time for this, dear."

"It is the time for it." She stared at her husband, unable to hide her anger. "The island hasn't been the same since they came back. Everybody knows that. If you have any doubts, just ask yourself why we're sitting here right now," she said, glancing at Jake, tears of exasperation filling her eyes.

Jake sipped his coffee, avoiding her look. He knew the futility of trying to defend his presence. He knew that words can do little for grief, less for fear. Private cops rarely bring good news; bearing bad news is part of the emotional cost of doing business. He put down his cup, buying time.

Steven Treadle reached over and took his wife's hand. He patted it gently, lovingly.

"I can't help it," she said to him. "It's how I feel, and now this business about murder . . . well, it's . . . I'm sorry," she said and stood, her eyes deep, teary wells. "I don't like it, that's all. And none of this happened before the Gorhams came. They should've stayed off the island." She looked squarely at Jake. "I just want to ask you one question, Mr. Eaton. Is my husband in any danger?"

"I don't believe so." He could see she needed something stronger, more definite, to help her out of her emotional quicksand. "No," he said firmly. "No, he's in no danger."

"Thank you," she said and turned away. Jake watched her ascend the stairs and felt sorry for her, as if his being there talking about Nate Cooper's death had undermined her sense that all was right with the world.

"I'm sorry," Steven said. "It's been quite a shock to us all. I don't really think she believes what she says about the Gorhams, it's just that Marjorie needs somebody to blame . . . somebody to yell at. Gloria Gorham's an easy target."

"I guess it helps to name the enemy," Jake said thoughtfully. "Even when you're wrong about who that enemy is."

"I suppose that's true," Treadle said and eyed Jake cautiously. "Except for someone like you. A professional, I mean. You can't afford to be wrong."

"No, I can't. That's why I asked to see you. I was hoping you might be able to help me."

"If I can, but you weren't very specific over the phone. What is it you think I can do?" Treadle asked reluctantly. "I mean, Nate and I were on the same board, but I don't have any notion whatsoever about why someone would want to kill him."

"Lucas Hendricks said the same thing."

"You talked to Lucas?"

"Yes," Jake answered.

"Out in his garden, I'd bet. Lucas takes all his bad news out back and buries it. Comforting, don't you think? All the flowers, the peace. I hide in old movies," he said sheepishly. "Musicals are the best. Old black and white musicals with production-number happy endings. That's the way life ought to be, Mr. Eaton. Production-number happy endings, not this terrible madness and murder. I guess that's why I prefer history to the present. When it gets too bloody, I just close the book."

"And if the book won't close?" Jake asked.

Treadle's face flushed. He got to his feet and paced uneasily about the room. Finally, he turned toward Jake. "I know what you must be thinking, Mr. Eaton. My friend lies dead and I do nothing. But what is it I'm supposed to do? I can't tell you any more than I told the police. To my knowledge, Nate had no enemies."

Jake nodded. "I think you're right."

"I'm right?" Treadle's brows furrowed. "I think you're playing tricks on me, trying to confuse me. How can I be right? The man died horribly. He's dead, for God's sake!"

Jake took another sip of coffee, put down the cup, and leaned back in his chair. "Believe me, the last thing I'm trying to do is confuse you. The truth is, I think you're one of the few men who can help make sense of this."

"That's what the police said," Treadle stammered. "But then they asked a thousand questions I couldn't answer and left me feeling like . . . like a stupid fool who let down his friend."

"You didn't let him down, Mr. Treadle, but you might if you don't give me a chance to explain." Jake waited as Treadle moved slowly back to his seat. When he was settled, Jake began. "Your wife said the island hasn't been the same since the Gorhams came back. Yet when I ask Gloria who from her past could hold a grudge against her or her family, she can't answer."

"I . . . I don't see the connection," Treadle said.

"The connection is, her life has been threatened."

"Threatened how?" He sounded as though he didn't really want the answer.

"To kill her," Jake said flatly. "She has no idea who, or why. All she knows is that by tomorrow, the Fourth of July, all hell is going to break loose."

Treadle was hunting for the thread. "And Nathan fits into this somehow?" he asked. "I can't imagine it."

"Then let me walk you through it. You're president of the Nantucket Historical Society."

Treadle nodded slightly. "That's right. Have been for ten years." Jake's expression coaxed him on. "I became a board member of the Nantucket Preservation Society five years ago when Nathan came to me with his idea about making the Island Basin reflect Nantucket's rich nautical history. That's my specialty, you know. Nautical history. I thought Nate's idea was a damn good one and still do, but I don't suppose anything will come of it now."

"Is that what your lunch meeting was about?"

"Yes. Nate, Lucas, and I were going to decide whether or not to come right out with it and ask Miss Gorham for space along Straight Wharf. Nothing much really. No property transfer or anything like that, just enough waterfront for a few working fishing boats. The little harbors in Maine still welcome the fishermen; we thought Nantucket ought to also. You ever been to Maine, Mr. Eaton?"

Jake nodded and watched as Steven Treadle slowly became more relaxed.

"Beautiful, isn't it? All those small, rocky harbors . . . islands everywhere . . . the cold blue water—and an amazing fleet of small fishing boats. A fishing boat in Maine would no more be unwelcomed at a dock than you and I could fly. But fishermen are not welcome here, and the Preservation Society wanted to change that. After all, this is where whaling started, and in 1723 Straight Wharf was literally the center of the whaling world. Can you believe that?" Treadle asked, his eyes sparkling as he spoke on his favorite subject. "The good people from this little island were sailing from here to England as early as 1720, delivering the whale oil they'd risked life and limb to get. Imagine it. A man of less than six feet rigged out in a wooden boat in an often miserable sea, hunting down a sixty-five-foot whale weighing one ton per foot. And these men did it, Mr. Eaton. They'd be gone for sometimes two years chasing the catch all over the world. I have great respect for the old sea captains. Great respect. That's one of the many things Lucas and I had in common with Nate Cooper. We all respected the island's beginnings."

"And what if in those beginnings," Jake asked eagerly, "were sown the seeds for Nate Cooper's death?"

Treadle sat upright, startled. "Where would you ever get such an idea?" he blurted. Jake handed him copies of the two threatening messages William had sent Gloria. As Treadle read them, his jaw dropped open. "My God," he said, unable to take his eyes from the pages in his hand. "I don't believe this."

"What I'm about to suggest may be harder to believe," Jake said. "Suppose, for the sake of argument, the phrase 'we go back so far' refers to something in the Gorhams' past that took place here on the island."

"Such as?"

"I don't know."

"Nantucket has a long history. The Indians were teaching the white man whaling in the early 1600s. I'd need something more to go on, something to narrow it down. Even if I started with the name *Gorham,* I'd be searching for a needle in a haystack," Treadle said, shaking his head. "Can't be done. Not in a matter of hours."

"You could try."

Treadle paused, sorting out these new facts in his mind. They didn't fall into place. "You've got to understand that the Gorhams go back to the founding of the island," he said. "I can't just begin at the beginning and start reading island history. I'm telling you there isn't time."

"Then start at the other end," Jake suggested. "When did the Gorhams leave Nantucket?"

"Ah, now *that* I know," he said, encouraged. "My wife asked that very question. The 1840s it was." He walked to a twelve-foot-high bookcase that lined one end of the long living room. "Nantucket's a funny place, Mr. Eaton. Not much has happened here that hasn't been written down. We can thank the Quakers for that. They were the first settlers, and a more compassionate, more charitable people never lived. But they also had an overblown sense of self-worth," he said as he took a heavy volume from the shelf. "They made records of everything, and I combined many of them in this reference for our use down at the Historical Society." He carried the book back to his seat, made room for it on the coffee table, and sat back down. "More coffee?" he asked.

"Please." Jake held his cup as Treadle poured.

"Besides old movies, I think being in a library and digging up odd facts is my second greatest pleasure," Treadle told him. "There's something very comforting and safe about it all." He opened the tome and ran his finger through the index. "Let's see here, G . . . G . . . G . . . Gorham. Yes, right. Libbeus Fitch Gorham, captain of the whaling bark *Zimmer,* left the island with his wife and three children in 1842." He tapped his finger under the name and scanned the page. "As far as the records show, they never came back to the island."

"Where did they sail to?" Jake asked.

"The mainland. New Bedford first, then in 1850, Boston. There are no entries after 1850."

Jake looked pensively at the historian. "Why'd they leave?" he asked.

"It doesn't say. The entry mentions Libbeus had a sale of property and belongings. That's all. But their departure isn't surprising. Many families left the island for other pursuits. I'm always amazed more didn't when you consider that if a captain were to make a profit, he had to sail the world, summer and winter, sometimes not coming home for three years, sometimes not ever. He chased the common right whale and bowheads around Cape Horn, across to New Zealand, to Japan, and even under the Arctic ice floes. It was an unimaginably hard life, and although I can't prove it, I think the demise of whaling was a blessing for some families. In the 1840s it was clear to many men that whaling was on the way out: petroleum was replacing whale oil, so they left the island. In some cases, there wasn't any choice. Like I said, Nantucket was the very center of whaling. The island was full of riggers, coopers, sailmakers, helmsmen, forecastle hands, and men with every other skill needed to prepare a ship for sea. When the fleet got smaller and the men's services were no longer needed, many families moved away. My guess is that Libbeus Fitch Gorham was one of those. When there was no use for his ship and his ability, he just sold out and left."

"What about his father?" Jake asked. "Was his father here on the is-land as well?"

Treadle again ran his finger down the list in the index. "Apparently so. His father, his father before him, his father before that, all the way back to when Mayhew Gorham arrived on Nantucket in 1697 from Plymouth. A lot of Quakers moved here from Plymouth back then. The Quakers couldn't stand the Puritans and the Puritans were well entrenched in the colonies. You know anything about that period, Mr. Eaton?"

"Not much."

"Fascinating, really," he said. Jake could see that Treadle could talk on for hours. "The Puritans left England for economic and religious rea-sons," Treadle continued, "but when they set up shop over here, so to speak, they were just as intolerant. Oliver Wendell Holmes put it best when he said that the Puritans drove a nail through the human heart and the Quak-ers wanted to pull the nail and dress the wound. Not believing in fighting one's fellow man, the Quakers would move on. Many of them came to Nantucket, as did Mayhew Gorham." Treadle was reading from the book again. "Mayhew married Rebecca Odem two years later. They had two boys, Obed and Zeke. Zeke died in childhood." Treadle looked up from the book with a gleam in his eyes. He reminded Jake of Watson on the trail of a rabbit. "Obed might be the one you're after."

"How so?" Jake asked as Treadle went back to the bookshelf and pulled down another smaller volume.

"Because of a scandal. If memory serves me, the Gorham name was associated with one of the island's first moneymaking scandals." Treadle flipped through the book. "Let me see . . . here. Here we go," he said and read momentarily to himself, moving his lips and mumbling as he did. He turned one page, then another and stopped abruptly, looking up at Jake curiously. "Good Lord."

Jake pushed forward in his chair. "What is it?" he asked.

"Not what—who." Treadle was staring straight at Jake. "Benjamin Cooper was involved as well. Nathan had spoken of him often."

"A relative?"

Treadle nodded as a smile spread across his lips. "A distant uncle," he said, his attention turned back to the book. "I'd forgotten all about this. Yes—Gorham, Brown, and Cooper." He looked hopefully at Jake. "This might be it," he said as he sat down. "Dear God, it just might be."

"You mentioned three names," Jake reminded him.

"Yes, Obediah Brown."

Jake let his hope rise. "If Obediah Brown accused the Coopers or the Gorhams—"

Treadle cut him off. "Yes, yes. There was finger pointing everywhere once the longboat went down. But let's start at the beginning. The trouble all began with a whale—only this whale was very special." Treadle closed the book and put it beside him. He clasped his hands together across his knees and began. "In the early 1700s a type of whale that had never before been taken was harpooned just south of here. Mostly common right whales had been hunted around these waters, but what was killed this day was a sperm whale—called by many the aristocrat of all whales because hidden in his bulky head was a reservoir two feet wide and six feet deep of pure oil. When exposed to air, this sperm oil turned waxy. It hardened right up and burned far cleaner than regular wax candles. Obed Gorham saw the means to making a better mousetrap, so to speak, and soon was making candles out of whale oil spermaceti, as it was called. In no time, spermaceti candles became a very important industry."

"Sounds harmless enough," Jake said.

"It was, until Obed and his partners Obediah Brown and Benjamin Cooper—recognizing the value of this sperm oil—made a deal with the Nantucket whalers not to sell the oil to anyone else but them."

"A cartel."

Treadle nodded. "Sort of. Today it'd be called an illegal monopoly. With Obed and his partners in control of all the oil, they could make a fortune manufacturing, selling, and distributing the finest candles in the world, all over the world. They'd be rich, all of them."

Jake sipped his coffee. "So what happened?"

"Obed bought hundreds and hundreds of barrels of sperm oil, driving up the price with each ship that tied up at the dock and unloaded." Treadle was back in the book, searching. "When the price was at its peak, one Nantucket captain—that's what I'm looking up here . . . Captain . . . Captain, yes Captain Winslow and the fifteen barks under his command—sailed to New Bedford and sold to the highest bidder."

"Down came the cartel," Jake said knowingly.

"That's right. Not immediately, but in a matter of months Obed Gorham, Obediah Brown, and Benjamin Cooper were broke," Treadle said and closed the book.

Jake finished his coffee. "What happened to Winslow?"

"He became a very wealthy man, although not very well respected, so the story goes. But," Treadle smiled slyly, "like most incidents in history, this wasn't the end of something, it was just the beginning. Not long after Obed Gorham went broke, a longboat with six men aboard rowing supplies out to the *Mary D* got caught in a squall. In the storm the load shifted and the longboat sank, killing all six men. The speculation was that Obed Gorham, Obediah Brown, or Benjamin Cooper had something to do with their deaths."

"Like tampering with the load?"

"Perhaps. No one really knows."

"Sailors drown, Mr. Treadle. Maybe there's nothing to it except bad luck."

"Maybe. Except that all six men had sailed with Captain Winslow on the New Bedford oil run that ruined Obed Gorham and partners, and the *Mary D* was Winslow's personal ship."

"Any formal charges ever filed?"

"None," Treadle answered. "There was nothing to go on but rumor and hearsay."

Jake nodded. "Everyone pointing fingers at everyone else, as you said. Who were the six men who drowned?"

"I don't know," Treadle said and felt the weight of the task sink in on him. "I'll have to look that up as well as what I have on Brown. He may have felt betrayed by his partners. I don't know where it will lead, but I'll do my best."

"Anything I can do to help?" Jake asked.

"There might be."

"Name it," Jake said.

"I'd like to talk with Miss Gorham. She might be able to help narrow the focus on her family's side."

"Done," Jake said and left Steven Treadle digging through the history of his island.

Chapter

——18——

William was looking out for the *Dolfin* in a thick fog that covered the island in a damp, eerie stillness. He motored slowly through the harbor in Gibby Bennett's stolen dinghy, his engine the only sound on the water. Once he saw the *Dolfin,* he hit the kill switch and drifted up alongside his tender. He transferred the bulky package from Gibby's dinghy to his own, then climbed aboard. Letting Bennett's small boat drift into the current, he pulled himself around to the *Dolfin*'s transom and took a speargun and two small bags of explosives from the aft locker.

Rowing hard in the quiet and foggy darkness, he headed toward North Wharf. With each powerful stroke, he made silent headway on the flat, calm sea. In minutes, he was easing past the cottages on North Wharf and gliding toward the lights on the Steamship Authority's cement docks. The passenger ferry *Eagle,* the largest of the line, was tied to the north side, bathed from the deckhouse to the waterline in harsh light. In the fog the huge, triple-decked white ship looked like a photograph taken through sheets of fuzzy gauze, a gauze that he hoped would conceal him from the guards he'd seen the previous night patrolling the ship from the mezzanine deck.

Fine with him. Let them guard all they want, get overconfident, he thought. He'd surveyed the ship closely when he'd sabotaged her fuel tanks, and found that he could get on and off in minutes through an opening in the aft hydraulic cargo hatch.

William rowed out twenty yards for one last look, then turned toward the ship. With each gentle stroke, he concentrated on the tasks before him, still finding it difficult to grasp the power he held. What happened in the next few hours would make him—William Rice—someone Nantucket would never forget.

With great care, he lifted the oars from their locks and slid alongside the *Eagle*'s steel hull directly under the aft cargo hatch. Huge, pistonlike arms would crank open the doors high and wide enough for cars and trucks to drive through. When the ferry was tied to the dock, the hatch was cracked open so fresh air could circulate. It was through that opening that William boarded the ship.

Without a load of cargo, the interior of the ferry looked like a long stripped tunnel painted white and lighted with glaring bulbs mounted along the bulkheads. William moved quickly. At each end of the ship was a confusion of wires and pipes coming down from the floor above; next to them were the engines used to open the cargo doors. William crawled behind the engines and set two charges at the waterline. One could blow the bottom out of the ship, scuttling her in minutes. The second he set for insurance, then connected them both to a remote timing device he carried with him.

He left the ship as quietly as he'd come and rowed toward the yacht club, threading his way through the fleet of small boats that club members used for lessons and day sails, until the dinghy slid gently through the shallows and up onto the sand of Children's Beach. Without a sound, he shipped oars, stepped from the boat, and pulled it above the high-water line so the tide wouldn't float it off. A nervous tension flashed through him as he removed the package and speargun and climbed the retaining wall.

It was just after four in the morning on July 3, and the streets and surrounding park were empty. Even so, William took no chances. He had come too far and was too close to his goal to screw it up now, so he waited and watched even though instinct told him that the way was clear.

Finally he crept through the fog to the Downyflake, an early risers' breakfast hangout. The flagpole that hung above the door was bare, the restaurant empty. It would normally open at 5:30, but Will figured that it would not open at all today. Not after the cook or the waitress or the owner came down the street and saw Gibby Bennett's bloody arm swinging gently above the door in the early morning breeze.

What would they think? Will wondered as he worked a line through the pulley and tied a double hitch around the exposed bone. When they saw a man's arm hanging there, its hand sculptured so the finger pointed in a splendidly accusing way, what would they think? He wished he could be there to see the horror on their faces, the shock of it all, followed by dreaded worry of what the murderer would do next.

Wait and see, thought William, smiling to himself as a cold, fat drop of sweat rolled down his back. He was having the time of his life.

When he'd finished tying the arm, he hoisted it onto the pole so it hung at eye level. No one had driven by, no one had seen him, yet a jangle of nerves pumped a stream of sweat from him as he made his way back to the dinghy to retrieve the bags. Each bag contained four powerful explosives, enough firepower to blow craters in the airport's runways, to make taking off and landing impossible. But before he set those charges, he had a bit of unfinished business with the soon-to-be-dead Eaton and his black dog.

Heading down Easy Street, William had never felt so powerful, so alive. He'd wrapped the speargun in the old blanket—now spotted with Gibby Bennett's blood—and moved swiftly down the docks, bouncing on raggedy strands of energy. In his mind he saw how it would happen. Eaton would be asleep in the forward cabin. The dog? He wasn't sure where the dog would be—that's why he carried the speargun. Even out of the water he could fire it true enough for a kill shot at fifteen feet or so. He'd nail the dog first. Eaton would hear the ruckus and come flying out of the bunk. Only this time, William Rice thought, there would be nowhere for Jake to run.

Past the gas dock William quickened his pace, anticipating the pleasure that would be his in minutes. With Eaton out of the way, he could play Gloria Gorham like a marionette. It will be pure joy, he thought, and ran toward the blue-hulled wooden boat.

What minutes ago was a thin ribbon of light floating above the horizon was now an early morning sun producing a muggy gray glow in the fog. Rice scanned the Island Basin, making sure he was alone before he stepped over *Gamecock*'s lifeline and onto the deck. The heavy sloop didn't move an inch under his weight.

Quietly, he slid his way aft. He was surprised that the dog hadn't noticed him. Not that it would have mattered. Rice was in complete control, overtaken by the same calm self-assurance he'd felt before he'd killed Nate Cooper and Gibby Bennett.

His worst fear had been that he'd be so jittery that apprehension would replace purpose and he'd be vulnerable even to someone smaller and slower than he was. But that was before. He knew now that no one could stop him. He jerked open the door just to prove it.

He leaped down the companionway to the cabin sole and rushed forward to the sleeping cabin. He yanked open the door, then froze in disappointment. The cabin was empty.

Rice's heart sank. "Sonofabitch," he muttered under his breath and roamed back through the yacht, his rage verging on madness. Angrily, he swung the speargun across the table and knocked a bottle of Remy Martin and a glass to the floor. A swift kick smashed through the louvered doors under the chart table. He was well on his way to ripping the old boat apart for the second time when he caught himself and stopped the carnage. He stood trembling, taking deep breaths.

Someone was coming down the finger pier toward him. He could hear the footfall on the dock. He eased toward the forward cabin, opened the door, and backed in, the speargun cocked and ready. He pulled the door shut and waited.

Come right on in, he thought as someone stepped onboard and moved into the cockpit. The footsteps came down the short companionway ladder and entered the cabin. William heard glass being stepped on, then silence. A crack of light appeared around the door as the cabin lights flashed on. Now's the time, he thought, and threw open the door.

The head of the foot-long arrow sank six inches into Sam Kingsbury's chest as a look of horrific agony crossed his face. He fell back against the navigation station, his hands closing around the arrow's shaft.

"You BAST . . . BASTARD!" Kingsbury gasped as William closed in on him. "Jesus Christ, help me!" he cried and held his chest with both hands. What was happening? Who was this madman coming after him?

In the tiny space they circled each other, Sam strangely aware of stepping on broken glass and of the fact that he very well might be dying.

"Whoever you are," he wheezed to the man, "help me. Please."

But William kept coming. In an instant, Kingsbury's survival instincts took over. Without hesitation he charged forward, the pain nearly unbearable as he grabbed his attacker around the neck. With all his strength, Sam bore down on the man in a death grip. William fell back heavily against the galley counter, gasping for breath against the relentless pressure. With his free hand, he grabbed the arrow's shaft sticking out of Sam's chest and pushed with all his might, lunging like a crude fencer until the razor-sharp point tore through Kingsbury's back.

Sam roared with blinding pain and fell across the table in agony. He was helpless. Will went after him again, grabbing his neck this time in a stranglehold. Kingsbury was too incapacitated to fight and too scared to die. He knew his only chance was to let the world know that someone was trying to kill him. With all the energy he could manage, he bellowed like a wounded animal until William mercilessly choked off his breathing.

Sam's face contorted from the lack of oxygen, his complexion turning a reddish blue. Rice tightened his grip until Sam slipped from the table to the floor, motionless.

William quickly turned his attention to those who might have heard the screams. After what he'd done to Nate Cooper, he was certain that most boats were filled with light, nervous sleepers wanting nothing more than to get off the island.

Let them try, Will thought. Just let them try.

In an instant, he was up the companionway and off *Gamecock,* carrying the two bags of explosives. As he moved down the finger pier toward Whales Way, small groups of men were beginning to gather along the docks, trying to keep alive the fragile camaraderie that the need for survival had stitched among them. Rice clutched the bags to his chest like bags of dirty clothes and stepped into the laundry room to avoid the men.

"Did you hear that?" one man said.

"Damn right."

"Jesus." There was fear in the voice.

"You think somebody else got . . . you know, got killed?"

"Where'd the sound come from? Which way?" The man was in a robe, looking around in the predawn light.

"Over there I think."

"Well?"

"Well, it's scary, that's all."

"Damn right it is. That's why we're leaving on the tide this morning."

"Us too."

"That scream. Just how it started the other night. Some woman screamed, and then there he was, harpooned to the dock."

"Coulda been any one of us."

"You think I haven't thought about that?" The man was shuffling his feet. "I can't get outta here soon enough."

"I'm never coming back. My wife wouldn't set foot back here if you gave her the place."

A youngish man yawned and ran his fingers through his uncombed hair. "Just let the sonofabitch try anything around me," he said. "Be the last thing he ever tries."

"Oh, yeah?"

"Believe it."

"Sure. How come you're not over there? That's where the hollering came from. Somewhere near that blue boat."

"Where's the cops?" another said. "Somebody call the cops."

"And get another day of the same old questions? My wife's gonna have this boat on the market if it comes to that. I'm gettin' the hell outta here." He moved off.

"I'm right behind ya."

"Me too."

"Don't ya think somebody ought to call the police?"

"And tell 'em what? Something scared you out of bed? I'm telling you man, just let that bastard near me. I'll break him in half."

William had heard every word and thought about walking up to the man— Sam Kingsbury's blood soaked through his shirt—and saying, Here I am, fuckhead. Start breakin'. But he didn't have time. Jake had just turned the corner in his station wagon and was sliding to a hard stop near the small group of troubled men.

"What's going on?" Jake asked. "What's happened?"

"Somebody needs help." The man wasn't looking at Jake, the voice sheepish.

"Who?" Jake demanded.

"We haven't . . . We don't know, but it sounded like it came from—"

Jake cut him off when the man pointed in *Gamecock*'s direction. "Call the police," Jake ordered. "Call the police and get back onboard your boats. Move it," Jake said, then told Watson to stay in the car.

He pulled his .38 and scanned the area, his eyes following the outlines of the docks, the cabins, and the masts. A thousand places to hide. But when Jake saw him, he wasn't hiding. He was running in a slow, half-leisurely gait down Straight Wharf.

Jake recognized the man immediately from his trip south—a tall, large-boned, slab-muscled man. Jake remembered his rough-looking face and a cruel, uneven smile that even in the Florida heat was chilling. Wilson Randall he'd called himself. Wilson Randall with those huge, dirty mechanic's hands, standing among the engine parts and denying he'd ever heard of anyone named Gorham.

At this early morning hour, the wharf and street were empty. Jake raised his revolver and sighted in the man, following him along just far enough so the feel of the gun was natural and easy. "One warning, Randall," Jake hollered out. "Stop right there."

William bolted at the sound of Jake's voice and ran even faster when the hollow-nosed soft-point splintered the edge of the wooden bench just in front of him.

Jake fired again, but Will ducked low and to the left as if he knew where the shot was aimed. Lucky bastard, Jake thought. His heart jerked with a frantic thump when he sensed that someone had moved up behind him. He whipped the .38 around and froze at the sight. Sam Kingsbury had crawled on all fours down Old South Wharf where he now knelt, rocking back and forth, side to side. Clutched in his bloody right hand was a speargun arrow.

Jake ran to him. "Don't try to talk," he said.

Kingsbury's voice was a raspy whisper. "Somebody . . . on . . . *Gamecock,*" he forced out. "Attacked . . . when . . . I . . ."

"Sam, don't talk," Jake said, vaguely aware of sirens and doors slamming and footsteps.

"Just doin' . . . my . . . my job . . . tell . . . Miss . . ."

"I will, don't worry," Jake said and cradled the poor man like a child. I'll tell her she's finally killed someone, he thought as he laid Sam gently down.

Sam moaned like a wounded bull, wheezed, and closed his eyes. Through his dry lips came puffs of parched sound. "Peh . . . pehrnns . . . prens . . . peh . . ."

Jake bent closer. "What?"

But there was no answer, nothing but the sound of Patrolman Shean—revolver drawn—running toward him. "We got the call," he said. "Gunfire at the Basin, we—" Sam's ragged chest wound stopped him in his tracks. He turned toward the railing as his stomach heaved. "Jesus Christ."

Jake stood beside him, quiet for a moment, then said with considerable sympathy in his voice, "There's no time for that now. The man we're after—the man who did this—ran down Straight Wharf. Take some men—"

The young officer gaped at Jake in astonishment. "Take some men? What in the hell are you saying?" he asked, nearly sick again.

"I'm saying we've got a job to do."

"No," Shean said. He shook his head, trying to force his mind blank and erase the picture of Sam's chest and the other horrors he'd recently witnessed. "I'm not taking any men anywhere. I'm not doing anything. I can't."

"If you don't, who will?"

"I don't care. I don't want to know about any of it, and if you want the truth, after this morning I don't think Mayor Tillis or Chief Sinclair does either."

"What are you talking about?" Jake asked. A prickly chill ran down his back even before Shean turned his stunned face toward him.

"A man's arm," Shean said without emotion. He was spent, gone. "That's what we found this morning hanging from a flagpole. A man's arm cut right out of the socket. 'Butchered' is what Andy Tillis called it. Somebody on the island's been butchered like an animal."

Chapter

——19——

"Butchered?"

The patrolman's head jerked a yes, his gaze fixed nervously on Kingsbury. "That's what Tillis said." He looked up at Jake. "He said to come get you—you'd know what to do—but the mayor didn't know about this," Shean said, dazed. "Is he dead?"

"He's dead," Jake said, his face set in determination. "Where can I find Tillis?"

The patrolman jerked his hand in the general direction of north. "The Downyflake, over on Children's Beach," he said as Jake took off.

"Get the medical examiner down here," Jake shouted back at him. "And keep the crowds away from the crime scene."

"I'm not in charge here," the officer called after him. "And neither are you."

Jake stopped, took a breath, walked back to the young officer, and stood directly in front of him. "It's time to grow up, boy," Jake said. "It's time for a lot of people around here to grow up. Sam Kingsbury is dead because he was doing his job. Now, you're going to do yours." Jake closed his fists tightly. "Do I make myself clear?"

Officer Shean nodded as Jake continued a slow, steady burn.

"Good." Jake was indignant. "Take care of the body and deal with the crowds. Help people get ready to pull out of the Basin or whatever it takes to keep it quiet down here. Understood?"

The young officer kept his eyes on Jake. "Understood."

"Fine," Jake said and again turned to leave. He pushed himself through lines of people staring at Kingsbury past misery. When Jake got into the car, Watson withheld his usual enthusiastic greeting. He could see the anger in Jake's dark face and sense the inevitable explosion.

Jake started the car and floored it, racing the few blocks to Gloria Gorham's apartment. He and Watson ran up the flight of stairs. Jake banged on her door with both fists.

When she opened it, Gloria asked bitingly, "Trying to knock down the house?"

"It's not what I'd like to knock down, but you haven't volunteered," he said and entered. Watson followed, his attention zeroing in on the tense current already circling the room.

"What are you doing here at this hour?" she asked curtly. "Let me guess— hurt pride." She stood rigid, challenging him as she pulled the white terrycloth robe tighter at the waist. "Sam thought better of it and phoned me about the fight you and he had earlier this morning. I figured if you were angry enough, you'd eventually show up."

"Had that figured, did you?"

She seemed proud of herself. "Yes."

"Just like the rest of it, right? Had it all figured down to the wire."

"I don't know what you mean."

"Of course you do. Whisking me off to Florida, then not wanting me to come to Nantucket so you could play your little games with the mayor. You two had it all figured, and you figured you could handle it. Nate Cooper's death was just an oversight."

Gloria bristled. "I think that's quite enough."

"Exactly what I thought," Jake said. "Seems to me we even had a conversation about it, when was that? Seems like a hundred years ago but it was just yesterday morning when I stepped off the plane. I was going to do my job and you were going to stay out of it. Remember?"

"I have stayed out of it," she fought back, adding, "You are in my employ, just as Sam Kingsbury is. I suggest you not forget it."

Jake gave her a cold look. "Why don't you fire me?" he challenged.

"Maybe I will," she shot back.

"And don't forget old Sam," Jake demanded. "You going to fire him too?"

"Not as long as he does what I say."

"Like keep an eye on the Island Basin?"

Gloria could feel Jake's anger. "Yes," she replied and stepped back. Like Watson, she too felt an imminent explosion.

"Wonderful!" Jake's arms shot out and slapped down against his sides. "I knock some sense in his head and you put him right back out there on the front line. Dumb, Miss Gorham. Stupid."

"I think you're upset because he was doing your job. A job I wasn't too sure you could do in the first place," she said bitterly, then cocked her head forward with an irritating smile. "Now, I'm convinced of it."

Jake angrily ignored her. "I knocked more sense into him than you've got, but he was right back out there sticking his big, ugly face where it didn't belong. You did order him back down there?"

"I did."

Jake didn't hesitate. "Then you killed him, Miss Gorham. Not an easy thing to do when you get right down to it. Most states have given up putting men to death, but you've managed to kill two."

She stiffened, her eyes on fire. "I don't have to take that," she said, her thoughts swirling. Sam dead? "I . . . I don't believe you." She turned to walk away.

Jake grabbed her wrists and squeezed until a look of pain settled in her eyes. "You *do* have to take it," he said, staring at her coldly.

"You're hurting me."

"He died at my feet, Gloria. Last night I sent him home where he belonged. This morning he's dead on the dock because he listened to you." Gloria tried to jerk her wrists away and failed. "Big, tough Gloria Gorham. You just can't stay out of it, can you?" Jake asked bitterly and abruptly let her go as if he couldn't stand to touch her.

Gloria stood facing him, rubbing the ache from his savage grip. "Is that all?" she asked finally.

"All except for the speargun," Jake answered. "It wasn't a quick death, Miss Gorham. It was hell."

Gloria stood unyielding, as if she'd been slapped. She looked at Jake for a long time before turning away and walking to the tile-covered counter that separated the kitchen from the living room. She kept her back to him and stared straight ahead for what seemed like hours. "Wou . . . would . . . ?" Her voice was in there somewhere. "Would you like some coffee?" she finally asked. For the first time in her life, Gloria Gorham felt like giving up.

"You've got to stay out of this," Jake said coldly to her back.

At first she was stone solid, then she hunched forward and put her face in her hands. Jake couldn't hear her, but the way her body shook, he knew she was sobbing.

He went to her and put his arm gently around her shoulders, as he'd done many times when his ex-wife's eyes burned with absolute frustration at the thought that the man she'd married was not the man she wanted to be with. An uneasy flicker swept through Jake. Such beautiful and fragile women, he thought. So beautiful and vulnerable. Even though he'd tried, he hadn't been much help to either one.

"Look . . ."

"Leave me alone," she sobbed. "I didn't want him to get hurt. I haven't wanted anyone to get hurt. I just want this to be over."

"Then you've got to stay out of it and trust me," he said. "We've got just under twenty-four hours, and I don't want to spend any of that time worrying about you out there playing detective."

She gathered herself, taking long, deep breaths. Was this what it felt like to surrender? she wondered. To fail? To be all the things that Gorhams were not supposed to be? Finally, she turned toward Jake, her eyes filled with sorrow and certitude. "I'm sorry about Sam. I'm sorry about all of it." She spoke with the quietness of people after a storm that had drowned out their voices.

Jake stroked her hair softly. "So am I," he said and held her closer. "You don't have to say any more."

"But I do," she said, tilting her head up toward his. "I've been lying awake nights wondering why I'm here. Why I'm really doing this."

"You're carrying on the family tradition. You're back on Nantucket."

"Those are my father's reasons for being here," she said. "Not mine." With the flat of her hand, she wiped the tears from her cheeks. She took a step away from Jake. Gloria looked him clearly in the eyes and asked, "Do you think people determine their own lives?"

"The small parts," Jake answered. "The big ones take care of themselves."

"Unless you have money." Gloria pulled in a deep breath that seemed to relax her. "Money lets people make plans that stretch far into the future. My mother had big plans for me. My father had big plans for me. The only time I heard them argue was over their big plans for me."

"You don't have to tell me this."

"No, but I want to. You don't have to listen."

He wanted to. "Go on. Please."

Gloria leaned back against the counter and folded her arms across her chest. "I told you that when I was at Harvard, I spent a lot of time walking along the Charles River thinking about *my* future, about my big plans—no one else's—for me. Do you know what they always came down to?

Happiness. I wanted to systematically practice the only thing in life worth learning: how to make myself perpetually happy."

"How'd it come out?"

Gloria paused. Finally, she said, "Not very well. I wouldn't be having an affair with a married man if I had all the answers. All I know is that for some moments, Richard Graham makes me very happy. But when I try to stretch the moment into hours and days, it collapses all around me. It's always been that way. I seem to have these involuntary and repetitive confrontations with love. Babies and marriage certificates seem like some faraway dream."

"Is that what you want?"

"Right now I want to stay alive."

"Then we should get you off the island where William can't find you."

"I already turned down Lewis Metcalf on that suggestion. I'm not leaving." Gloria ran her fingers through her hair. "I know you don't understand," she said, "but the reason I'm on the island in the first place is because I want to run my own life. No one is going to run it for me, least of all William."

"I can understand that," Jake said.

"Then you can't expect me to run and hide." There was a strange calmness in her voice. "I *won't* run and hide and that's all there is to it."

Jake looked at her curiously.

"What are you thinking?" she asked.

He wasn't certain himself, yet he stepped forward and took her face in his hands. At that instant, it became the only thing in his world; her head was tilted back with cheeks winged and wide as if a sculptor had been at work. Looking deep into her eyes, he felt something nearly palpable pass between them. She put her arms around him and held tight.

"I'm not very good at making people happy, Jake."

"Neither am I."

"I try."

"We all do."

"Why doesn't it ever work out?" The question stuck in his mind like glue, clogging his brain. "Jake?"

He was a thousand miles away.

"Jake?" Gloria unwrapped her arms after three loud rings. "The phone," she said, picking it up. "Hello?"

"Miss Gorham? Steven Treadle here. I know it's early, but a private detective—"

"He's right here," she said.

"Oh, then you know why I'm calling and understand its importance."
No, she wanted to say. No, at the moment I don't understand a thing.
Treadle kept talking.
"Who is it?" Jake finally asked.
Gloria told him.
"Tell him to add one more name to the list: Wilson Randall."

Sylvia Fine lowered her voice, but it still carried her anger and fear.
They were free to go, Officer Shean had announced over the bullhorn
to all Island Basin guests. Free to go whenever they wanted, but as always Murray wasn't fast enough, and Sylvia had a feeling they'd never
get out.
   "*Right now,* Murray," she said. "Not one more minute. I want out of
here now or I'm taking a cab to the airport!"
   "And leave me to single-hand this thing?" Murray said and tried to imagine
how he'd manage thirty-eight feet of charter sailboat by himself. Judging
boat speed in and out of slips was not one of his strong points. "I can't
do it by myself, so don't get any ideas about running off. This is *our* vacation,
remember? Ours."
   "Whose?"
   "Ours."
   "Not anymore, Murray. Not after this morning and that man dying right
there before my eyes," she said, throwing a few things in an overnight
bag. "You can have Nantucket. I'm going back to New York where the
odds of staying alive are better."
   "Sylvia—"
   "This trip wasn't my idea anyway. Who wanted the mountains?"
   "Italian mountains, Sylvia. You wanted Italian mountains."
   "So?"
   "You didn't want American mountains, Sylvia. You wouldn't even consider
American mountains at fifteen hundred a week."
   "I'm not talking money, Murray. I'm talking life," she said. She climbed
out into the cockpit, where she saw families in other boats coiling lines,
stowing fenders, and getting ready to leave the Island Basin. "Looks like
I'm not alone," she commented as Murray stepped up beside her.
   "I'm hurrying as fast as I can," Murray said.
   "Not fast enough. Like always, Murray. Not fast enough." Sylvia slapped
the ignition key into her husband's chubby hand. "Start the engine," she
ordered. "If you won't take us out of here, I will."

Twenty minutes later Murray Fine was the first captain backing his boat out of an Island Basin slip. Sylvia stood on the bow and fended him off the portside pilings as the sleek yawl eased gently into the IB's interior turning basin. Once clear, Sylvia gave Murray the okay sign, and he slid the transmission lever from reverse into forward. In seconds the twenty-five-ton yacht stopped moving back and lay calm in the protected waters. Before Murray gave the thirty-horse Yanmar more power, he was aware of people standing on their decks waving.

"Be right behind ya, cap," someone hollered as Murray increased power. "Place'll be empty before noon."

"Good sailing."

"You too," Murray said, waving, his confidence rising as it always did when he made the boat do what he wanted instead of the other way around. When Sylvia got back to the cockpit, he put his arm around her waist. "Nothin' to it," he said, smiling.

Sylvia smiled back. "You're my captain, Murray. Sometimes it takes a mutiny to get you to realize it, that's all."

He nodded sheepishly and turned the big boat to port, staying well in the middle of the turning basin. Off to starboard were the last finger pier slips at Old South Wharf. Straight ahead was the opening between the two bulkheads that led to the main harbor, the channel, and home.

"More power," he said, and Sylvia throttled up the diesel.

The opening was twenty yards away, and Murray kept looking around for someone else to wave to, but most were too busy getting ready to follow him out.

"Maybe we'll get out of here after all," Murray said and pushed the throttle forward once again.

The big yawl was about to pass between the two bulkheads when she shuddered violently, rose up on her board as if she'd run hard aground, and came to a crushing halt, blocking the only water exit from the Island Basin. Murray cut the engine and looked over the side.

"Jesus Christ," he muttered.

His wife's face was ashen. "What is it? What's happened?"

Murray couldn't believe his eyes. "There's a boat down there," he gasped.

Sylvia was staring down at the water. Below their sailboat, which was now teetering on its centerboard, she saw the vague outline of a large power cruiser. "It *is* a boat, Murray." She said it but she didn't believe it.

"A what?" It was the voice of another captain making ready to pull out.

"A boat, goddamnit!" Murray Fine shouted. "We've run over a fucking boat! None of us are going anywhere!"

On board the *Dolfin* looking through his binoculars, William Rice could almost read the captain's lips. Not just any boat. No sir, mister pleasure boat captain. What you have run over is my ticket to paradise. I thank you very much, Rice thought, as he watched the docks fill with anxious, and trapped, onlookers. With the *Betsy* sunk between the bulkheads, there was no way out.

Content, William lay back, listening to the water lap against the hull of the *Dolfin*. The sun had finally burned away all the fog. It had turned into a bright and beautiful July morning after all.

Chapter

—20—

The Downyflake was closed for the day, wrapped like some horrible present in yellow barrier plastic with Nantucket Police Department stamped across it every foot or so. Jake ducked under the tape and opened the screen door on an empty takeout counter. The kitchen was behind the counter to the right; from the left in the dimly lit eating area came the heated voice of the man Jake was looking for.

"Come on, Roger," Sinclair shouted at a man sitting across from him in a wooden booth painted with black enamel. "We need it now! We need it fast! Those folks at the Basin aren't going to wait all day!"

"Best I can do," Roger Dolby said firmly. He removed his baseball cap and scratched his tanned and wrinkled forehead. He was a small, chunky man with a passion for bad cigars. He tapped the ash of the one he was smoking into the tray and popped the wet end back into his mouth. "These ain't airplanes, Russ," he added. "These are tugboats."

"And this is police business," Sinclair barked, his hands clasped in front of him across the table.

Roger Dolby, of Dolby's Nantucket Fuel, put his cap back on and spoke as if Chief Russell Sinclair weren't there. "Tugboats are slow, Russ. Slow and booked solid. I don't carry 'em around in my hip pocket. They're all over the damn place."

"Where's the closest?"

"The closest with a crane is in Chatham, dredging, and you need a crane, Russ. The only way you're gonna get that boat hauled is with the right equipment, which means a barge crane, a tug to pull her over here, and divers. I got all three, but you're gonna have to wait," Dolby said, puffing on his cigar.

"Where are the divers?" Sinclair wanted to know.

"Oh, they're here on the island somewhere."

The chief freed his hands and slapped them on the table. "Get 'em," he said. "Get 'em down here right now."

"Can do," Roger said calmly, "but it's still gonna take time to haul that boat."

"How much time?"

"Ten to fifteen hours," he said behind a cloud of bluish smoke. "The divers can be ready anytime, but it's gonna take a good ten to fifteen hours to pack up, secure the crane to the barge for hauling and then pull her over here. A few more hours to set up . . . better say fifteen to be safe. Fifteen to twenty hours oughtta do it," he said, looking at his watch. "If we push it, we might be in here and ready to haul by midnight."

Sinclair shook his head. "Not soon enough. Tonight is the Fourth of July."

"Can't be helped, Russ," Dolby said.

"Then don't waste any more time. Get to it."

"Okay, chief," Dolby said and stood. "I'll put the call into the Cape."

"Have the divers stand by," Sinclair said. "I'd like them to take a look at what's down there before we do anything else."

"Will do. I'll have 'em wait off the float on Commercial Street," Dolby said as he walked past Jake with a nod. At the door, he stopped. "You sure you got a handle on this, Russ?"

"Yeah, Roger. I've got a handle on it."

"Folks are worried. Some of 'em are damn scared," Roger said. "What's next—you know?"

"What's next is a good arrest, Rog. We're closing in. Anybody asks, you tell 'em I said we're closing in and fast."

"How fast?" Dolby wanted to know.

"Twenty-four hours," Sinclair said without hesitation. "Before you get that boat hauled and the channel open, we'll have the man who killed Nate Cooper. Anybody asks, you tell 'em that."

Dolby considered it and seemed satisfied. "Okay, Russ," he said and left.

"More trouble?" Jake asked.

"The channel's blocked," Sinclair answered, his hands living a separate nervous life. "Nobody goes in or out of the Island Basin until Roger brings over his equipment and hauls out whatever's down there. A boat of some kind, from what it looks like, but the water's not all that clear."

The water may not be, Jake thought, but it was clear that William was tightening the noose. "What about the folks in the Basin?" he asked.

"Trapped and mad as hell. They're going to do something, Eaton. What, I don't know. But something. I can feel it like I can feel this whole damn mess closing in around me," Sinclair said, his eyes puffy from lack of sleep.

"How'd you discover the sunken boat?" Jake asked and sat in the booth across from Sinclair. Watson paced, his nose to the floor in search of tasty crumbs.

"Charter boat ran into it. Doesn't anything ever go right anymore? I tell those people we're through with 'em—they can leave, go home, get the hell out of my hair—and then this. We damn near had a riot over there when that sailboat blocked the only way out. Nasty," Sinclair said. "Nasty seems to be what your boy William specializes in."

"Or Wilson Randall," Jake said.

Sinclair's voice turned hopeful. "You mean Treadle came through and identified him?"

"No. I saw him."

"When?"

"This morning, on the dock. Just after he killed Sam," Jake answered.

"You mean right after his second attempt on you. When I didn't see you around, I stopped by *Gamecock*. It looks like a slaughter went on down there. My guess is that Wilson Randall or whoever the hell he is, set a trap and the wrong man sprang it. Too bad Sam didn't listen to you the first time," Sinclair said. "Any idea why he didn't?"

Jake thought of anwering the question but decided that Gloria had suffered enough. "No," he told Sinclair. "I don't know why he went back. How'd you make out with the Land Rover?"

"A lawyer from New Jersey with his wife and four kids parked it in the town lot and went shopping. When they got back, it was gone."

"Any prints?"

"A million. Most of them sticky. Candy keeps the kids quiet," Sinclair said. "But since you've identified him, we don't need prints."

"I identified the man, not his name. Wilson Randall is as bogus as the others."

"You've already run it?"

Jake nodded. "In Florida. It turned up clean, I still had my doubts and went back to the marina where he was a mechanic. If he was who I was looking for, I figured the second time around he'd be a little shaky . . . maybe even bolt. But he didn't. He was right there tearing apart engines, answering every question, admitting nothing."

Sinclair absently picked at his thumb nail. "No law in changing your name," he said and looked carefully at Jake. "'Course it wouldn't make any difference, would it? He breaks every damn law on the books and throws it up in our face. The guy's sick," he blurted. Sinclair looked overwhelmed. "I still don't believe this. I don't."

"Think you're going to wake up from a dream?"

"I wish." Sinclair looked sincere.

"And the arrest you promised Roger Dolby—is that where you're going to make it? In your dreams?"

"What else was I going to say? A public official has to make some gesture of reassurance, and it certainly won't come from our illustrious mayor," Sinclair said and flicked a wadded paper ball to Jake. "Go ahead, open it."

Jake did and read, "Having a wonderful time." William had signed it.

"Andy found that when he checked his shop last night out at Madaket. It was slipped under the door. Now he thinks he's a target. He thinks William might be after him next."

"Why?"

"For being friends with your client, for supporting her move down here." He shrugged. "Who knows?" Sinclair said disgustedly and took back the note. "If you ask me, Andy Tillis has finally showed his true colors to the folks of this island. If he doesn't get his butt in gear, he won't be elected dogcatcher next time."

"Where is he?" Jake asked.

"Hiding in his house. Oh, to hear him tell it, he always takes a few days around the Fourth, but I can see it in his eyes, hear it in his voice. He's shaking in his boots and if you want to know the truth, I don't blame him. I shook all over too."

"You're talking about the arm," Jake said.

Sinclair nodded and bit his lip. "One of my officers on patrol found it and called it in. I thought he was kidding at first. An arm dangling from a flagpole—come on."

"Where is it?" Jake asked.

"Thought you'd want to have a look," Sinclair said and stood.

Jake followed Sinclair past the takeout counter, past the closed cash register, and into the kitchen. Boxes of cereal stood on shelves above the sparkling clean work areas. Sinclair opened one of the walk-in coolers.

"It's in here," he said and flicked on the light. Wrapped in a towel amid the cheeses, eggs, milk, and meats was the arm. Sinclair brought it out and set it on a butcher's block. "Go ahead," he said.

With his thumb and two first fingers, Jake pulled back the cloth and looked on with ghastly facination. The arm was bluish white, bent slightly at the elbow and crudely cut on both ends. Streaks of nearly dried blackish blood contrasted with the white flesh.

Jake's attention focused on the hand. The thumb and three fingers had been amputated. The index finger pointed right at him, as if to accuse him mockingly of something untold.

Jake folded his hand so his index finger was pointed at Russell Sinclair. "That's exactly how a hand looks when a man is being accused," Jake said, then added almost inaudibly, "Banker, accuser, and Gloria."

The way he said "Gloria" made Sinclair's ears perk up. "You taken a sudden liking to her, have you?" he asked, frowning.

Jake covered the arm up. "I'm trying to understand her," he said, adding, "Nothing's going to happen to her regardless."

"Regardless of what?"

"Regardless of anything William does." Jake's expression was thoughtful. Something in his mind was inching its way forward, teasing him by being so close, yet he couldn't catch hold of it. Finally, he said, "I want you to assign one of your men to Gloria Gorham."

"I thought that was your job," Sinclair said then wished he hadn't. He needed Jake Eaton and he damn well knew it. "Not that I wouldn't like to, but I can't spare a man what with increased security at the airport and ferry dock. Even Shean's all alone at the Basin."

"He won't be for long when Gloria finds out her guests are trapped inside. She'll be down there running the show in no time. I don't want that, Sinclair. She'll be a sitting duck out there on those docks. I don't think you really want to deal with her either," Jake said.

Sinclair considered it for a moment. "Special Summer Forces," he said almost to himself. "About the only thing they're good for is guarding a woman, if they haven't already all run home to momma. I'll see what I can do."

"I appreciate it," Jake told him. "Think those divers are ready?"

"Let's find out."

Chapter

———21———

Joe Macy was at the wheel of a thirty-foot multipurpose fiberglass boat powered by two 150-horse Yamaha outboard engines. Painted on the sides of the craft in bright red block letters was Dolby's Dive Boat/Nantucket Fuel. Macy pulled back the throttle and glided up to the small float off Commercial Street that was used mostly for sailboat rentals. Ron Katish cleated a line to hold the boat steady as Chief Sinclair, Jake, and Watson climbed aboard. The early morning sun was already glaring down, sparkling off the water.

"Chief," Katish said, then extended a hand to Jake. Katish uncleated the line, and Macy backed away from the float. He gunned the engines and turned the craft a tight 180 degrees. The IB gas dock was on their left as they moved out to where Murray and Sylvia Fine had grounded the sailboat and sat there embarrassed for all to see. The boat was high and dry, listing heavily to port.

"I've seen pleasure boaters do a lot of stupid things, but this takes the cake," Joe Macy said. "Some stupid sonofabitch, if you ask me. Ought to have his ass kicked." Macy's tone of voice matched his appearance. He was an angry-looking man with purple veins threaded across his fat, wide nose.

"What'dya think?" Ron asked as Joe Macy pulled his powerboat closer. Katish was a few years younger and in better shape than Macy, with a tough, lean body. His eyes were hidden behind reflective aviator glasses.

Macy, obviously the boss, ignored the question and yelled up to Murray Fine, who was eager for company. "What's she look like down below? Any leaks?"

"No leaks," Murray answered self-consciously. He was living every captain's nightmare—running aground in full view of everyone—even though it wasn't his fault. Murray wiped his brow with a hankie, wishing with all his being that he'd gone to the mountains. "Hung up on something, though . . . I couldn't back her off."

"How much power you got?" Joe asked.

"Thirty horse."

"The prop?"

"Two bladed."

"Figures," Joe Macy said to Sinclair. "Thirty horses and two blades won't whip eggs." Then he yelled back up to Murray. "You're out here in the middle of the goddamn ocean, man. Why don't you get yourself a real boat?"

"I hate boats," Murray Fine shouted over the roar of Macy's powerful engines. "You can have this one if you'll get us off the island."

Sylvia Fine's pinched face said the very same thing. She was behind Murray, her hands firmly on her hips. She wasn't good at suppressing her emotions and snapped at her husband. "*You* hate boats!" She turned, exasperated, to the dozens watching her from the docks. "He says he hates boats. Well, that's not all *I* hate. Let me tell you, that is *not* all I hate!"

Macy ignored her, thankful he was married to someone more normal. "We've got to see what she's caught on, Ronnie. Probably nothin', and if she's free, we'll pull her off."

"What kind of keel you got?" Macy called.

"Retractable," Murray said. "I pulled up the board and we're still stuck."

Again Macy turned to Sinclair. "Centerboard boat that size can't draw more than three feet. Ain't a boat in the Basin that can clear that obstacle," he said.

Sinclair knew what he meant. It didn't really matter if the Fines got their boat off or not, no one was leaving the Basin until that sunken boat was towed away. Sinclair seemed to sag, resigned to his fate. "Do what you can," he said and watched the two divers go to work.

Macy throttled back twenty feet and dropped a red dive flag over the side. When he eased forward, Ron Katish already had his wet suit zipped, weight belt fastened, tank on, and regulator in place. He spit on the faceplate glass and rubbed it with his fingers before swinging his legs over the side. There he wrestled with his flippers and dropped into the water.

Watson looked startled as the man disappeared underwater and thousands of bubbles floated to the surface. When Jake did nothing to help, the dog barked as if to signal him that something was wrong.

"It's all right," Jake said and patted him. "He'll be back."

Macy already knew the answer but asked it anyway. "Your dog?"

"He is."

"You the guy who found Sammy? Sam Kingsbury?" he asked, his voice not wavering in its unfriendliness.

"I am," Jake said.

"He was a friend of mine," Joe Macy said, his voice low and menacing. "I didn't like the idea of you knockin' him around the other night."

"You didn't?"

"I didn't. No, I didn't. We were gonna correct that, me and Sammy was," Macy threatened. "Now I'll have ta do it myself."

"Don't count on it," Jake said as Sinclair stepped between them.

"Macy, I've got enough trouble," he said, grimacing.

"Only trying to help, Russ."

"Sure, Macy. Just like always. Do your fucking job, will you?" Sinclair snapped and looked back at the bubbles. They were coming toward him now and in no time, Ron was back onboard.

"Ought to pull right off, Mace. Nothing's holding her," Ron said, unstrapping his single tank and weight belt.

"What's she sitting on?" Sinclair asked.

"An old cruiser."

"Gibby's?" Jake asked.

"Looks wooden, but I didn't go down for a good look." Katish kicked off his flippers. "Didn't want that sailboat gettin' loose and sittin' on me," he said and took a line from Macy.

"When I pull forward, throw that to the captain," Macy said and inched forward so Ron could almost hand the line to Murray. "Snub that line to your biggest stern cleat," Macy directed Murray Fine. "We'll pull you right back to your slip."

Sylvia was waving her arms frantically. "I don't think you understand. We want out, not in."

"Sorry lady," Macy said, not sorry at all. "If we pull you forward, we'll rip that rudder right off. The only way to go is back."

"Murray?" Sylvia whined. "Murray?"

Murray didn't want to fight in front of docks full of people. "Whatever you say," he told Joe Macy with a sheepish wave and cleated the line. "Ready anytime you are."

Ron Katish walked the line back to a stainless steel support that cleared the engine cowlings by a foot and was mounted to the floor and braced with steel struts. As Joe Macy eased his boat into the Basin, Katish tied off the bitter end and used hand signals to inform Macy of the line's tension. When all the slack was gone, Ron dropped his hand like a man starting a race.

With full throttle, the back of the workboat dropped as the propellers chewed away at the water. Joe Macy kept his eyes dead ahead with an occasional glance to the rear. Ron's were fixed on the line and the struggling sailboat. She was moving. First the bow lifted, then she began side-to-side shudders as if trying to walk out on her own. Finally with a muffled roar of something underwater tearing away, the big sailboat floated free and Macy cut back his powerful engines.

"Put some fenders out to starboard," Macy hollered up to a relieved Murray Fine. "We'll back you right to your slip," he said as Katish hauled in the tow rope and coiled it on deck. "You got dock lines out?"

"They will be," Murray said scrambling past his wife, who sat in the cockpit fuming. "Care to help me?" he asked sarcastically. "Damnit, Sylvia."

"I hate this, Murray. Every bit. I hate it!"

Murray was white with rage but too busy handling the boat to do anything about it. He cleated a bow and stern line and handed them down to Macy, who tied them snug to the workboat for towing.

An expert at handling his craft, Macy eased the big sailboat into the slip. Murray tossed a second stern line to a concerned onlooker and ran forward with another for the bow. He was paying out his spring lines when Joe Macy made his first wide circle around the sunken boat. He took one last look back at Sylvia and said to Katish, "I'd throw the bitch overboard."

"Please," Katish joked. "I'm about to go in that water."

"All right, guys, come on," Sinclair said as the men prepared to dive.

Katish picked up the twelve-pound Danforth and eased it over the side, letting the line slide freely through his big hands. Macy backed the boat until the anchor held, then he backed up another eighty feet and Katish dropped a second anchor over the stern. Ron Katish now took the controls and eased the throttle forward to set the stern anchor. The two men worked without a word, comfortable in their routine and skill.

"Keeps the boat in one place," Ron told Jake. "The current won't move 'er with two anchors set. When you're diving, you always want to know where your floating base is case you get in trouble."

"We gettin' paid extra for running commentary?" Joe Macy cut in.

"That's it Joe, keep it light. One of the reasons I always like to work with you," Russell Sinclair said. "A laugh a minute and that sweet, sweet smile."

"Just trying to help," Macy said.

"Then get your ass in the water."

"You got it, chief." Macy sucked in his gut so he could zip up his wet-suit top.

"You need to lose a few," Jake said.

"That what I need?" Macy glared back. "Glad somebody told me. I always thought I needed more exercise . . . like kicking ass. Yours, maybe?" Katish shut down the two engines, and in the following silence Jake stepped toward Macy. "I always thought divers were trained to be careful," he said without emotion. "You must've missed that lesson."

Macy puffed his chest. "You threatening me?"

"Warning you." Jake smiled dismissively and turned away.

"Here, Joe." Ron Katish held the tank harness open for his partner to slip on. "We've got a lot ahead of us if we're gonna get done." Grudgingly, Macy put on the harness. "What else you gonna need?"

"Depends on the chief. What exactly do you want from down there?" Macy asked.

"Identification of the boat."

"Easy enough."

"Reason why she sunk," Sinclair added.

"Also no problem."

"And a good look around inside," Sinclair said.

"A look for what?" Macy asked.

"Just a look, Joe. Come up and tell us what you find."

"Piece o' cake," Macy said. Then to Katish he added, "I'll take a pry bar and the battery-powered light. That oughtta do it."

"Right." Katish went forward to get the items. While he was gone, Macy occupied himself by carefully inspecting his regulator, air lines, and every buckle and strap. He was an asshole, Jake thought, but he certainly wasn't stupid.

Jake motioned to Sinclair, and the two stepped away from the divers. "You thinking what I'm thinking?" Jake asked looking Sinclair straight in the eyes.

The chief shrugged. "That there might be a body down there?"

"Yeah," Jake said. "Be a great place to hide it."

"Could be."

"Why didn't you tell Macy what you think he might find?" Jake asked, wondering if Sinclair had deliberately not mentioned this.

"I don't know what he might find," Sinclair answered and glanced at Macy. "Besides, Joe's an all right guy, but he does have an attitude. There might be something down there that takes a little of the bullshit out of him."

"It wouldn't hurt," Jake said.

"Just what I was thinking," Sinclair said with a grim smile.

Katish handed Macy the light. "Ready to dive," Macy said, and Katish helped him over the side.

Chapter

22

Macy went down in a roar of bubbles and the glow of bright light from the hand-carried lamp. Watson looked on nonchalantly. Apparently he'd learned not to be concerned, or maybe, like Jake, he didn't like Joe Macy either and didn't really care if he came back.

While they watched the diver's slow descent, Jake said to Ron Katish, "It's curious that a fuel company has ready access to divers and a dive boat. You'd think they'd be more concerned with tank trucks and land deliveries."

Katish kept his eyes on his partner down below. "You might think so on the mainland," he said, "but not on an island, where the first thing you've got to do is get the fuel over here. Dolby's got barges carrying up to eight hundred thousand gallons of gas and diesel all through these waters. And there's one thing about a boat—anything can happen and it's usually bad. Just ask the Fines," Katish said glancing over at Sylvia, who still had not moved to help her husband. "Takes all kinds, I guess."

Jake's eyes followed the air bubbles coming up from below. "Boats or people?" he asked.

Katish shrugged. "Both, I guess. Me and Joe's worked on just about everything that floats. Barges run aground, tugs foul their prop, a shaft gets bent, pilings need to be replaced, a boat sinks and blocks the channel . . . you name it and me and Joe have worked on it. But this beats all."

"How we coming?" Sinclair wanted to know. "Can you tell anything, Ronnie?"

"Not from here, chief. Have to wait for Joe to come up."

Swimming near the top of the wreck, Joe Macy felt at home. The bright sunlight at ten feet formed pale green columns that tiny school fish swam through as one. They were fearless, dancing here and there, exploring like Macy was exploring the sunken hull. At twenty feet, his lamp took over as he felt his way against the current along the painted white sides.

Starting at the bow, Macy moved along the outer skin looking for any sign of an explosion. Old boats usually fired their cookstoves with unvented propane that often leaked into the bilge. A spark from the engine could blow apart a boat. But not in this case. The outer skin was fine. There was no sign of an explosion or a fire.

Macy kicked farther along, his light illuminating small particles suspended in the water. Out of habit, he checked his air gauge, then ran his light left and right across all the ports for a look inside. He saw nothing. The curtains were closed and swayed with the motion of the water like small trees in a light breeze. It was an eerie sight, as if someone were inside breathing in and out, in and out.

Macy used a strong kick and swam toward the stern, checking the hull below the waterline stripe as he went along. That part of the huge old boat had to be sturdy enough to take the strain when the wide nylon straps were put on her ribs and planks to refloat her. With one strap fore and one strap aft, they'd pull her right up to the surface.

Macy let the light hang from the tether around his neck and tapped the boat's planking to test for rot and weakness. She sounded strong enough to survive the lift to the surface. Macy also wanted to make sure the boat wasn't resting on any obstructions or buried cables that would make it difficult to slide the straps under her. She wasn't.

When Macy reached the transom, he read the boat's name: *Betsy*. That was Gibby Bennett's boat, he thought to himself. How'd you get down here, old girl? He shone the light in the cockpit. If anything was in there when she went down, it had floated away. Except for the line cleated aft that now moved gently in the current, the cockpit was empty. But why a stern line? he wondered. She wasn't close enough to the dock to be tied in a slip; besides, there weren't any fenders out. Then he remembered what he'd seen when he first entered the water. *Betsy* had a bow anchor out. Anchoring in the channel? It didn't make sense. Only a lunatic would anchor in a channel, or a drunken and lost Gibby Bennett.

Once in the cockpit, Macy tilted his head back and cleared his mask of the water that had seeped in around his nose. Had he been down deep enough, the water pressure would have forced a tighter seal, but then his ears would have ached. He'd rather have the leak.

At the door to the inner cabin, he again tried to shine his light inside—with the same result. A closed curtain. Only this time he got a glimpse of something floating behind the curtain. Something large. What, he couldn't make out. Bunk cushions, most likely, he thought and tried the door. It was locked.

Strange. When the boat's going down, who locks the damn door? Same guy who closes the curtains, he thought, and jabbed at the lock with the metal pry bar. It was an action in slow motion. Thunk. Thunk. Thunk.

The door wouldn't budge. Locked and jammed, he thought. He put down the light so he could use both hands and ram the bar home.

Thunk. Thunk. Thunk. Thunk.

The wood splintered, and Macy pushed the door open against slight water resistance. The closed cabin was pitch black. He put down the metal bar and reached for the light hanging from its tether. Something bumped against his leg and an icy chill ran up his back as he pushed it inside the cabin. He didn't want it to float out the door. Might be what Chief Sinclair wanted him to find.

What do I look for?

You'll know it when you see it.

Thank you very much, Russ. Everybody knows how much Joe Macy loves games.

Macy grabbed the light and shone it inside the deep, watery pool of the cabin. As expected, the cushions were floating on top like limp, cloth-covered planks. He stepped under them and closed the door to keep everything inside. It was an odd feeling, like closing the door on your own casket.

Probing with his flashlight, he saw the opened doors under the galley sink. He bent low and leaned in as far as he could without banging his tank and damaging his air supply. It was far enough.

Sonofabitch, he thought looking at the cut water lines and open sea cocks. She's been scuttled. That explains the anchor. Somebody got her right where they wanted her and opened the dam. She probably sank in five minutes.

Again, Macy felt something bump into him. Slowly he backed out of the galley, pushing away whatever it was as he moved. Then he swung the light forward—onto the dead man floating beside him. His heart pounded like a jackhammer and he felt the cold lifelessness of an underwater grave.

"Jesus Christ!" The words came out in bubbles as he kicked through the water, pushed open the door, and swam frantically toward the surface. When he broke through and spit out his mouthpiece, he yelled at Russell Sinclair, "That some kind of fucking joke?"

"You find a body?"

"Thanks for the warning, chief. I really appreciate it," Macy hollered.

"Who is it?"

"Ought to make you go down and find out for yourself."

"Who is it?" Sinclair snapped.

"Gibby Bennett."

"You sure?"

"Goddamnit, Russ, he used to work for Dolby. I saw him every day. His arm's gone, Russ. Somebody cut off his right arm."

"Bring him up," Sinclair said as Joe Macy treaded water. Macy wasn't in any hurry to go back down. "Sometime today, okay, Joe? Bring him up."

"I'll help," Ron Katish said and jumped over the side with a coil of rope. "Let's go, Macy. Nothin' to it. Ready?" In seconds, they were both under.

Sinclair was dumbfounded. "Gibby Bennett?" he mumbled under his breath. "Why'd anybody want to cut up a harmless old drunk?"

"I don't know," Jake said. He looked out into the harbor at the hundreds of masts gently rocking on the small waves like metronome arms ticking the time away. William was out there; Jake knew it. He was out there planning his next move. And time was running out.

William Rice was there all right, but he was taking no chances after being spotted and shot at. No point in screwing everything up now, he told himself, so he stayed out of sight in the *Dolfin*'s cabin, wishing he could be in the control tower high above the airport's main runway when the charges went off. It would be a good show—a small detonation line formed from the explosives he'd taken ashore with Gibby's severed arm. But a show he'd have to miss, just like he was missing the divers and Jake and the chaos on the docks. Ah, well. Good things come to those who wait. Besides, he could occupy his time building a little surprise for Jake Eaton. Something really special.

What he'd told Gibby Bennett stuck in his mind as he worked: You shut up or you do. Yeah. Shut up or you do. Ummm. Shut up or you do. Yo. Shut up or you do. Brother.

Song filled the cabin as William Rice soldered the delicate wires.

*   *   *

Sylvia Fine looked on wide-eyed as the poor man's body was being lifted onto the dive boat. Her defiance and frustration turned to uncontrollable fear.

"Mur . . . Murray." Suddenly, she was crying, her eyes squeezed tightly shut and tears streaming down her cheeks. She was pointing, her hand shaking violently at the end of her outstretched arm. "My God, Murray! Another dead man! Look!"

Murry Fine was trying to make sense of what his wife was blurting out. Dead man? What dead man?

Suddenly the docks were alive with groups of men and women hurrying their children away from the dive boat, scrambling toward some sense of safety. Murray felt excitement mixed with despair race through the crowd. He felt his legs go rubbery as the possibility settled in his mind that no one in the Basin would ever get off the island.

"Come on," he snapped at Sylvia, grabbing her arm. "Now, come on."

They jumped to the dock. He was nearly dragging Sylvia as they stumbled toward Whales Way.

"Where are we going?" She was still crying, struggling to keep up with Murray, who rushed past Morton and Janice Colder, ignoring them.

"We're going home," Murray said, heading for the taxi stand near Straight Wharf. He jerked open the door of the waiting cab. "Airport," he ordered and climbed inside.

They rode to the airport in a daze as Sylvia's stomach twisted into knots. She dabbed at her eyes with a tissue and turned to Murray. "I tried to tell you," she sniffed, blowing her nose.

"Not now."

"Well, I did."

The cab wheeled into the airport entrance. "Maybe you'll listen to me next time," she said as the first explosive blew a huge crater along the east side of the runway. The cab shuddered as a second, then a third, followed by more explosions tore huge holes in the tarmac.

Back on the *Dolfin,* William Rice was wiring his last bomb.

Chapter

—23—

Outside on the runway, Andy Tillis surveyed the damage with Rodney Paul, the airport manager. Rodney was a tall, nervous man with thin, pinched features and a high, whining voice lowered an octave by years of cigarettes.

"You said you were going to take care of this, Andy." Rodney was anxious, smoking. "When my training flight went down, you said you were going to take care of it. Now look." He couldn't take his eyes off the cement and asphalt rubble, the deep craters that ruined what was minutes ago a serviceable landing strip. "What kind of monster are we dealing with, Andy? Answer me that," he demanded as the gray smoke fell from his mouth.

Tillis turned away. "Not now, Rod. Jesus." Tillis was weary, his face chalky from lack of sleep. "Find anything?" he asked Jake, who was down in a crater, an oblong hole three feet deep and ten feet wide. There were six holes just like it spread out fifty yards apart in a zigzag fashion, making it impossible for any plane to land or take off.

Watson had sniffed out a timer hidden in the grass. Jake gave it to the mayor who held it in his right hand as if it were a rotting fish.

Jake climbed out of the hole and gazed at Tillis, a man he'd not liked from the moment they'd met, and liked even less now.

Tillis looked at Rodney Paul, then back to Jake. He felt exposed, embarrassed by Jake's unforgiving glare. "Nothing else down there?" Tillis asked.

Jake moved past him with Watson at his heel.

"Eaton?" Tillis's voice wavered.

Jake stopped and turned back to him. "He's closing in. You didn't want to hear that before. Now," Jake said holding in his anger, "you don't have a choice."

"What are we going to do?" Andy Tillis pleaded.

"I'm going to look after my client," Jake told him and walked inside the terminal. He put a quarter in the phone and punched in Gloria's apartment number. In three rings, she picked up. "Are you all right?" Jake asked.

She answered without hesitation. "Yes. Has something happened?"

"William's closed down the airport and blocked the exit from the Island Basin," Jake said, concern for her apparent in his voice.

"I . . ."

"Don't talk."

"But I've got a business to run."

"And you'll run it, but you can't do one thing for those people right now. I want you to stay put," Jake urged. He felt he could almost hear Gloria's heart pounding through the phone. "Did you and Treadle solve anything?"

"I don't know. I answered a million questions." She paused. "He seemed to think I was of some help."

"Good."

"He said if you wanted to see him, he'd be at his office."

"I'm headed in that direction," Jake said and added, "When Sam was dying he tried to tell me something I've not been able to make sense of. He kept saying 'friends' or 'prens' or something like that. Mean anything to you?"

Gloria thought for a few seconds. "No. I can't think that it does."

"Well, if it comes to you—"

"Of course." There was an awkward silence. Finally, Gloria spoke Jake's name in a way she'd never done before. It was softer, filled with caring. It almost made him step back from the phone.

"Stay put," Jake said suddenly and hung up. There wasn't time to wrestle with his feelings, not now. There was never time. Emotions could blow up in your face and affect your sanity. Jake bent down and roughed the hair on Watson's neck. "I keep you fed, you keep me sane. Fair?"

Watson spun after his tail and barked twice. It sounded like a "yes" to Jake and they were off.

Gloria put down the receiver, frowning at this new tug of emotion for the man trying to save her life, and frowning at her predicament. She could deal with Jake later, but what could she do about that young guard posted outside on the landing? She hesitated, thinking of how she might get away, then went to the door and pulled it open. "Would you like some coffee?" she asked with a sweet smile.

Turner Reese, full of nervous energy and troubled thoughts, shook his head, then changed his mind. "I would, yeah. I guess so," he said and stepped inside. He was a twenty-year-old college student majoring in criminal justice at Northeastern University, looking taller and more spindly in his Special Summer Forces uniform than he ever looked in sneakers and jeans. "Cream and sugar," he said. "Three sugars."

"I'll just let you fix it," Gloria said and carried the tray from the counter to the coffee table in the living room. "Care to sit?"

"I . . . I really shouldn't."

"Of course," she said and sat. "Guard duty, isn't it?"

Turner Reese tried to smile but could only manage to squeeze his lips together. "Nice place you got here," he said and let his eyes gaze over the luxury. He didn't know exactly what he was looking at—elaborately carved crown moldings and leaded glass windows—but he sensed they cost money and lots of it. "Real nice."

"Thank you."

"I mean it."

"It's comfortable," she said. She was wearing a pale green cotton blouse, matching slacks, and open-toed sandals. She forced a yawn, then stretched halfheartedly. "I don't know," she said. "It seems a little different when you're locked in here. Smaller or something. I haven't quite put my finger on it."

Stay outside. Keep an eye on her. Make sure she keeps an eye on you. And don't talk to her. You understand?

"I shouldn't be in here," Turner said, remembering Jake's specific instructions.

"Then you know how I feel," she said, and knew as soon as she had said it that she'd tipped her hand.

"I . . . I'd better get outside, Miss Gorham," he said, backing away from her. "I'll take that coffee later, if it's all right."

The disappointment showed in her face. "Of course," she said as he closed the door and locked it from the outside.

When the tumbler clicked, Gloria's anger and frustration rose. It was less an emotion than a physical need to do something other than look out the window and pace. Exactly the same thing she had done last night when she couldn't sleep.

She was a light sleeper anyway, and whenever she drifted off, nightmarish dreams closed in. At first she saw herself driving her car. It was a foggy night, and when she stopped at a red light, a frightening feeling made her throat burn. She was not alone. Someone was in the backseat waiting for the green light when he would slice through her neck.

Waking in a sweat, she had fought off that image and tossed and turned her way into a dark and empty dream house. There were no lights, no sounds. Slowly and carefully she moved toward a door, feeling her way along the cool plaster walls. She was not inside herself. She was certain of little else, but she knew that she was not inside herself. It was as if she'd lost consciousness and had drifted away to a point just beyond her body where she floated, looking back at her physical self with an abstract knowledge of some terrible fear. Was this the beginning of death? A time of no physical discomfort, only this oddly strange view of yourself lying there inches away?

Suddenly and without warning, the entire house had come alive and burst toward her. The swayback couch moved in the air; the old andirons and scuttle bounced toward her; ashtrays, harpoons, old newspapers flew at her with frightful speed. There was no escape, but she had to get away. She ran toward the tapping, toward the pounding sounds that seemed to draw short charges of breath from her.

The tapping—those insistent double raps—had come from the front door, which she stared at until her hand was steady. Slowly she opened the door onto Jake's seething face and knew at a glance—without him even saying a word—that Sam Kingsbury had been killed.

"Trying to knock the house down?" she'd asked, when what she really wanted to say was, "I'm sorry. I am so terribly sorry. Will you please hold onto me? Please?"

And Jake held her willingly, feeling like some poor, lonesome ghost released from his past of longing and desire that had no name.

Steven Treadle's office—overflowing with stacks of paper and piles of books—was on the second floor of the Historical Society on Independence Lane. Jake opened the white wooden door and let Watson go in first. They climbed the curved staircase and followed the worn carpet tracks to Treadle's office. When Jake and Watson entered, the historian was hunched behind his desk with an expression on his face that begged for a few more working minutes. Jake understood and sat, Watson curled up beside him. Finally, Treadle made the last of his notes and closed the book.

"Sorry," he said. "But I wanted to make sure I had the last detail exactly. This is very exciting, Mr. Eaton. Very exciting."

"Then you've got something?"

"Not all the *i*'s are dotted, no. But the field has narrowed considerably," he said with pride. "Miss Gorham was very helpful. She has a flair for family history. Saved me hours digging through the stacks. She jogged my memory a bit about one recorded connection between Obed Gorham and the Cooper family. Very helpful as I said, but not what we were looking for. Obed Gorham—come to find out—had a perfectly legitimate, uncomplicated business transaction with Benjamin Cooper. It had nothing whatsoever to do with sperm whale oil. The good news was her addition of the name."

"Wilson Randall?" Jake asked.

"Correct," he said with a professorial air. "Now this is fact, Mr. Eaton, not speculation. My staff and I have checked all the references in the library, and there is *no* connection between the names Randall, Cooper, and Gorham. None."

Jake wondered why Treadle was smiling. "Doesn't sound like very good news to me," he said.

"Bear with me. It get's better when we add the fourth name of Mr. Bennett. Terrible what I heard about his demise. Just terrible." The reality that he was dealing with death sidetracked him, made him think of those wonderful black and white movies.

Jake pressed him. "The name of Bennett," he reminded Treadle.

"Oh, yes, yes. That name I didn't cross-check until last and I was just finishing up when you arrived." Treadle let the moment build, then said, "Again, nothing."

"I don't get it."

"At first I didn't either. For certain we have three names—Cooper, Gorham, and Bennett. There can be no question about that. Even if we don't know the true identity of the fourth person involved—that is, assuming he's using an alias of some sort—we still ought to be able to identify him by finding the connection between the three names we do know."

"But you didn't," Jake said.

"Correct. I didn't. Turns out the reason's very simple. The truth be known, Mr. Eaton, there *is* no connection between the names. The connection is between the roles each played. It wasn't Nate Cooper this fiend was after. It was—like the message says—a banker. It wasn't a Bennett he was after; it was a town drunk."

"But he *is* after Gloria Gorham," Jake said.

"I'm afraid so." Treadle paused, looking at Jake. "You were quite right about there being a historical connection in all of this. Enoch Gorham was the second person to accuse an innocent man of bank robbery. The first was Joseph Mardy, the town drunk. The innocent man was Randall Rice."

"And when did this robbery take place?"

"1795."

"Are you sure?"

"I'm positive," Treadle said firmly. "If I had the slightest doubt, this eliminates it." He handed Jake a worn folder.

Jake opened it. Inside were two pencil-scrawled notes stating that if the Gorhams ever came back to Nantucket, he—Oliver Rice—would do what it took to guarantee they never enjoyed a second of their stay.

"Where'd you find these?" Jake wanted to know.

"In with the history of the robbery. My guess is since the Gorhams weren't on the island, it wasn't a threat the local police would take seriously. The notes ended up here in the Historical Society's files. You can see the dates on the notes. They're more than twenty years old."

Jake picked up the phone and punched in a number. "This is Eaton," he said to the dispatcher. "Let me speak to Sinclair."

"I'm sorry, Mr. Eaton. The chief's not in."

"Where is he?"

"Double-checking the tank farm."

"Any trouble?" Jake asked.

"Not yet."

"Good. I want you to check a name for me. Oliver Rice. See if he's got a record, and a son—William. Think you can manage that?"

"I'll get somebody right on it."

"And fast." Jake hung up and asked Steven Treadle for the rest of the story.

Chapter

24

Percy (Buck) Thurmon wasn't an average fireman. Many on the force thought him a misfit, but Buck was quick, bright, and innovative. He was smarter than most and was more than willing to prove it by referring to his ever-present clipboard. It was no surprise five years ago when Mayor Tillis wanted to improve the safety regulations of the tank farm, he tapped Buck for the job. It had been his responsibility ever since, and Buck looked after it like a major general.

When fuel arrived by tug, Buck assigned two firemen and water trucks for every barge off-load. He initiated new environmental regulations for the loading rack area where land deliveries begin, and he installed speed bumps inside the farm to slow down traffic. His crowning achievement was a se-ries of alarms from each of the four fire zones wired directly to the depart-ment. As far as Buck Thurmon was concerned, the tank farm couldn't be any safer in principle and—as he was explaining to Chief Sinclair when Jake and Watson arrived—it couldn't be any safer in practice.

Buck Thurmon had a wide face and a tall, thick frame. His head of longish, curly brown hair was thinning at the front and slicked down with a per-fumed tonic to keep the wind from tossing it in his eyes, which would bore right through you with their seriousness.

Buck nodded a greeting in Jake's direction and continued with Sinclair. "You don't need to worry about a thing, Russ. The farm's foolproof, but just in case," he said, "I check 'er every day." He ran his finger along a series of checkmarks on a chart attached to his clipboard. "The tanker pier's clean, as are the storage tanks and the loading rack. Not a thing's been tampered with. The electrical power plant has its own security and they've reported all is tip-top. Besides," he added, looking at Jake as if he didn't like being doubted, "that chain-link fence is twelve feet high. Nobody gets in there unless I know about it."

Jake leaned against Sinclair's car, thinking. "Maybe he doesn't need to get in," he conjectured.

"Fine with me," Buck Thurmon said, relieved. "But let him try in any case. He won't make it."

"The airport had security," Jake reminded him.

"The airport's out in the middle of nowhere. Any fool could've set a few explosives on the runway."

"What about the fuel feeder pipes under the street?" Jake said, remembering the videotape and the grainy images of William crawling through the timbers.

"I saw the tape," Buck said flatly and looked at Sinclair. "He doesn't give up, does he, Russ? He must think we don't have a brain in our heads." Buck turned his unfriendly gaze on Jake. "I checked every inch of that dock myself. All clear. Believe me. If you don't, ask Russ—I just gave him the tour."

Sinclair nodded his head. "Clean as a whistle."

"Like always," Buck said in his defense. "See, Eaton, everybody on the island knows that the tank farm is a potential bomb, and we've made safety preparations for it long before this goon showed up. The storage tanks might not be pretty, but the farm's probably the safest place on the island. Now, if you'll excuse me," he said and confidently walked away.

"Thanks Buck," Sinclair called after him.

Jake straightened up from the car. "Testy," he said.

"Buck's under a lot of pressure. Besides, he was pretty close to Gibby. Went fishing together from time to time. Which reminds me, Lucas Hendricks did a preliminary on Bennett. His neck was broken just like Nate Cooper's."

Jake sat on the cement retaining wall beside a panting Watson. The noonday sun was blazing, the breeze shifting so the air was near calm. Jake pulled a blade of grass. It was at times like these, when men such as Russell Sinclair struggle for peace of mind, that Jake was at his best. "Things are beginning to make a little sense, Sinclair," he said. He summarized what Steven Treadle had told him.

On Friday, June 26, 1795, sometime after dark, the Nantucket Bank was broken into and $20,963 in gold and currency was stolen. Three robbers had sailed over from the mainland, made a key out of a pewter spoon, opened the door, cleaned out the bank—which had been open only one week—and sailed back to the mainland that very night.

Many Nantucketers didn't want the bank in the first place, and when it was stripped clean and their savings wiped out, quick action was demanded. If they couldn't get the money back, they at least wanted the robbers brought to justice. Two men stepped forward to do just that.

Joseph Mardy and Enoch Gorham were constant—if somewhat odd—companions. Joseph was the legendary town drunk and Enoch was mentally retarded. They both swore that on the night of the robbery, they saw Randall Rice, a well-respected local dry-goods merchant, step from the bank carrying an unidentified bundle. They didn't actually see any money, and they never said they actually saw Randall Rice enter the bank. Not much to go on, considering the nature of each accuser, but it was enough. Rice was arrested and brought to trial.

Walter Prescott, president of the bank, felt that a speedy guilty verdict was in his best interest. What better way to restore confidence in an infant business? So he hired an expert in physiognomy—the popular science of the day whereby a man's motives and actions were predicted based on his facial expressions and head shape—to testify against Rice.

Randall Rice admitted that he had walked by the bank and that he'd even spoken to Joseph Mardy and Enoch Gorham. He also admitted that twenty thousand would come in handy since he was interested in investing in Obed Gorham's new spermaceti candle business. He did not, he said, rob the bank and to prove it he willingly let the authorities search his home and business.

Money was never found. But it didn't matter, because the shape of his head and the look on his face were proof positive. On the testimony of the drunk, the idiot, and the banker's scientist, Randall Rice was found guilty and locked up in jail. While he spent every penny trying to prove his innocence, the three who'd actually robbed the bank split the money and went their separate ways. One went to Canada and one to England; the third—while robbing another bank on the mainland—was arrested and ended up in prison.

"The one in prison," Sinclair said. "must've been the one to tell who'd actually robbed Nantucket's bank?"

Jake nodded. "Yes, eventually. But by that time Randall Rice was a poor and broken man. When he got out of prison, the people responsible for sending him to jail were too ashamed to welcome him back. Rice was a constant reminder of a terrible mistake. No one could live with it. Finally, Rice took his family off the island and was never heard from again."

Sinclair took a minute to collect his own thoughts. "And now," he said, "all these years later, one of the family has come back to get his revenge."

"That's right."

"But why now?"

"Some things eat at a man. It doesn't make any difference how irrational that thing is, how far back in his past it happened, some things just eat right through you until there's nothing left but one last crazy act. He's a man on a mission, and that makes him very dangerous."

Sinclair removed his hat and wiped the beads of sweat from his brow. "Did Steven come up with a name?" he asked.

Jake nodded. "I've already called it in to your men: William Rice. We should get something back within the hour." Jake paused a moment then asked, "How many ferries are now on the island?"

Sinclair looked at his watch. "The eleven-forty is long gone. That leaves one, the *Eagle*."

"Incapacitated?"

"Not anymore. They got her engines up and running late last night. Why?" Sinclair asked warily. "What're you thinking?"

Jake absently pulled another blade of grass. "That he'll do the same thing he's been doing. More teasing, a little slight of hand. He's the cat, we're the mice. Will Rice likes to play with his food before he kills it."

"That's disgusting," the chief spit out.

"But true. The classic shell game. Only the pea is a carefully designed explosive and the three shells are a ferry, an airplane, and the Basin. Think about it, Sinclair. He's moved against every possible way off this island. Is the ferry safe? Is the airport? And now he's blocked off the Island Basin so no one can get out."

Sinclair's insides rolled into a slow knot. "We've got a crane coming."

"I'm sure he's aware of that," Jake said reading the question in Sinclair's eyes. "One of the divers said Bennett used to work for Roger Dolby. I'm sure William got all the information he wanted before he killed Gibby. Besides, Roger Dolby said this morning it would take twenty hours to clear the channel. In less than twelve hours it'll be the Fourth of July, chief. That's the day Will Rice has been aiming for."

Sinclair pulled in a deep breath. "Damn," he said with a sigh. "I told Andy Tillis before you ever got here, we oughtta get these damn people off the island. He wouldn't hear of it."

"And now it's too late," Jake conceded.

"We've still got the *Eagle*. Load her up top to bottom. No cars, no cargo. Just people."

Jake shook his head. "And maybe walk right into a trap?" Jake let the thought linger. "What if he blows her up out in Nantucket Sound? Hundreds of people would drown before help ever arrived. You willing to take that chance?"

Sinclair didn't answer.

"I'm not," Jake told him. "Not until I find out more about William Rice. The more we know, the easier it will be to predict where he might attack and how. Once I know what kind of man he really is, I'll pick up the shell. Until then, the odds are still in his favor."

"We can't just sit around and wait," Sinclair said abruptly.

"I don't intend to. We'll beat him to the punch on this one."

"How?"

"Call the ferry lines on the Cape. Tell them we've got an emergency down here and to stop service. That'll cut off one option before it starts. He can't go after what isn't there."

"What about the *Eagle?*" the chief wanted to know.

"She stays right where she is. Just in case, have your men go over every square inch with a fine-tooth comb."

"Done." Sinclair walked back to his car. "What about you?"

"I'll be around," Jake said and headed in the direction of *Gamecock*.

As he had done in Florida when he was about to board a craft and rob it, William Rice had been keeping track of the twenty or so small boats moored in the shallows off of Monomoy Beach. Some were used daily, some only on weekends, and some—in the ten days he'd been watching— had developed no predictable pattern of use. The one he'd locked on was a twenty-seven-foot fiberglass Bow Rider with twin ninety-horse Evinrudes to power her. She was quick and stable—the plaything of a man in his middle fifties who hit the popular fishing grounds every morning for three to four hours, then blasted back to his mooring for a few beers while he cleaned his catch.

William Rice had watched him for days until he was certain the man was punctual and predictable. When the time was right, Rice rowed his dinghy alongside the powerboat. He cleated a bow and stern line and transferred his gear from the dinghy to the Rider. He worked calmly and slowly, just like he belonged there. After he boarded the boat, he walked his dinghy forward and tied her to the mooring ball.

It was just after two o'clock on July 3.

Rice looked around. As expected, everything was locked in a reasonable attempt to discourage vandals and pranksters who might make off with a few life jackets. But there was nothing anyone could do to keep the boat itself from being stolen. It was something that amazed Rice: a thirty-thousand-dollar boat sits there locked up and all anyone has to do for a free boat is board her and drop the mooring line over the side. Isn't America wonderful? Yes indeed. Thank you very much.

Rice took his time and checked the two twenty-gallon fuel tanks. One was half empty, the other full. Perfect. He then bypassed the ignition and hot-wired the engines, which roared to life. While they idled smoothly, he walked forward and removed the mooring line from the bow cleat and dropped it over the side.

He walked back to the cockpit, moved the throttle forward, and slowly powered out to the *Dolfin* for his good-byes. He'd owned the old boat for several years, and knowing he'd never see her again touched him the way having your house burn down would. That done, he sat in the driver's seat of the Rider and headed toward Brant Point and the channel leading out of Nantucket Harbor. The waters of Nantucket Sound lay straight ahead. He powered up and raced out of the harbor.

In the driver's seat, he thought as he roared off. In the driver's seat. Finally.

Chapter

—— 25 ——

Gamecock was still a mess when Jake and Watson climbed on board. Broken glass was on the floor, blood—now dried—was everywhere. Jake hadn't returned since he'd gone to Steven Treadle's home hours before and he wouldn't have come in now if he hadn't wanted his Smith and Wesson .44 Magnum. Something told him to get it, and when he saw what Sam's fight for life had done to F. Gordon's boat, he knew what that something was: William Rice.

Jake unbuckled the .38's shoulder harness and removed it. He took the .44 from his overnight bag, checked the load, and slipped the barrel between his belt and his pants near the small of his back. The .38 would stop a man nine times out of ten. The Magnum—too large and heavy to always carry—would stop a man every time, and would do pretty well with a car. He stuffed some extra shells in his pockets and picked up the phone to call Gloria.

When she answered, he said, "How are you holding up?"

"How do I like being locked up, you mean?" Her voice held an icy brittleness. "I don't like it."

"I didn't expect you would," Jake said and got immediately to the reason he'd called. "I need the keys to *Gamecock*'s tender."

"What for?"

"The keys. Where are they?"

"On a hook to the right of the chart table."

Jake looked where directed and found the keys. He put them in his pocket. "Is there any place to hide in the harbor?" he asked.

"How do you mean?"

"Island Basin clients pull into a slip, then sit out on their deck chairs in the cockpit so everybody walking by can give them an approving look. 'Nice boat' and all that."

"There's a good deal of that," Gloria conceded. "My clients work hard; they want people to see how well they're doing. A cocktail on a million-dollar yacht is a nice way of letting others know."

"Say you were on the opposite end of the social scale and didn't want to put on a show. Where would you go?"

Gloria didn't like the put-down. "As far away from the I-B docks as possible," she replied.

"It's a big harbor," Jake said. "There must be more than a hundred boats out there."

"Closer to two hundred," Gloria corrected.

"There isn't time to search them all."

"Is that what you're planning?" She sounded indignant but hadn't meant to. She twirled the phone cord around her finger, thinking about the attack on the beach when William came after Jake in the Rover. "I don't think that's such a good idea," she said.

Jake ignored her. "If a man wants to hide out on a boat, blend in, be left alone, where would he go?"

"You're not going to listen to me, are you?" Her answer was silence. "There are two places in the harbor where you can be left alone," she said reluctantly. "One is the northern edge of the anchorage on the east side of the harbor. The second is near Monomoy."

"Which is . . . ?"

"A bit of water off a public beach of the same name. You can't miss it—it's directly across from the gas dock on the other side of the harbor. You'll see a lot of dinghies and other small boats moored right off some wooden steps."

"Anything else?"

"Both areas shallow up very fast. If the boat you're looking for is William's home, it won't be close to shore. It'll be farther out, and the farther out you go, the more crowded it gets. Finding his boat won't be easy," she warned.

It never is, Jake thought, and heard in the background the faint knock on her door. His skin prickled. "The only person I told to contact you was Steven Treadle," he said. "What happened to the guard?"

Gloria felt her heart quickening. "He was out there." Her voice was a whisper.

The knock came again. "Don't answer it," Jake ordered but Gloria was already at the door. "Gloria!" he shouted into a dead phone, then heard the man's voice. "Sonofabitch," Jake mumbled angrily.

Gloria was back on the line, sighing with relief. "It's Andy Tillis," she said.

"I heard."

"You don't sound too happy," she replied.

"He's a man I can do without," Jake said, about to hang up.

Gloria sensed it. "Wait. There's one more thing. If you're on the water looking for as much privacy as you'll ever get on a boat, you anchor. You don't pick a mooring."

"Why not?"

"They're rentals. Collectors come by every day for the rental fees. Not much privacy when that happens. Anchoring's free. And nobody bothers a boat at anchor." Gloria paused. "Look, Jake, I can help. Just let me out of—"

"No."

"Please."

Again, he ignored her. "And do me a favor. Don't listen to Tillis. He's a slug. Maybe less than a slug."

"What are you saying?"

"I'm saying I want you to kick him out. He's bad news, believe me."

She recognized the tone and knew there was no use in defending the mayor, a man who'd always been helpful to her since she'd come to the island.

"Be careful," she said and hung up.

"Thanks." Jake was again talking into a dead phone. He put it down and bolted out of the companionway.

Watson waited on the dock wagging his tail. His clear hazel eyes followed Jake from the boat to the dock. He cocked an eyebrow, then yawned.

"Don't start that," Jake said, fighting off his need for sleep. "We've got work to do."

The twelve-foot, hard-bottomed Avon inflatable was tied bow and stern to *Gamecock*'s port side. Jake climbed down the metal ladder and caught Watson, who jumped into the red rubber dinghy on command. Jake put the key in the ignition and fired up the twenty-five-horse Johnson before untying the lines and bringing them aboard.

With the Basin entrance blocked by the sunken *Betsy*'s flybridge, Jake eased the small boat through the pilings until he found an opening wide enough to let him out of the Basin and into the harbor. Then he gunned the engine until the little craft set up and planed. In no time, he'd covered the half mile of open water and was closing in on a cluster of boats in the northeastern portion of the anchorage. He backed off on the throttle and cut his speed to a crawl.

There were boats everywhere, of every size. He worked his way through them slowly, trying to find some indication that William Rice lived there. He looked for the common white dinghy he'd seen in the video. He looked for Rice himself. He found nothing and kept going.

A windsurfer raced by as gulls flew overhead. On the beach, a gull hovered in midair trying to open a clamshell by dropping it on the pebbles below. The gull swooped down, picked up the clam, and soared back into the air, focused on its own moment of survival. For the clam, either the shell would hold or it wouldn't. There was nothing it could do but rise and fall, live or die at the whim of the bird of prey. It was a terrible, helpless feeling—one that Jake was trying to avoid.

He spun the boat around, the engine chattering behind, the smell of exhaust rising about him. Waston shook his head and sneezed at the odor.

"Any ideas?" Jake asked.

Watson cocked his head and looked up at his master.

"Find William Rice," Jake said to his partner. Just then a man popped up from down below his fiberglass ketch and gave him a curious wave. The man looked to be in his early forties with a head of sandy hair. He was well tanned and holding a coffee cup in his hand. Jake motored over.

"Afternoon," the man said lifting his cup slightly in greeting.

Jake waved and shifted into neutral. "I'm looking for a friend of mine," he said and described William Rice.

The man listened intently, wondering why Jake was lying. "Out here on a boat, is he?" he asked.

"He is."

"What kind?"

"That's the thing," Jake said. "He didn't describe it all that well, but he's towing a white dinghy. A ten-footer. Wooden."

The man sipped his coffee and scanned the harbor. Of the two hundred boats anchored or moored, more than half trailed white dinghies. "Not much to go on," the man said and tucked in his shirttail. "By the way, if I were you, I'd be careful," the man told Jake. "Word out here on the water is that some kind of nut is loose in town."

"So I've heard," Jake said and shifted into forward, powering slowly past other captains who eyed him with suspicion. None seemed to welcome his presence, but why should they? They were in this part of the harbor to escape the world, and he was a reminder that they still had a connection.

Jake gently increased his speed and swung in a wide circle, keeping the anchorage to his left and Monomoy to his right. He tried to imagine how far out Rice would anchor. In which direction? What would the boat look like? How would it reflect the man?

"Point him out, Watson," Jake said, smiling at Watson's intensity as he stood firmly near the bow, his sturdy legs bending slightly to absorb the shock of the waves that rippled under the dinghy, his ears flapping in the wind. "Point him out and get on with it."

One hundred yards from the Monomy shore, Jake came off ten degrees to starboard and started to slowly zigzag around the boats, changing speed and direction just enough to make him less of a target. He didn't like being so exposed, so vulnerable, but if he was going to stop William, he couldn't let the gorilla make his next move uncontested.

And what was the next move? Where would he strike? A reflection caught Jake's eye and he squinted in the bright sun, trying to catch sight of it again. Thirty yards up ahead, a pair of binoculars were zeroed in on him, the man's free hand waving vigorously over his head. Jake glanced around quickly in case it was a trap, then drove toward the flush-faced man. He looked about sixty, and from the way he stood rigidly with his binoculars hanging from a strap around his neck, Jake guessed him to be retired military with little to do but varnish his old cabin cruiser and knock back a few rum and cokes. As he got closer, Jake could see that rum and cokes seemed to be the man's primary occupation.

"Glad somebody's paying attention," the man said as Jake pulled up alongside and held onto the cruiser's cap rail. "I would've called the harbormaster, but my radio's broke." The man peered over the side. "Nice dog."

"Thanks."

"Yours?"

"That's right," Jake said feeling he was wasting his time. He picked up his marine radio. "What do you want me to call in?"

"No, no, not now. The name's Mitch Tobey," he said, extending his hand. "I've been watchin' you. You and the dog. You been lookin' for somebody."

"A friend," Jake said, ready to push off.

"How'd you like ta find him?" It stopped Jake cold.

Jake pulled up closer to Tobey. "Who?"

Tobey half smiled. "This friend of yours. He said a man with a dog'd be along sooner or later. He guaranteed it, you might say."

Jake's muscles tightened across his shoulders. "You know where William is?" Jake's eyes were hard on the old man, boring straight through him. Tobey shook his head. "I didn't ask his name, for God's sake. Although I've had the opportunity. I've been watching him ever since he anchored off over there. A real loner. Keeps to himself. I rowed over once and offered him a beer. Worst hour I've spent in a month."

"What's this man look like?" Jake asked and heard his heart pounding as he listened to a description of William Rice. "You're sure?"

Tobey nodded, proud of himself. Too proud, Jake thought and instinctively grew more cautious.

"Which boat?" Jake asked.

Tobey pointed to a thirty-five-foot wooden sailboat not more than twenty yards away. She was rigged as a cutter but only carrying a main- and headsail. From the bangs and dents and discolorations along her sides, it was clear she'd been well used but certainly not neglected. When her transom swung around, Jake could read her name: *Dolfin*.

"Where's the captain?" Jake asked.

"That's what I was gonna tell you. He just made off with my friend's boat. A twenty-seven-foot Bow Rider . . . fast as lightning. Jimmy got her last year so he could spend his time fishing, not getting to the fishing grounds. Then that unfriendly bastard comes along and hot-rods 'er right off the mooring."

"When?"

"Half an hour ago, an hour maybe. Fast as that boat goes, he could be anywhere now," the old man said bitterly. "Probably on his way to the Cape."

"What makes you think he isn't coming back?" Jake wanted to know.

"Because he stopped by the *Dolfin* and loaded up."

"Loaded what?"

"Couldn't tell. Bags of stuff. Real heavy, like he'd packed everything he wanted to keep, and then took off."

Jake pushed the tender free and drifted aft. "Have you got a horn of some kind?" Jake said.

"Sure do. Foghorn. Every boat's got one."

"If he comes back, blow it."

"Will do. Will most certainly do," Mitch Tobey said. He raised his binoculars to watch Jake pull away.

Chapter

—26—

Jake drove the Avon hard to the *Dolfin*, circled her once, then eased off on the throttle as the dinghy glided alongside. He grabbed the lifeline and held fast. Watson climbed to the seat, then jumped onboard and into the old boat's cockpit. He slowed down to an alert and mincing walk along the cockpit seats, then stopped.

"What?" Jake asked and watched the dog take a few more cautious steps. "What is it, boy?"

Watson answered with a crisp warning bark, deeper and lower in his throat than normal. He then lowered himself and bellied forward across the teak.

The security guard at Boston's Logan Airport had made a joke of it— drug sniffer is he? Tracker? I'll bet tracker. Watson did have the uncanny ability to sense danger. In the wild where fights were for survival, all animals had that working sense but Watson's ability somehow went beyond that, as if he were a gifted child with psychic powers. Jake had long ago stopped trying to figure out what made Watson tick, and simply trusted him.

Jake cleated the bow line and slowly climbed aboard. Watson hadn't moved. He was staring straight ahead, his eyes locked on the wooden slats and closed hatch that separated the cockpit from belowdecks.

Jake followed the dog's eyes and moved toward the hatch as Watson whimpered anxiously. When Jake touched the hatch, Watson half whined, then rolled out a throaty growl that turned into one bark after another. It was then that Jake noticed the hatch wasn't locked, it was only closed. Damned odd behavior for a man leaving his boat and not coming back, Jake thought.

He moved closer and examined the hatch, paying particular attention to the strap hinge that hung down from it. Jake saw that behind the upper slat, a double copper wire had been tied to the hinge. Rice had obviously wired his own boat. If the hatch were slid back, the strap hinge would be raised high enough to close the circuit.

Watson sprang to his feet and offered a few angry yelps at the two aft lockers built into the seats on either side of the pedestal steering wheel. On most boats of this size, the lockers led to the engine compartment, which in turn led to the main cabin. Jake was not a small man, but if he could snake his way, he might be able to get into the cabin, disconnect the bomb's triggering mechanism, and have a look around inside Rice's boat.

"What do you think, Watson? These lockers wired too?"

Watson was still on full alert, shifting his weight from one front paw to the other. When Jake bent low and examined both locker doors, Watson squelched a nervous yawn with an undulating growl. Jake too felt uneasy, but he remained calm and steady even when he saw that each locker was spring loaded and wired. Open either one and the cockpit would explode. If he was going to get inside the *Dolfin* and maybe inside the mind of William Rice, the forward hatch in the bow was the last possible option.

"Come on, Watson," Jake said and led the black dog along the deck. Forward of the coaming was a square hatch opening built of teak and covered with Plexiglas to let in light. The hatch was built into the deck over the forward sleeping compartment. When the hatch was open, a man could lower himself through it, stand on the bunk, and step down into the cabin. The hatch was closed, but Jake could see through the Plexiglss that it was neither wired nor locked from the inside.

A trap? Jake wondered. Wire the cockpit but leave one entrance free? Or was it a safe way for Rice to come and go if he needed to return to his boat? But where was he? Jake wondered. And why go to all this trouble?

"Something isn't right," he said to Watson with a reassuring pat. Watson wasn't reassured and shook with a spasm of fear. Carefully—feeling the underside for any surprises—Jake opened the hatch and rested it against the base of the mast.

Still on deck, he leaned over into the opening for a cautious look. The door separating the forward compartment from the main cabin was ajar, providing a partial view of the *Dolfin*'s musty insides. She was narrow and low ceilinged, dressed out in yellowy brown bunk cushions that looked worn and tattered. A sleeping bag was bunched in one corner, and dishes from the last meal or two sat in the galley sink. There was no navigation station, no bank of electronics such as filled *Gamecock,* but Jake hadn't expected that. He wasn't certain what he'd expected, but what he'd hoped for was a clue to what Rice had in store. And he wouldn't find it unless he went below for a thorough look around.

He swung his legs over the opening and, supporting himself with one hand on each side of the hatch frame, lowered himself down. Watson sat and peered into the opening as Jake stretched his legs, hunting for the bunk with his foot. As soon as his right foot eased down on the cushion, he heard the quick crack of gunfire and a dull whack as the bullet splintered wood in the cockpit behind him.

Quickly, Jake pushed himself back on deck, staying low. He pulled the .44 from his belt and looked out over the water for the location of the shooter, his vision snapping from boat to boat to boat. But nothing stood out. Nothing moved on the water.

He pushed Watson behind him and turned toward Mitch Tobey's boat to see if Tobey might have been watching. But Tobey was doing more than that. A rifle barrel flashed in the low evening sun as Mitch Tobey took dead aim at Jake.

Jake raised the .44 and pulled off two fast rounds. They missed high as the *Dolfin* rolled up on a swell. In a fraction of a second he compensated and fired again just as the old man's weapon flashed another round. Jake's shot struck Tobey in the chest, killing him instantly. Tobey's bullet hit one of the cockpit explosives. The back of the *Dolfin* burst into a white-orange brillance and exploded in a loud, crackling bang, throwing Jake and Watson hard over the bow and into the water.

Jake gulped for air and swam away from the raging fire. He called Watson's name and kicked hard to keep his own dizzy head above water. "Watson!" he called again frantically and swam toward the rubber dinghy, which was slowly floating away.

From his post outside Miss Gorham's apartment, Turner Reese watched in awe as a fireball rose up from somewhere out in the harbor. The higher the smoke went, the lower his spirits fell. Something terrible had happened, that he knew—*another* terrible thing. As before, he was unprepared for it.

Not unprepared to stop it. That was out of the question. Turner Reese was unprepared to accept it, to acknowledge it, to deal with it in any way. What he wanted now more than anything was to go home, but he'd heard from other Special Summer Forces who'd stopped by to razz him about pulling rich-woman guard duty that that was impossible. The airport was shut down, the IB dock blockaded, and the ferry service closed. Twenty miles out in the ocean and the only way home was to swim. Jesus.

"Open this door!" Gloria Gorham commanded and pounded her fists hard against it. "Right now, do you hear me?"

Turner Reese had no fight left and opened it.

"What was the explosion?"

Turner shrugged and pointed toward the harbor and the rising smoke.

"My God," Gloria said as the sky turned a hideous lurid color.

Turner didn't even react as Gloria took off like a rabbit toward the Island Basin, running down the stairs and outside, darting between cars and slow movers. She reached the Basin the same time Sinclair did and fought her way through the stunned crowds listlessly lining the docks.

She raced up to the chief and grabbed his arm. "Jake's out there," she panted.

Sinclair's voice sounded as gruff as a bear's. "What did you say?"

"He's out there looking for the boat . . . for William's boat," she said as an inner voice began a silent prayer for Jake to be found alive. After what happened to Sam . . . "Do something!" she demanded.

"I will but don't help me, you got that?" Sinclair barked. "I don't give a damn what you do, but *don't help me!*"

"Fine!" she yelled back and followed the chief as he bulled his way past the onlookers.

What is the fascination with another man's misery? Sinclair wondered. A car wreck, a house fire, a burning boat. At times like this when gawkers blocked his every step, Sinclair wished all of them would go straight to hell.

"Get out of my way," he growled and charged on, Gloria still in tow. "Stand back, for Christ's sake . . . let me through . . ."

"Chief?"

"Not now."

"Chief Sinclair?"

The voice was not penetrating his consciousness as he and Gloria made their way to the end of Old South Wharf. Sinclair needed a boat to get out on the water; he'd hoped to find the dive boat and either Ron Katish or Joe Macy, but they were gone.

"Chief Sinclair! CHIEF!" Officer Shean's voice finally crashed through.

Shean was standing on the bulkhead nearest the sunken *Betsy* and pointing out into the harbor where the red Avon—the portside pontoon partially deflated, the engine barely running—pushed its way unevenly through the water.

It was Jake. The closer he got to the IB docks, the quieter the crowd became as they clearly saw the blood smeared across his chest and a limp black dog at his feet.

"Dear God," Gloria whispered. Nothing else would come out. She wanted to say more, to be of some comfort. She needed to say something to release the tension of those around her, to reassure them and herself that no matter what had happened these past few days, everything—somehow—would be all right. Would be fine. It was not only her job as IB manager, it was what she wanted to believe. What she needed to believe. But a small lump of flame had burned her throat dry and she—like the others—was speechless.

William Rice never heard the sound of the explosion over the roar of the stolen Bow Rider's engines, but he saw the puff of smoke and grabbed the wheel of the Rider with such joyful glee, he nearly ripped it out of the steering column. Billowing smoke from that part of the inner harbor could mean only one thing: Jake Eaton had found the *Dolfin,* and the old boat on her own—or with the help of Mitch Tobey—had ended the career of the Cambridge detective and his black dog.

It was a glorious thought. Rice could just imagine Tobey sitting out there with his binoculars and his .22-caliber peashooter playing military man. That's how Gibby Bennett had proudly introduced him. Military man. Battle wounds to prove it. Good drinkin' buddy, too.

Just hours after Gibby's body was recovered, Rice had paid Mitch Tobey a visit.

"Me and Gibby was best of friends," the old military man had said, his eyes going all misty. "Real good friends. Do you really think Gibby would want me ta do this?" the military man had asked.

"Don't you? Here, let's toast to ol' Gibby," Will Rice said and poured the Southern Comfort, Gibby's favorite. Turned out Mitch Tobey had a yearning for it too.

"Gibby's brand, you know. Always drank Comfort, Gibby did. Me too."

"That a fact?" Will Rice said and wondered if it was normal not to have any feelings at all about cutting off a man's arm. None. Zero. He needed the arm and he took it.

"It is, yes sir. That's a fact. Always drank Comfort."

"Then to Gibby."

Tobey raised his glass. "To Gibby," he said, thoughts circling the edge of his mind. "Let me get this straight. You wanna give me a hundred dollars to keep an eye on your boat."

"That's right."

"Why don't you do it?"

Rice nodded approval at the question. "I'm gonna take me a little trip. Point some folks in the direction of a killer."

Tobey thought for a moment, then said, "You know somethin' I don't?"

The hook had been baited, the line paid out. The military man bit. Now to reel him in nice and easy with the help of the Southern Comfort.

"I know corruption when I see it," Will Rice said. "This island is full of it. If there's ever any justice to be done, it's gonna have to come in from outside. The Vineyard, maybe. I know the state police real good on the Vineyard. They could wrap this up in no time."

Mitch drank his glass dry. "Wrap what up?" he asked confused.

"Who killed Gibby and sank his boat. Can't have that sort of thing. It's goddamned anarchy, that's what it is."

"That's what it is, all right," Mitch said, his chest puffed a full six inches wider. "And, by God, you can't . . . *cannot* . . . have that sort of thing." He let his chest sag and added, "No, sir, you can't. That's a fact."

"Ought to at least hold the suspect for a day or two," Will Rice said, pouring more into their empty glasses. "Even if he is tied into the big money. Big money ruins us all."

"What's that?"

"The Island Basin."

"Ohhh, them. Gibby hated them . . . what's her name?"

"Gorham. Ol' GG herself."

"Gibby hated her. She fired him, you know." Tobey was on a roll. "And you say this suspect works for the I-B Gorhams?"

Will Rice nodded. "Man with a black dog. Jake Eaton. If he comes snooping around my boat . . ."

"Why would he?"

"He knows I was a friend of Gibby's. He knows I might go to the police over on the Vineyard and tell them if they'd open their damn eyes, they'd see that Eaton was their prime suspect in Gibby's killing."

Tobey nodded instant agreement. "But," he said slyly, "like you said, I could take care of it myself. For Gibby."

"That you could. That you could."

"Say no more, my friend. I'm military. Old military. I'll take care of it. Be a pleasure. And what about you?"

"Think I'll borrow a boat. Just for the day, you understand."

Tobey crinkled his brow knowingly. "You're going for reinforcements," he said, slurring his words. "Over on the Vineyard. Your friends over there."

"Exactly," William Rice had said. "I'm going for reinforcements."

For one last look, Rice swung the Bow Rider around. Curls of black smoke hung over the harbor. Was it possible? he wondered. Could the old bastard have done what William hadn't been able to do—blown Jake away? It was a marvelous thought. Simply wonderful.

It was a thought Rice kept with him as he swung back around on course and laid the throttle down. The powerful boat opened the blue water like a knife.

It was 7:15 P.M. Less than an hour of daylight remaining, and only a few hours until his Fourth of July celebration hit the island.

Chapter

—27—

An hour after he got Jake to the hospital, Russell Sinclair and his men were scouring the *Eagle* looking for an explosive device. They began in the deckhouse and wearily worked their way down. They were weary of death. Weary of the sleepless hours. Weary of the doubt knotted in their chests.

Searching the *Eagle* was a huge job. The ferry had three large decks and room for nearly 2,000 passengers and sixty cars. She was a miniature football field of floating iron, and Sinclair hated every inch of her because he feared, as did Eaton, that she was wired to blow, and it was his job to stop it. Suppose they couldn't find the explosives?

Sinclair moved quickly, his eyes scanning for what didn't belong, be it wire or color or shape. He was looking everywhere, feeling with each step that he had lost control of his life. And then it hit him—the reason he disliked the Gorhams, the mayor, the big money, Gloria herself. She was the embodiment of what was bad for Nantucket. He, and to an even greater extent Nate Cooper, had a dream for the island, a dream for a new start. But Mayor Tillis had traded that dream to the Gorhams, sold it right out from under them. Property for dreams.

"Damnit all," Sinclair muttered to himself. Then the call came up from below.

"Chief? Chief Sinclair? We've found them, sir. We found the explosives."

The phone on the mayor's desk rang ten times, then stopped. It rang ten more times, then quit again. Long after Mayor Andrew Tillis concluded they were never going to leave him alone, he picked up the phone.

"Yes?"

The mayor's voice was so weak that Sinclair had to restrain himself from shouting "Boo!" heartlessly into the mouthpiece. "We've found explosives on the *Eagle*," Sinclair said louder than normal, trying to overpower the nervous flutter in his voice.

Tillis was slow, his thoughts pawing through cobwebs, but that news broke through the haze. "A bomb?" His voice sounded far away.

"We've got to talk, Andy. My place or yours? Just name it."

"We *are* talkin'."

"Face to face. You've got to own up to your repsonsibilities, Andy."

"Look, Russ—"

"No, you look. You can't hide from this any longer, Andy. Get your ass down here, or I'm coming over. Name it."

The line was quiet for nearly a full minute before Mayor Tillis managed to speak. "I'll be right there."

In twenty minutes, Andy Tillis pushed through the swinging glass doors of the police station and walked into Chief Sinclair's office. Even though it was a warm night, he rubbed his arms as if he were cold. He smiled uneasily at Sinclair, who looked up from his desk with unfriendly eyes.

"Why the nasty look, Russell?" asked Tillis. "I didn't plant any bombs."

Sinclair put down his pen. "That might be a point we could argue."

"Oh, really?" The mayor's voice shot up an octave. "I suppose you're going to throw my opposition to the Preservation Society back at me. Is that your agenda, Russell? I support island progress, and the devil shows up at our doorstep? The logic is inescapable—I'm responsible for this entire mess. Bullshit."

Sinclair eyed him coolly. "Sounds to me like you feel a little guilty."

"Then you don't hear very well, Russ," the mayor said and took the chair opposite the desk. "What I am responsible for is the safety and security of the people on this island. It's a responsibility I take very seriously."

Sinclair said nothing.

"I know you don't believe that," Tillis continued, "but the fact remains, I am in charge. I have to decide what's best, and then I have to act."

"Decide what's best for who?" Sinclair asked.

The mayor had settled in his seat, his elbows resting on the arms of the chair, his fingers together forming a steeple. "For all of us," he said. "As mayor, I never think otherwise. Can't afford to."

"You're playing games, Andy," Sinclair told him. "I can hear it in your voice, and I don't like it one damn bit."

The mayor's steeple collapsed. "Now, hold on."

"No, you hold on," Sinclair said and leaned forward on his desk, his eyes boring through the man across from him. "We're under attack, damnit! You saw what happened out at the airport this morning. And the Basin's closed down and will be until the tug arrives. In addition, that ferry was wired with so much explosive it would've torn the bottom right out of her, and you sit here playing games."

"Are you through?"

"No." Sinclair's anger was rising. "I've canceled all the incoming ferries."

Tillis's eyes popped wide. "On whose authority?"

"Mine. Eaton said—"

"Oh, the hell with Eaton." Andy Tillis's voice was shrill. "He's no good to us now. We've got to work our way out of this on our own, and those ferries were how we were going to do it."

"You never mentioned that to me."

"So?"

"You said 'we,'" Sinclair said suspiciously. "Who've you been talking to, Andy? Or do I venture a wild guess?"

The mayor took in a deep breath. "I don't know what you mean."

"Missy Gorham—and don't lie to me, Andy. You don't know what you're dealing with . . . but I do." Sinclair took a folder from his desk and opened it. "We got the report back on William Randall Rice," he said. "If we get out of this alive, we can talk about why he came to Nantucket, but for now it's enough to know that he's a navy demolitions expert dishonorably discharged with a police record half the length of the Florida coast."

"I don't see what difference it makes, Russell. You told me yourself Rice is gone, that he stole a boat and took off."

"That's what Eaton reported. He thinks Rice wired his own boat then hired Mitch Tobey to blow it up once Jake got onboard."

"I'm not doubting the source or the truth of it. All I'm suggesting is that this Rice fellow has finally gotten a stomach full and left."

"Not likely."

"Not if he'd just walked away, but he didn't," Tillis said, his voice warming to the task. "Look at the facts, Russ. You said yourself Rice placed charges on his own boat, that he'd arranged for old Mitch Tobey to watch over it, blow it up if need be. What made him do it, I don't know, and we never will now that the old fool's dead. But the point is, William Rice wouldn't do that if he were planning on coming back. It doesn't make sense. The only way it does is to assume that Rice has done what he came for, and then left."

Sinclair shook his head. "Impossible."

Tillis lost control of his voice again. "It is not impossible," he squeaked. "Gloria Gorham is still alive, Andy."

"And under guard. William Rice is not a stupid man. He knew he couldn't get to her. Why risk it? He's off the island, Russell. He's gone. That's the only way it makes sense."

"Wishful thinking."

"Have you got a better idea?" Tillis waited, then filled the silence. "God knows he's killed enough people, sunk a boat, blown up his own, set a charge onboard a passenger ferry. That's enough," Tillis said, as if saying it actually made it true. "Mission accomplished. He can't do any more or doesn't want to. Bored, maybe. People like that get bored too, I suppose."

"So he calls it a day?" Sinclair mocked.

"Far-fetched?"

"Yes."

"I don't know, Russell. Think about it."

"I have."

"Then you come up with something better."

"I don't have anything better, Andy. All I know is that this man promised fireworks, and I don't think he's the type to leave with only an hour to go before the Fourth of July," Sinclair said as Tillis glanced at his own watch.

The mayor's shoulders sagged as if a weight had been placed on them. "So what are you saying?"

"I'm saying he's going to hit us big. Eaton's convinced me that it's bigger now than just an attack on Gloria Gorham. It's Nantucket—the whole island—that he's after. Sometime between midnight and sunup, sometime when the fireworks will be seen best, William Rice is going to make his move."

"And we're just going to sit here and wait?" Tillis shot back. "Is that what you call a plan of action? To sit here and wait?"

"Eaton said—"

"Eaton's not here!"

"Eaton said—"

"Eaton's in the hospital, Russell. If he's so smart, how is it he damn near bought it from an old fart like Mitch Tobey? Come on, use your head," Tillis coaxed.

"He's been right so far," Sinclair warned.

Tillis leaned back in his chair as if he'd given up. "All right. Say he is right. Say this Rice fellow is out there somewhere waiting for one last shot at us. If that's the case, Russ, it's all the more reason to get some of these folks off the island."

"I told you the ferries aren't running," Sinclair reminded him. "You can't get off the island."

"Unless we sail on the *Eagle.* No, no, don't say anything, Russ. Just listen. Her engines are up and running. You and your men have gone over her with a fine-tooth comb. She's perfect for a little run over to the mainland. Perfect and safe."

"You're crazy!" Sinclair shouted.

"I'm using my head. Look, Russell, Nantucket needs us and we need to help one another come to grips with this little mess we've gotten ourselves into. Maybe we should've done some things differently, but we didn't. Now," the mayor stressed, "is not the time to turn our backs on one another."

Sinclair was wary of the political "we." "Careful, Andy. I'm not going to do anything else stupid."

"Of course not. You're going to do what's best. When you first told me that this man Rice was on the island, I told you that Nantucket could not afford a tragedy. It would ruin us."

"I know that," Sinclair said, still keeping his distance.

"What's happened so far is terrible, don't get me wrong. But if you are convinced that this Rice fellow, this madman, is a few hours away from something bigger—something worse—we can't stand by and wait for it. We can't."

"I can't stop him, Andy. I'm trying." Sinclair shook his head. "I'm so damn tired of this," he said.

"You can't do more than you've already done," Tillis reassured him. "I know that. No one can expect you to do more than you've done."

Sinclair could feel the trap closing. "What are you after, Andy?"

"I'm not after anything. I'm simply owning up to my responsibility as mayor of this island." He paused, thinking. He ran one hand over his chin. "I had a meeting with Miss Gorham this afternoon, Russell."

Sinclair was afraid to ask but did. "And?"

"And plans are already in place to get her Basin guests off the island. We didn't know at the time it'd be on the *Eagle,* but that's just how things work out. When you canceled ferry service, you saw to that."

"The *Eagle* stays on the dock, Andy."

"I don't think so."

"She stays on the dock," Sinclair repeated in a firmer tone, then added, "You're always trying to rub up to Missy Gorham, aren't you, Andy? You backed the Gorhams instead of the Preservation Society, and you haven't gotten off the scent yet."

"So? I did what was good for Nantucket," Tillis defended. "We're a tourist town, Russ. Any dumb-shit tourist can drive to Disneyland, but when you sail into Nantucket Harbor, you're a captain. Captains pay, Russell. It's part of the privilege."

"And the privileged move out on the ferry?"

"That's how I see it, and I would imagine that the privileged—as you put it—will be eternally grateful," Tillis answered.

"And when this is all over, you think they'll rush right back? Pocketbooks wider than ever?"

"I'd hope," Tillis said.

"Nothing doing, Andy. The ferry stays on the dock," Sinclair said. "I won't do it."

"Of course you will."

Sinclair let his voice rise. "In my professional opinion, I agree with Eaton. Everyone stays put. When the tug brings the crane over and the channel is opened, those people can leave under their own power."

"When's the crane due?" Tillis asked.

"Anytime."

"Roger Dolby and his outfit?"

Sinclair nodded.

"Roger Dolby hasn't been on time for anything in his life," Andy Tillis said, but he sensed his chief's resolve. "Look Russell," he said, looking him straight in the eye, "you were in the army. You've got a good feel for the pecking order, and you know that now and again, everybody gets pecked. So I'm telling you: get those people out of here and keep your job, or I will get them out of here and you will lose it. Understand? Now you take a little time and figure out how best to proceed while I go tell Miss Gorham that if she wants her people off the island, we've got a ferry for her."

Chapter

——28——

Cottage Hospital was a little over a mile from police headquarters, but it seemed to take Russell Sinclair forever to drive it. A gray feeling welled within him, slowing him down. Once again Andy Tillis held all the cards, and he had rubbed in that fact with the smug look of a gambler. It was the look that ate at Sinclair as he turned down the hospital's driveway.

He pulled to a stop, got out, and slammed the cruiser door. Entering the hospital, he tried to think of some suitable explanation for Jake once he got around to telling him that the ferry was loading and would soon be on her way. A suitable explanation wasn't necessarily the truth: the truth was, with his job on the line, he hadn't stood up to Mayor Tillis.

At the nurses' station, Sinclair tried to grin. "I'd like to see Jake Eaton," he said.

The duty nurse busied herself with some papers, trying to avoid looking directly at the chief of police. She'd never seen him look so bad. Finally she turned to him. "Are you all right, Russell? You look like you haven't seen a bed in years."

"I'm fine. Never better," he said.

"You don't look so fine," she said. She thought he looked like her son did when he struck out in Little League.

"How's Eaton?"

"Sore. A few stitches. He tried to leave once, but Dr. Kenton wouldn't hear of it. He wants him overnight for observation. Possible concussion."

"Is Dr. Kenton here now?" Sinclair asked.

"Gone home," the nurse said. "He's already put in his eighteen hours."

Lucky guy, the chief thought. "Room number?"

"Two hundred," she said, pointing to the stairs.

Once upstairs, Sinclair paused outside the room, then went in without knocking. Jake was sitting on the edge of his bed studying his copy of William Rice's background while carefully working his shirt over his hurt shoulder.

"God, am I glad you're here," Jake said, and grimaced at the pull of the stitches. "I know what he's going to do, chief. I know what Rice is going to hit. Think about it," he said, hurriedly buttoning his shirt. "A navy demolitions expert but not part of any attack team."

"So?"

"So? Is that all you can say?"

Sinclair shrugged.

"Didn't you read the report?" Jake snapped.

"Most of it," Sinclair said. It was a weak defense. "I was in a meeting with Andy Tillis."

"And?" Jake tucked in his shirt and studied the man in front of him. "What is it, Sinclair?"

Sinclair struggled to return Jake's look but faltered. "The passenger ferry," he said. "They're taking everyone from the Island Basin and loading them on the *Eagle*."

"Who?"

"Andy Tillis and your client. They're going to take them off the island."

"But that's suicide!" Jake exploded. "Didn't you try to stop them?"

Sinclair hesitated, then added awkwardly. "I couldn't. I wanted to but—"

"Get out of my way." Jake ripped his .44 Magnum out of the top chest drawer. Without saying a word, he stormed out the door and down the hall.

Sinclair ran up behind him. "What are you going to do?"

Jake grimaced as the stitches in his shoulder and pulled back. "Where's Watson? I talked to the vet and he . . ." Jake leaned against the wall as his world began to spin. He tried to stand on his own and wobbled.

Sinclair held him up. "You can't go anywhere," he told him. "You're going to get yourself killed."

Jake's head throbbed. "Where is Watson?" he demanded.

"Gloria picked him up. She's taking care of him."

Jake put his hand against the wall, then marched off down the hall.

"Eaton? I told Andy what you said." He was with Jake step for step. "I told him the ferry stays on the dock. Bomb or no bomb, she stays."

Jake stopped. "You found the explosive?"

Sinclair nodded. "*Explosives,* all disarmed," he said, then hesitated. "Eaton, please. I know I should have stood up to Tillis, but I couldn't. Please let me help."

Jake continued for another twenty feet, realizing with each step he wasn't going to make it on his own. "Come on then," Jake said. "Drive."

"Where to?"

"The Island Basin. Maybe we can stop some fools from killing themselves."

First the orange ball sunset; then the evening mist hanging over the island; then the patchy night fog blowing in on southwesterly winds, causing the island to disappear behind the heaviest rolling banks. William Rice had watched it all with gritty, impatient eyes, but what he was looking for had yet to appear. Could he have missed it, as he'd apparently missed spotting the *Eagle* sail out? Or, had the ferry never left Nantucket? The doubts and questions darted through his mind, and he had to force himself to ignore them.

You shut up or you do, he told himself. Even if they're your own thoughts, shut them up. Blank them out. There has been no mistake so far, and there would be none.

And how could it be otherwise? Every vessel entering or exiting Nantucket Harbor had to pass between the lighthouse on Great Point and the red flashing navigational bell buoy marking the beginnings of the harbor channel. There was no other way in or out. Beyond the flashing bell they would run aground in the shallows, and past Great Point there was nothing but open Atlantic Ocean. Every craft of any size had to pass between these two points, and that's where Rice had been waiting after he'd scattered some clothing, life jackets, and enough fuel to create a slick a few miles farther out into the Sound for the Coast Guard to find. He'd radioed in a distress call, vessel going down, and watched the Guard race off after phantoms.

Then to save his own fuel, he'd anchored the Bow Rider close to shore halfway off Great Point and watched until the mist thickened and the sun went down. At night when the fog had begun to move in, he had set off, hunting through the dark waters like a hungry shark. Back and forth, back and forth, leaving trails of swirling phosphorescent curls in his wake.

What he wanted was out there. Close and closing. He could feel it as surely as he felt the long roll of the Sound pass beneath him. Then he saw it—the tug broke through the dense fog patch and he could make out the red and green running lights coming toward him a half mile away.

Rice's spirits rose. It was the moment he'd been waiting for, planning for all along. He knew he could never get away with stealing a tug, but sinking the *Betsy* meant one would be delivered to him. Brilliant. His heart pounded like that of a heavyweight fighter on the night of his comeback.

But this wasn't a fight for money. This was a fight for glory and honor and revenge. Old Randall had been screwed, and the son of many sons was about to step into the ring for the entire Rice clan and make up for it.

Who can stop me? Rice thought as he turned off his running lights and throttled hard for one hundred yards in the foggy darkness. No one can stop me. Zero. Just rack the balls, baby, this game is about over. But to make certain, he monitored channel 16 and listened to the Coast Guard. They'd found the oil slick and the clothes and the life jackets he'd scattered over the water. They wouldn't stop looking for survivors until it was too late for even the Coast Guard to stop him.

Running the Bow Rider hard on instinct and skill, Rice shot through the tug's prow wake and came up beside her. The tug captain was in the pilothouse, drinking coffee and paying attention to his radar screen as Rice came aboard.

The crane operator never had a chance. He was checking the towing bridle when Rice slid the knife in and pushed him over into the path of the towed barge. The captain didn't hear the scream—the engine noise was too loud. Nor did the captain hear William Rice enter the pilothouse and come up behind him. All he saw was large pink bubbles blow from his lips as he tried to speak. All he felt was a sharp, shallow pain as something cool ripped across his throat.

Rice threw the captain over the side and checked the tug for additional mates. There were none. He then went back inside the pilothouse and eased off on the throttle. It would take time to slow the following barge.

It was 2 A.M. on the morning of the Fourth of July and Rice was five miles from the entrance of Nantucket Harbor. Five miles from the knockout blow.

Chapter

29

The fog was so thick, the headlights were useless. Sinclair was feeling his way along the road, seeing only a few feet ahead.

Jake grew impatient. Nothing had gone right, and now this slow crawl. "Can't you go any faster?" he blurted, his exhaustion not helping his temper.

"Not if you want to get there."

Jake slammed his fist against the dash. "Damn it!" A pain shot through his shoulder where a splintered piece of the *Dolfin*'s planking had cut him. He hadn't noticed it in his desperate attempt to find Watson, who'd been thrown clear of the burning boat. Jake had swum and hunted until his arms became numb with fatigue. Finally, he had seen the black dog struggling weakly between swells. Jake had carved through the water with powerful strokes, using the last of his energy to hoist his barely breathing partner and himself into the dinghy.

"The Island Basin," Jake said evenly to Sinclair. "We need every man we can get down on those docks."

Sinclair took his eyes from the road and glanced at Jake. "Now?"

"Right now," Jake said and pointed to the radio. "Start with Buck Thurmon. Get him out of bed and tell him to meet you down there."

"Me? Where are you going?"

"To the ferry."

Sinclair reached down for the radio just as the deep, rumbling sound of the *Eagle*'s horn blasted through the wet fog. Once, twice, three times she boomed her warning to clear the channel. She was hauling lines and leaving the dock.

*   *   *

Standing on the edge of the now empty ferry dock, hearing the screeching tires and seeing the flashing blue lights of the police car, Gloria Gorham felt unaccountably chilled. Even Watson's warm, grateful eyes—she'd taken him to the vet and watched after him—didn't help this empty feeling, nor did they soften Jake's biting, sharp voice.

"Proud of yourself?" He didn't wait for an answer and pushed open the passenger side door. "Get in."

Gloria didn't budge. But Watson, bursting with happiness at seeing Jake, obliged. Jake gingerly hugged him, relieved he was all right.

Jake gunned the accelerator, then hit the brakes. The police car jumped forward ten feet and slid to a halt. "Get in!" he said again to Gloria with such force there was no denying him.

Gloria shut the door after her and glared at him. "What did you want me to do? There was a ferry offered. I had people who wanted off the island. What would you have done?"

Jake winced as he spun the police car around and headed back toward downtown. "Where's Tillis?"

"On the ferry with the other passengers."

"Figures."

"What's that supposed to mean?"

"It means he looks out for himself, nobody else. Just like any other politician. After finding a bomb, I'm surprised the captain agreed to leave," Jake said. An uneasy silence followed as the car blasted across Main Street. "Well?"

"I paid him," Gloria said, looking down at her hands.

Jake gripped the steering wheel, his knuckles showing white. "We've got to get them back," he said.

"Back?"

"Back," Jake said, his face grim. "They're sitting ducks out there."

"I don't understand," she said. "Andy told me—"

"Andy Tillis is a fool. You two make a good pair," Jake said more disappointed than angry. "What the hell did you think you were doing?"

"I was doing what I'm in business for! I was taking care of my guests," she snapped.

The police car roared through the A&P parking lot and bumped to a stop against the curb on Whales Way. It was then that Gloria saw the swarm of police on the IB docks, their tiny flashlights glowing in the mist as they pierced the darkness under the docks.

"What is all this?" she asked. "What are those men doing?"

"Looking for explosives."

"Here? My God."

To their right and left, fire trucks blocked the entrance to Commercial Wharf. Jake threw open the cruiser door and eased his sore body out of the car. Gloria and Watson followed after him into the flashing red- and blue-tinted fog.

"Where are we going?" Gloria asked.

"You open the office on the gas dock, and I'll be right there," Jake said and turned his attention to a fireman pulling hose from a ladder truck. "Have you seen Chief Sinclair?"

The fireman pointed in the direction of a tall man wearing a yellow rubber raincoat. He was standing next to Russell Sinclair, and pointing at something that appeared to be blueprint schematics.

"You got the prints?" Jake asked.

"Right here," Buck Thurmon replied.

"This way," Jake said, and the three men raced down the wharf to the gas dock and upstairs to the office, where Gloria waited nervously.

"I thought," she said, carefully keeping her voice in check, "that is, the mayor told me . . . told all of us that this . . . this attack on us was over with. He said William Rice had taken a boat and left the island."

"The attack hasn't even started," Jake said. "William Rice left the island to load up, and if I'm right, when he sees the *Eagle* and discovers his plan to scuttle her won't work, he'll make a run on her."

Gloria stood her ground. "With a little boat?" she asked. "What can he do in a little boat against the biggest ferry in the fleet?"

"If we're lucky, the little boat is all he'll have. He has a way of getting what he needs. Remember, that tug's out there."

Gloria's jaw dropped. "You don't think he's going to ram the ferry?"

"I do. Now, you get on the radio," Jake said to her. "Talk to the captain, talk to Mayor Tillis, talk to anyone who'll listen, and tell them to get that ferry back here. Then reach that tugboat and tell them to turn around for home, to keep their eyes open but don't come near this island. Rice is out there waiting for them."

Buck Thurmon wasn't sure what he'd heard. "Waiting for them?" He looked at Jake questioningly. "A run on her? What's this have to do with us breaking out all our fire equipment at this hour of the morning?"

"Everything," Jake said. "How much have you told him, Sinclair?"

"Just enough to get him down here. Potential fire hazard in Zone One, I said."

"Right," Jake replied. He laid the blueprint of the Island Basin on Sam Kingsbury's wooden desk.

In broken parallel lines running from the tank farm, under Whales Way and onto an off-loading dock, three sets of eight-inch fuel lines were indicated. Smaller four-inch lines branched off and ran to the Island Basin gas dock just below them.

"This is the fire of Will Rice's fireworks," Jake said tapping his finger along the lines. "This is the target—what he's been building up to all along."

"Like I told you before, Eaton, that's impossible," Buck Thurmon said incredulously. "The town, the fire department, the fuel supplier—all of us have worked on safety for years. Each year we take another step to prevent an accident and there hasn't been one since I took over."

"But this won't be an accident," Jake told him. "Will Rice knows as much as you do about this tank farm and the lines running underground and the shutoff valves and the docks they're all connected to. He's studied it."

"How could he?" Sinclair asked. "He'd need a set of plans."

"He's got a set," Jake said and turned to Gloria, who was still trying to raise the *Eagle*. "Isn't there supposed to be a set in this office?"

"Of course," she said. "Sam's. They're in the desk."

Jake opened all four drawers. The plans were gone. "The bottle of Southern Comfort with the message inside? All dressing," he said. "A diversion. The reason Rice delivered that message here was to get those prints."

"Jesus Christ," Sinclair said, astonished.

"That's what Sam tried to tell me. He wasn't saying friends or fins, he was trying to say prints. These prints. My guess is Bennett helped Rice to get back at you for being fired," Jake said to Gloria. She had switched to channel 69 and was trying once again to call the ferry.

"Island Basin calling the *Eagle*. This is the Island Basin calling the passenger ferry *Eagle*. Over." Gloria waited. "I-B calling the *Eagle*, come back."

"Say he's got plans," Buck Thurmon said. "What's he going to do with them?"

"He's going to pick the most vulnerable point—the point where he can do the most damage—and he's going to ram the dock . . . smashing everything in his path."

Thurmon glared at Jake. "You can't be serious."

"I am serious. I've never been more serious. William Rice is out there right now in his element. The fog won't bother him. He's perfectly capable of running the tug. Picking his way through the dark will be a walk in the park."

Sinclair's face was a picture of confusion. His brain was approaching overload.

"It's in the report, chief," said Jake. "Rice was a Seabee. He spent two years in Vietnam building bridges and docks, repairing landing strips, removing wrecked tonnage from the shipping lanes, running cranes and tugs up and down the rivers. He knew what would happen when he sank Bennett's boat. We'd hand deliver to him the one thing he needed—a tugboat and a six-hundred-ton barge with a crane on top."

"A floating battering ram," Sinclair said. "My God, if that hits the ferry, they could all be killed!"

"And when he crashes into the dock? You're the expert, Buck. What would you do if you wanted to wreck the Island Basin?" Jake asked.

Thurmon didn't hesitate. "We're standing on it," he said and pointed to the schematic. "Everybody knows the gas dock is a terrible design, but there was nothing else we could do. She's exposed on the west side to a direct hit. If that were to happen, well . . . you've got a thousand feet of fuel lines running from here back to the tank farm. There's always fuel in those lines even when the system's shut down. There's no way to get it out. If the lines crack or break in two, the gasoline and diesel in the lines will run right into the Basin."

"How many gallons?"

"Enough to burn the waterfront to the waterline once it catches those fiberglass boats on fire. You ever see fiberglass burn? Water won't put it out. If those fuel lines crack and he starts a fire fed by three hundred fiberglass boats and a half a mile of creosote-covered pilings, we're in big trouble. There's not enough fire equipment on the East Coast to put out something like that, that's assuming you could even get close to it. The heat would be intense." As Thurmon described the worst-case scenario, worry spread over his coarse features. "She'd burn hot and she'd burn for days. But I don't believe he's going to do it."

"Why not?"

"Too much risk of an explosion. There's an electrical trunk line under that dock too. He's been down there crawling around. If he didn't see it on the prints, he saw it under the dock. If he crashes into the dock and spills a few hundred gallons of gasoline, then sets it off with an electrical spark, it'd blow up everything . . . including him."

"And if he doesn't care?" Jake asked.

The question froze Buck Thurmon. "What do you mean, doesn't care?"

"Just what I said. What if he doesn't care that he dies as long as he gets even, gets his revenge? A man like that is capable of anything. I think he's proven that, don't you?"

"But that'd be suicide," Thurmon protested.

"Sometimes suicide is an act of creation. The person makes something happen larger, more powerful than they could ever achieve while they were alive. Rice is carrying around two hundred years of family failure," Jake said. "Do you think for one minute he's going to do this halfway?"

Thurmon's face twisted uncomfortably. "I don't think I like what you're saying."

Jake was unmoved. "He's going after the tank farm."

"Impossible."

"There's no bigger target around. No bigger bang for his fireworks. I'm not sure how, but that's what he's going to do," Jake said. "Imagine. He rams the dock, the fuel lines snap and fall into the harbor, then he gets those big, full fuel tanks in the tank farm to open up and spill their contents into the Basin." Jake paused as he saw a look of horror settle in Buck Thurmon's eyes. "What's the matter?" Jake questioned.

Thurmon seemed unable to speak. Finally he said, "That's not what would happen. There's more than a million gallons of fuel in that tank farm, and if Rice really did steal a copy of these plans, he'd know that not a drop of it would run into the Basin from an accidental spill. We designed a failsafe to make sure that would never happen." Thurmon turned to a different schematic page. "I'm not denying that the ruptured feeder lines would spill enough gas and diesel into the Basin to start a fire. But if the fuel tanks go, it's the *town* that's at risk," Thurmon said, banging his hand on the desk and turning on Sinclair. "Damn it, Russ! Damn it! I told you and I told Andy that this could literally blow up in our faces. Jesus!"

"What's he talking about?" Jake asked.

"A way of protecting the harbor from an oil spill," Sinclair offered sheepishly.

"A way of lying about protection is more like it," Thurmon snapped. He ran his finger along the blueprint and stopped at Nantucket's Main Street. "Look at this," he said jabbing at notations for manhole covers buried among the cobblestones. "Underground downtown Nantucket is a drainage system so old and decrepit that an inch of rain in the summer floods Main Street. The drains are totally inadequate. But a major spill at the tank farm is designed to run into that very drainage system to protect the harbor from any possible environmental damage. The idea is that we'll contain the fuel there and later pump it into trucks and get rid of it."

"You don't look too confident," Jake told him.

"Confident? Oh, I'm confident all right—confident it won't work," Thurmon said, his voice low. "I've told Andy Tillis for years what would actually happen if we had a major spill. Have you ever seen a diesel fire burn? It creates a heat so intense that only hard metals won't melt. Everything else—wood, rubber, flesh—you name it—doesn't stand a chance. But that's not the worst of it. Half of those million gallons of fuel are gasoline. Once gasoline gets down in those tunnels, the fumes will spread everywhere. Anything—the spark from an engine, a match to a cigarette—anything will set them off. A million gallons of fuel will literally blow downtown Nantucket off the map. What isn't blown away will be burned beyond recognition."

"Just the sort of bang Rice would look for," Jake said as Gloria came to life.

"I've got them," she said. "I've got the ferry."

"This is the *Eagle,* over. What can we do for you, Island Basin?"

"You can get back here," Gloria said breathing short, quick breaths.

"Sorry, Miss Gorham," the captain said. "This is a one-way trip. You had your chance and turned down the ride."

"Captain, I am serious. I want you to turn around and come back."

When the ferry captain came back on, Mayor Tillis's voice was heard in the background. "Gloria? What is it? What's going on?"

"You're in danger . . . all of you," she said as Jake took the microphone.

"Now you listen to me," Jake said and started to explain about the tug and barge. But the captain didn't seem worried.

"I've had that barge on radar since we left the dock." The captain's voice was the height of confidence and calm. "In this fog, visual sightings are out of the question. She's just sitting there about a mile off Great Point, most likely hauling in her tow cable and rigging herself up for push. More control that way. Most tugs make that change out there—plenty of sea room, plenty of water. Over."

"Which probably explains why you haven't been approached, captain," Jake said. "When Rice is ready to roll and he makes you out on his radar, he'll come after you. Can you outrun him? Over."

There was a burst of laughter crackling over the marine radio. "In this tub? Never happen. Over."

"Then use your head," Jake urged. "Bring her back home."

In the pilothouse of the tugboat, William Rice damn near tap-danced when he heard the quiver in the woman's voice. "You're in danger . . . all of you," she'd said, but she didn't know the half of it. He'd already picked up the green radar blip.

Rice was leering when he cradled his radio receiver and called the *Eagle*.
"Why don't you do that, cap? Take her back home. Nantucket's famous for
her open arms, the little island where everyone is welcome. Right, GG? That
was you, wasn't it? Sweet little voice that doesn't know what danger is."

Rice calmly played with the remote detonator device in his hand as he
keyed the mike again. "The *Eagle*'s full, I hope. Two thousand or so Island Basin folks out for a foggy night's swim." He flipped the toggle to
"on," then pressed the detonate button. "Bye-bye," he said, his eyes on
the screen, waiting for the *Eagle* to disappear. When she didn't, the grin
on his face widened, and he spoke on the radio again. "You found the
explosives? You don't know how glad that makes me. It gives me a chance
to spar with the ferry before the main event."

"Give it up, Rice." It was Jake. "We've called the Coast Guard."

"I'll bet they were busy," Rice said, then altered his voice into that of
a frightened and panicky man. "Mayday! Mayday! Two women and five
children onboard. Going down fifteen miles east of Nantucket . . . power's
out . . . pumps are not working. Mayday! Mayday!"

"You bastard," Jake fumed into his microphone. The Coast Guard had
told him they were unable to help him. Now he knew why.

Rice was unfazed. "I'd like to say a few words to little Gloria, if you
don't mind." He checked his instruments while he waited, and turned his
attention to the *Eagle*. "I'm gaining on you, cap. Do you hear me? I'm
gaining. What do you think?"

"This is the *Eagle*. There are people onboard, sir," the captain said firmly.
"Nearly two thousand men, women, and children."

Andy Tillis grabbed the *Eagle*'s microphone and shouted into it, "Now
you listen here, you—"

"Who's this?" Rice interrupted.

"The mayor! I want you to—"

"Better make yourself useful, Mr. Mayor. Hand out the life jackets, what
say? Now, I want to talk to GG before I decide not to give you all a sporting
chance."

Jake came on. "What chance?"

"Put GG on," Will Rice ordered, his voice brooding with menace. "I
know she's there. Probably looking out the window like she was the night
I axed the banker. I waved, GG, but you didn't wave back."

"What do you want?" she asked with a voice full of loathing.

"Is that any way to talk to me? My, my. Thanks for the hundred grand,
but I never had time to spend it."

She hesitated, then asked, "Were you going to kill me?"

"I was. I still am," he said with an icy certainty.

Gloria turned away and cupped her face in her hands.

"Put on the private cop. . . . Say cop, how'd you ever get away from the *Dolfin?*"

"I saw the wires," Jake answered evenly.

"Well, you won't see them this time," Will Rice threatened imagining the reaction of those in the gas dock office. "Feeling sorta bad, folks? Good." He screeched in roaring laughter. "Explosives, my boys. You've got less than an hour to find them."

"Where are they, Rice?" Jake demanded.

"Good question. I'm gaining on you, captain," Rice said to the *Eagle*. "Slowly, but gaining. Too bad the fog's thick and you can't see me. This is a real sledgehammer I've put together here. Just like the sort of thing we jerry-built in Nam all the time. A real battering ram."

"Maybe we can make a deal," Jake tried. "You, me, and Gloria."

"Sorr-rry." His voice was full of glee.

Jake wanted to reach through the microphone and drag him back, pounding him every inch of the way. "Listen—"

"No, you listen. I'm trying to give the mayor a picture of what I'm gonna do. Something for him to visualize while he's wetting his pants. This barge I'm pushing has this crane on it, see? I backed up the crane toward the front of the tug, then I lowered the cantilevers so they're parallel with the deck—everything's in perfect balance. But the kicker is that one of the cantilevers sticks out in front of the barge maybe fifty feet. It's like a big arm, you understand? A big, closed fist of cold steel coming right at you. In Nam we'd knock down bridges with a rig just like this. One little bump and down she'd go. You ready for a little bump, Mr. Mayor?"

"Why the games, Rice?" Jake snapped. "Where'd you set the bomb?"

"Did I say there was just one?" Rice teased.

"It's somewhere in the tank farm, isn't it?" Jake asked and looked at Buck Thurmon.

Rice paused. "Is it?" He burst out laughing, a vicious jeer that broke Buck's resolve.

Thurmon grabbed the mike from Jake's hand and shouted into it. "You're a lying bastard! The tank farm's clean and you damn well know it."

"I do?" Rice mocked. "Who's this, the skinny little chicken man? I saw you running around over there, chicken man. Up and down, up and down, just like some mother hen. You don't think I'd be dumb enough to leave it where you could see it. Come on, now. Credit where credit is due. I'm smarter than that. I'm smarter than all of you put together."

"Then you're smart enough to know that those tanks are impregnable," Thurmon defended.

Rice didn't say anything, and the doubt in Buck Thurmon's mind grew. Finally, Rice came back on: "You looked right at it, chicken man. Right at it. You even ran your hand across it. So close yet so far away, what say? Hey? Pluck . . . pluck . . . pluck . . . pluck . . . pluck . . ."

"What are you talking about?" Thurmon demanded, his voice out of control.

"I'm talking about why I harpooned a man. You figure it out," Rice said, looking at his watch. "You've got forty-five minutes."

Gloria couldn't stand any more. "Why are you torturing us?" she shouted into the mike. "Why?"

"That's what Nantucket's all about, GG," William Rice said. "A little pain. A little hurt. Welcome back."

Chapter

——30——

It was in moments of crisis that Jake knew he was different, and this knowledge kept him going in the face of his pain and exhaustion. As Chief Sinclair and Buck Thurmon looked on nervously, wondering what to do next, Jake turned the gas dock office into a command center, issuing orders to prepare them for the attack.

Thurmon was to turn off the island's electrical power supply, then he was to take his men and check every inch of those twelve massive fuel tanks. Sinclair was to see to it that the town of Nantucket was evacuated in case Thurmon's men failed. When Sinclair and Thurmon had gone, Jake concentrated on the puzzle pieces laid out in his mind. All he had to do was match the pieces and fit them together. Easy. Watson could do it.

You looked right at it. Why I harpooned a man. You ran your hand across it. Why I harpooned a man. Why are you torturing us? Why?

Rice's jeering taunts and Gloria's weary and cracked voice bounced around in Jake's mind. He'd come to Nantucket to keep Gloria alive and had seen her nearly break apart right in front of him while William Randall Rice grew more powerful, more cunning, more dangerous. There was no doubt now what Rice was after and no doubt what Jake must do to stop him.

"Are you going to be all right?" he asked Gloria.

She looked Jake full in the face. "I'm fine," she said, but her trembling hands betrayed her. "Why won't he let it end? Why?"

"He probably can't answer that himself." Jake stepped to her and held her gently in his arms. "I didn't thank you for taking care of Watson."

"That's all right. The vet said he has a concussion."

"You told me."

She looked at him. "I did? I don't remember much of anything." She laid her head on his chest. "I'm scared, Jake."

"No need to be. Watson's going to stay right here and take care of you."

"You're leaving him with me?"

"I think he wants to stay." He bent down and rubbed Watson's neck. "You're in charge, pal," he said, looking directly into Watson's huge eyes, then he got up to leave. "Now, remember. You've got five minutes before Thurmon shuts down the power. The whole island will go dark, but at least an electrical spark won't blow us up. It's one less thing to worry about."

"Do you really think Rice is going after the town?"

"I do," Jake answered as Russell Sinclair's amplified voice broke through the night.

"We have a Zone Two emergency, a Zone Two emergency," Sinclair bellowed over the loudspeakers attached to his patrol car. "This is a storage tank emergency. All electricity in town will be off in five minutes. Five minutes. Turn off any open flames and proceed to the high school until the all-clear is given. I repeat, we have a Zone Two emergency. All residents within ten blocks of the tank farm are ordered to evacuate the downtown area."

Farther in the distance, Jake could hear Officer Shean's voice announcing the same warning.

"Five minutes," Jake cautioned her. "Take what you can't live without and go. Is that clear?"

"Yes," Gloria said absently. She was thinking about the *Eagle.* "Those people on the ferry. I'm responsible, aren't I?"

"You did what you thought best."

"Which isn't good enough when someone might die because of it." She looked past the window into the fog. "Is it?"

Jake didn't answer.

"Hey, Eaton," a deep voice boomed up from the dock. "You looking to take a boat ride?" It was the scuba diver, Joe Macy.

Jake stepped out onto the landing. "Are you the driver?"

"Dolby said you wanted the best," Macy replied with a forced smile.

"Be right down," Jake said and turned back to Gloria. "Five minutes."

"Five minutes," she repeated. When the door closed behind Jake, she reached for the marine radio receiver and made the call she felt she had to make. "Brant Point Coast Guard, Brant Point Coast Guard, this is the Island Basin. Over."

"Coast Guard, Brant Point, I-B. We monitored the three-way conversation between you, the *Eagle,* and the tug," the official-sounding voice told her. "The Mayday vessels have been contacted about the possibility of a rescue hoax."

Her hopes soared. "Then they're coming back?"

"Negative. Debris was spotted near the caller's location. The search will continue for possible survivors."

"But it's a trick. You heard the man admit it!"

"Roger, Island Basin, but debris in the water means we've got to confirm there are no survivors. Coast Guard regulations. Could be that the second call was the hoax and people really are out there in trouble."

"By then it'll be too late," she protested.

"I have my orders, Island Basin. We'll do what we can. Switching back to channel sixteen," he said and ended the transmission.

Gloria's entire body sagged. Waston padded forward and rested his head on her lap. It was the perfect kindness, a heartfelt gesture that brought tears to her eyes. She hugged the black dog and got ready to leave the office.

What should she take? What was there she couldn't live without? What would she miss if the Island Basin broke apart like so many toothpicks?

"Nothing," she told Watson. She caught a glimpse of Joe Macy running past *Gamecock* on the way to his boat, Jake trailing behind with a limp.

Maybe there is something I can't live without, she thought, and looked into Waston's dark eyes. "Tell me this," she said. "Who's taking care of whom?"

Watson whimpered.

"All right," she said. "I'll follow you then. Let's go."

"You ready?" Macy asked Jake as he fired the engines. It was the dive boat used earlier to pull the sailboat off the *Betsy,* and Jake felt comfortable with the vessel. It was the man he wasn't sure about. If Joe Macy still had in mind evening the score on Sam Kingsbury's behalf, now was not the time.

Jake pulled his .44 Magnum from his belt and double-checked the load. "This is no game. You understand?"

"If you're talking about this afternoon, forget it. I know you didn't have anything to do with Sam getting killed. Spoutin' off's all. Blowin' steam. And it wasn't just because of Sam. I'm an islander, and what's been happenin' down here turns my stomach," Macy said bitterly. "Then when Roger Dolby told me about the tug and how most likely that bastard killed two of our men, you couldn't keep me away. No matter what Russ Sinclair says, sometimes I fight for the right causes." He uncleated the dock line.

"All right," Jake said as they powered out into the harbor. In minutes the soft glow that had been island lights went out. They were in total darkness, with visibility in the fog ranging from zero to fifty feet, depending on the constantly moving banks.

"I take it we're going after him," Macy said.

"Sort of," Jake said and tucked the .44 back in his waistband. "We're going to let him come to us."

"How so?"

"What are our odds of finding that tug in this fog?"

"You want the truth? We'll be lucky if we don't get run over."

"Could Rice lock us in on his radar and come right at us?"

"Not in a small boat like this. Radar wouldn't pick us up. That's probably how he got aboard the tug in the first place. The captain didn't see him."

"But we might see the ferry." Jake, his face set, studied Macy's eyes. "It's big, it's slow, and it's the only target we know for sure Rice is going after. Let's find the ferry, then you've got to get me onboard that tug."

Macy didn't flinch, but he didn't like what he'd heard. "You're going to use the *Eagle* as bait?" he asked.

"I don't like it any better than you," Jake said, "but that's our one chance to get to him and we're going to take it."

"And the people onboard? What about them?" Macy's face was grim in the dark. "There are kids on that boat."

"That's why you've got to get me on that tug."

Jake held tight as Macy roared out of the harbor.

It was 3:25 when they began their hunt. At 4 A.M. the tank farm would blow.

Chapter

——31——

Onboard the *Eagle,* the navigator stared at his instruments. The tug pushing the barge was steaming nearer. "Closing, captain. Less than one hundred yards dead aft," the navigator reported.

"Steady, steady," the captain repeated, trying to sound calm and confident.

The water churned as the ferry plowed on at top speed. She was a half mile from the entrance to the harbor channel, making a zigzag course to fend off the attacking tug.

"Seventy-five yards, sir."

The captain turned to the first mate. "Sound the order to prepare lifeboats."

"Yes, sir."

"Tell the men this is not a drill. I want every passenger wearing a life jacket. Break them out."

"Yes, sir." The first mate switched on the ship's intercom and relayed the captain's orders.

The captain nodded imperceptibily, his eyes on the global positioning system screen giving him cross-track steering data. He moved the wheel ten degrees left and straightened the ferry's course. Fifty yards ahead on her starboard beam was the lighthouse at Brant Point. The captain gripped the wheel firmly, the skin on his knuckles stretched and white. He was grinding ahead full speed at fifteen knots.

The navigator glanced at his captain. "Twenty-five yards, sir," he said, unable to hide his fear.

With an even motion, the captain tried turning the giant ship toward Steamship Wharf, but she was too top-heavy to carry the speed in such a tight turn. He corrected quickly and ran her straight for the dock at North Wharf some three hundred yards ahead.

"We're not going to make it, are we?" the navigator said as his insides rolled. "We're making too much speed, and if we don't back off soon, we'll be aground or run into the dock. People live on that dock, captain. What if they haven't been evacuated?"

"Sound the alarm!" the captain shot back.

"But captain . . . !"

"We're being pushed, damn it! I've lost control of the ship. Sound the damn alarm! All hands on deck!"

The shrill alarm rang through the night. The crew prepared for their worst nightmare and scrambled to their posts as the vessel raced forward pushed by the tug.

Andy Tillis—white as a ghost—ripped open the pilothouse door and entered just as the foremost part of the crane rammed hard below the bridge deck and the giant ferry lurched sideways. A tremendous shudder ran through the ferry and knocked the mayor to the floor.

"Do something!" Tillis cried, crawling around on his hands and knees. "Do something, for Christ's sake!"

The crane struck again, and a deeper, meaner vibration rumbled through the entire vessel, mixed with horrible, panicky shouts for help. The captain's body tightened. He felt as if someone had hold of his heart and was crushing it into a bloody ball.

"We're being *pushed!*" the captain shouted. "The tug's locked onto us and is driving us right onto the wharf!"

The noise of the terrified passengers below was unbearable, but the navigator yelled above it. "Bring her around, captain! Bring her around!"

But it was too late. The huge vessel stumbled and rolled. No one could stand on the sloping decks, and bodies flew as the *Eagle* pitched and yawed out of control. She slammed hard against North Wharf, breaking windows in the wharf buildings and tearing doors loose from their hinges. The ragged swell of frightened voices reverberated throughout the helpless ferry, punctuated by the shocked screams pouring out of the cottages below as they rocked precariously on their pilings.

But Rice hadn't had enough. Slowly, he backed the tug away, circled, and rammed the *Eagle* once more hard in the side until the sound of twisting metal and straining engines filled the night air.

Joe Macy had followed the noise and was moving toward the chaotic scene. His insides knotted when he heard planking snap and saw shingled cottages fall into the surging water. "That rotten bastard," Macy hissed under his breath. "Let me have your gun. I'll shoot him right now."

"Get me on that tug!" Jake demanded. "Now."

Macy gunned the dive boat over the tug's propeller wash. He closed to within twenty feet, then backed down on the throttle. The tug was still driving the ferry forward, grinding her into the docks. Jake strained to see, but the fog and the darkness prevented all but the faintest outline of the tug and the barge. But something with the outline wasn't right.

"She turning!" Macy yelled and cranked the dive boat hard to port. The engines revved to a whine as he sped out of the crane's way.

Jake looked up in awe at what appeared to be the iron fist of a giant looming over him. Slowly the rest of the barge came into view. It was a fighting machine like none he had ever seen. Macy saw it too. He looked up, breathless.

"Are you all right?" Jake asked.

Macy answered with a jerky nod. "Fine," he said. "Could use a drink."

Jake listened with half an ear, his mind focused on the tug and the opportunity to board her. "Sorry," he said. "All out."

"Too bad Gibby isn't here," mused Macy. "He had emergency bottles stashed all over the island. Sam once found a half pint of Southern Comfort tucked away inside the body of a shutoff valve."

Jake took his eyes off the tug. "What did you say?"

Macy corrected course and commented, "Nothin'. Just talkin'."

"No, no, about the shutoff valve," Jake said as if he'd been caught off guard.

Macy shrugged. "When Gibby worked for Miss Gorham, one of his jobs was to repack the tank farm shutoffs. They're big, ya know. About ten times the size you find on a water hose. Sam said he once found a half pint inside one."

"Thurmon told me he locked up the valves."

"The wheel's locked so you can't turn fuel on or off, but you can get inside the valve body by removing the access plate from the outside. Nothing to it. Just unbolt six or eight nuts and the plate comes right off. But Thurmon's been like a guard dog over there since Nate Cooper was murdered. Your man Rice couldn't have gotten near one of those valves."

"Why not?"

"Someone would have seen him."

"Under normal circumstances," Jake said as William Rice's voice sounded in his memory. *Why I harpooned a man. You figure it out.* "There was nothing normal about Cooper's murder and how it stung the people on this island. Even Sam said when he picked me up at the airport that he was only good for spotting big black dogs. He was in shock."

"Who wasn't?"

"Will Rice wasn't, and when he saw his chance to set his explosive, he took it," Jake said. He picked up the marine radio's microphone. "What channel would Thurmon monitor at the tank farm?" he asked Macy.

"Sixty-nine. But what if Rice is listening in?" Macy asked. "He'll know we're out here, and I'll never get you close to that tug."

It was 3:41 A.M. In less than twenty minutes, the tank farm would blow. "We're running out of time," Jake said, and called the tank farm.

Buck Thurmon answered immediately, his voice full of frustration. "We haven't found a damn thing."

"Check inside the valve bodies."

"Inside?" The weight of what he'd just heard settled on him. "My God, Eaton. If he blows the valves, there's no way to keep the fuel from flooding downtown! She'll go up in flames."

"Can you stop it?"

"There isn't time, man!"

"Look," Jake said, trying to calm Thurmon. "Get Sinclair over there to disarm it."

"It? There are twelve tanks!"

"Watson can point out the ones that have been tampered with. Get him. He and Gloria ought to be off the docks by now."

"Ought to be," Thurmon told him, "but she and that dog of yours are still down there."

Jake's blood turned cold. "What?"

"She's moving *Gamecock* to a slip on the other side of the Basin out of the way of a possible direct hit."

"Goddamnit!" Jake exploded.

The tug's loud and heavy horn blasted into the night. The horn sounded twice more, then a brilliant white flare with a six-second burn was launched right over their powerboat. Macy slammed the throttles forward and spun the boat away from the tug as the throaty, nasty voice of William Rice spoke to them from the radio: "It's the Fourth of July, gentlemen. Welcome to the fireworks!"

Jake grabbed the microphone. "You're not going to make it," he shot back. "We know where you set the explosive."

"So I heard." Rice gave a scornful laugh. "But the chicken man's right. There are twelve tanks and twelve valves. Question is, how many have I wired and which ones?" Rice paused, then teased, "Too bad. You lose." Menacing laughter crackled over the radio as Jake switched channels and called Buck Thurmon.

"When Sam picked me up at the airport, he'd just finished repacking one of those valves," Jake told Thurmon.

A flicker of hope was evident in Buck Thurmon's voice. "So not all are wired."

"That's right."

"Gasoline," Thurmon blurted. "Tanks nine through twelve are gasoline!"

As Jake and Joe Macy raced back to the Island Basin, Buck Thurmon and Russell Sinclair worked furiously to remove the access plates on valves nine and ten. The massive fuel tanks towered a hundred feet above them.

"What am I going to find inside when you get it open?" Sinclair asked anxiously.

Thurman was drenched in sweat. "What time is it?"

Chief Sinclair looked at his watch. "Three forty-five," he said. "I need to know what's inside, what I'm looking for."

Thurmon had two nuts to go. "A threaded shaft connecting an on/off wheel at the top and a gate valve below it. When the gate's down, no fuel gets into the line. The gate's locked in the off position," Thurmon said, putting the wrench on the last nut.

"What's behind the gate?"

"Eighty thousand gallons of gasoline. Chances are there're enough fumes trapped in the valve body to ignite every gallon of it if we don't get to the explosive."

Sinclair worked the wrench in his clumsy hands. Eight stainless steel bolts held the faceplate to the housing. The last nut dropped to the ground. He pulled the bolt through and removed the plate, then shone his light inside the opening on a smaller version of what he'd disarmed on the *Eagle*. Deliberately, without hurrying, he reached in and removed the device, a detonation cap wired to a timer. The gasoline would explode when the detonator went off. Sinclair snipped the wires.

"Got one," he said. Sweat poured down his face.

"Me, too." Thurmon was on his way to tank eleven. "Hurry!" Buck Thurmon yelled at Sinclair. The tension was now thicker than the fog. "Hurry, damn it! Hurry!"

At 3:52 A.M. Joe Macy dropped Jake off on the gas dock and went back to help those on the *Eagle*. He didn't offer to stay, and Jake didn't ask him to. Jake had enough on his mind without worrying about Joe Macy getting himself killed. At the top of his list was Gloria Gorham.

Helpful little Gloria, Jake thought as he forced his aching body to run down the finger pier toward *Gamecock*'s old slip. It was empty, and thanks to Buck Thurmon's announcement over the marine radio, William Rice knew that Gloria was onboard the boat somewhere inside the Island Basin. One boat out of more than three hundred—a dark blue hull on a pitch-black night. Just perfect, Jake thought, suddenly aware of a faint glow out in the harbor. It was moving left to right, then appeared to stop. Jake watched the pattern of running lights and knew at once it was the tug and barge. It hadn't stopped at all; it had turned straight at him. Rice was setting off flares, which were rising into the night sky like so many dim and silent fireworks, covered by the blanket of thick, wet fog.

Jake guessed at the tug's distance by sound, not sight, as the barge pushed water and the engine labored for speed: 300 yards . . . 250.

More flares shot up in the murky night, but still Jake could not see either the long arm of the crane reaching out or *Gamecock*'s new berth. I'll have to find Gloria later, Jake thought, and ran past the gas dock office as fast as his lame leg would carry him.

He pulled his .44 and waited as the glowing halos got nearer. One hundred yards, he guessed, and fired three rounds at the unseen crane just to let Rice know that someone was waiting for him. He held in a breath and fired three more rounds before reloading and moving farther down the dock.

He could only guess at the position of the pilothouse in the fog. He raised his revolver one more time and was about to fire when a muffled explosion, followed by the sound of twisting metal, went off behind him. He looked at his watch. It was four o'clock. The tank farm had been hit by one, then almost immediately a second, violent explosion.

Jake ducked reflexively and hunched his shoulders in anticipation of a gasoline fireball that didn't come. What did come was the huge barge—dark now, no flares to announce its arrival—bursting out of the dense fog at full speed. In seconds the massive cantilevered arm, which reached out in front of the barge like a club, smashed into the gas dock office and ripped it from its pilings. The office—what was left of it—fell back into the Basin waters.

Moments later the barge hit with incredible velocity and strength. Jake was knocked from his feet as the dock sagged and strained against its bracing, but the tug's unrelenting power was too much. First the planking began to peel away, then the pilings snapped off under the tremendous pressure. The dock was breaking apart.

Jake got to his feet and ran down the wobbling pier toward the barge, which was continuing its attack. Each step was like balancing on a tightrope; if he fell, he'd be crushed against the pilings. But it was the only way to stop the assault, the only way to stop William Rice.

The pressure on the dock where Jake was standing was fierce, and the dock gave way—taking with it the fuel lines—just as he jumped onto the barge deck. The smell of gas and diesel fumes was instantly everywhere.

Flares! The realization hit Jake as he ran along the slick barge deck. Got to stop him. One flare and it will all be over.

Frantically, he raced ahead, his battered body no longer registering pain. He dodged coiled ropes and cables as the crane moaned and rattled above him. The barge had a notch in her transom where the tug's bow rode for better push control. An enormous rope bumper that looked like a hemp mustache separated the two and kept them from banging into each other. Jake climbed the bumper like a rope ladder and dropped onto the tug with his Magnum drawn.

The lighted pilothouse was before him and he broke for it. The door to the companionway was open. He whirled in and took the steps two at a time, only to find the pilothouse empty. The tug had been set on automatic pilot, and to make certain she held steady after the first driving hit, the wheel had been tied into position with rope.

Jake's heart sank. Where is he?

Gamecock.

Gloria Gorham. *The banker, the accuser, then you.*

Jake pulled back the throttle and killed the tug's 3,000-horsepower engine. The silence, the lack of the pulsing vibration, startled him. He needed time to think but there wasn't any. He had to move. He had to find Gloria.

Where was she? Where inside the Island Basin had she moved her father's boat? Where, goddamnit? But the only answer that came to him was to get off the tug and search. Find her before Rice made good on his promise.

The night seemed to grow colder as Jake made his way off the tug and down the splintered dock. The broken planking was undulating, and negotiating it was like walking across the top of a wet circus tent. He struggled to keep his balance, aware that his gyrations and the fog made him less of a target for Rice—if he were out there in the dark, waiting.

Jake bent low, ignoring the pain shooting through his leg, and ran to the solid end of the pier near Whales Way. A pool of shimmering fuel covered the cobblestone road and poured into the harbor in tiny rivulets.

Jake turned right past a small service cottage and stopped behind the closed chandlery. As if for the first time, the enormity of the Island Basin settled upon him. More than three hundred slips, piers jutting out every which way and all he had to do was find one blue-hulled boat in the foggy dark. Damn, he muttered, and sped down South Wharf.

Seconds before the tug struck the dock, Will Rice had gone over the side and swum the fifty yards to the far end of the gas dock. He carried with him a watertight flare and a rigging knife. At the end of the dock, he swam the opening between the two bulkheads, gliding effortlessly right over the *Betsy* and passing the very piling on which he'd brutalized Nathan Cooper. But a man's severed arm and a harpoon through a chest were nothing compared to what his barge crane was doing to the gas dock.

What a perfect machine, he thought when the gas dock office plummeted into the water. What a perfect match of man and machine. Fantastic! World champions!

Soon the barge would break through and rupture the fuel lines, and he'd have the sense of satisfaction he'd worked so hard for. It didn't matter that he hadn't heard the tank valves explode. They had, he knew it. There wasn't time to disarm them all. Had there been, he wouldn't have taunted Eaton with the prospect of Nantucket's downtown going up in flame.

Yes, he thought. What a perfect match of man and machine. But then the machine stopped grinding, slowed to idle, then stopped completely. What the hell? Rice wondered as he climbed up into the bracing under the dock to avoid the fuel that was just now coating all the boats in the Island Basin. But Rice was only after one. The pretty blue one.

"Where are you?" he mumbled to himself. He climbed up on a cross brace so he could pull himself onto the bulkhead's planking. The farthest away Gloria could get and still be inside the Island Basin was Straight Wharf. That's where Rice headed, running like the wind to where he knew she had to be. It was inevitable. It was destiny. There was never any doubt in his mind that the blue hull would appear. And it did. Resting in a slip not twenty feet away.

Rice sucked in a deep breath and tried to relax, but he couldn't control his heart-thumping joy. He was going to snap little GG like a twig, then torch the fuel-soaked Basin. By the time the fire burned back through the broken fuel lines and set off the gas and diesel mixed in the storm drain, he'd be far away from the impending explosion.

Yes, sir, baby. Rack the fucking balls! This game is just about over.

Rice stepped aboard *Gamecock*. With a voice low and breathy, he said into the companionway darkness, "You can't escape your past, GG. You know that. No one gets away from their past."

Watson growled.

"Now I'm scared," Will Rice teased. "Scared to death, GG. Shame on you. I suppose you got that big detective down there too, huh?"

"No," Jake said and carefully stepped into view from his position on the dock. "The big detective is right behind you. With a .44 Magnum aimed right at your back."

"That a fact?" Rice's voice was emotionless.

"Turn around and find out."

Rice did, holding the flare in both hands. "You know anything about flares?" he asked coolly. "They ignite as soon as you pull them apart. Any idea what would happen if I pulled this apart? The Basin would go up in a ball of fire. Wouldn't bother me to burn up the little lady," he said.

"And you too?" Jake said.

"The price of victory. Somebody's got to pay it. You hear that, GG? You want to go out real crispy? Or do you want to come out of there so I can have a good look at what I've been chasing all my life? Kick the dog out too. Now!"

"Do as he says," Jake told her.

"Hear the man?" Rice continued. "Sounds like good advice to me. Come on, GG. Out."

Slowly, with Watson leading the way, Gloria climbed on deck. She held Watson by the collar, the dog's muscles like steel springs, ready to launch at William Rice.

Rice's grip tightened around the flare. "Call off the dog, Eaton," he snapped. Jake did. "Very good," Rice said. "Now the gun. Toss it in the water."

Jake didn't budge, and for a long second their eyes locked. Eyes that told Jake that he, William Randall Rice, was going to kill them all. Shoot now, Jake thought. Shoot now. "One question," Jake said.

"One," Rice answered, and in that briefest instant, Jake killed him.

Chapter

——32——

When the sun came up on the Fourth of July and burned off most of the fog, the Island Basin was still there but it wasn't very pretty. Neither was downtown Nantucket. The gas dock needed replacing, as did the office, which now housed a few hundred curious fish. The tug and the barge and the crane had done a thorough job.

The tank farm survived because of the heroic efforts of Buck Thurmon and Russell Sinclair. Rice had set four charges in four valve bodies. In the short time they had, Thurmon and Sinclair concentrated on finding the explosives set in the valves controlling gasoline, knowing full well that even an explosive charge wasn't enough to ignite diesel fuel. They'd found and disarmed explosive charges in valves nine and ten and were working on eleven when they ran out of time. Diesel valves six and seven exploded.

When the diesel valves blew, Thurmon was ready with an emergency flange to cap both lines. Instead of 160,000 gallons of fuel running through the storm drain, only about 20,000 gallons actually made it. A mess but not a disaster. The last Jake heard, Nantucket had voted to move the tank farm inland, miles from the town and the ocean.

He also heard from Gloria about a month after they'd both left the island. She phoned him and asked if he'd like to meet for a walk along the Charles River. There was something she had to know. So they met and walked and tossed sticks for Watson in the warm August evening.

The Gorham Corporation, she told him, had reconsidered its investment on Nantucket and scaled down its plans. For now it was quietly funding

The Preservation Society's attempt to make the waterfront more hospitable to local fishermen and to honor the island's nautical history. Cruising yachtsmen would have to anchor out in the harbor or rent a mooring. The Island Basin had been closed and renamed Cooper's Landing. It was now a place for tourists to walk among the old fishing boats and enjoy the summer weather along the public piers.

Even Andy Tillis supported the effort wholeheartedly once his broken leg had mended and his black eyes faded so he wasn't embarrassed to go out in public. A door had shut on his leg when he tried to get off the floundering ferry; as for his eyes, Russell Sinclair had blackened them when he broke the mayor's nose. An accident was the story they agreed to, just like they'd agreed to tell no one about William Randall Rice when he first came to Nantucket. As for the *Eagle,* she survived better than the wharf and the two cottages that fell into the harbor. Fortunately, no one died.

After Gloria closed the island's Resorts Management office, she came back to Boston, broke up with Richard Graham, and started looking into other resort management opportunities. Her mind wasn't really on business, however, and the thought crossed it daily that she ought to take some time and sail *Gamecock* up to Maine. She'd always wanted to try that on her own. A new challenge, something different. Something relaxing after being hunted by William Randall Rice.

"Sounds like a good idea," Jake told her.

"And I might do it, if you'll tell me what that question was," she said.

"What question?"

"The one you were going to ask Rice."

Jake took the stick from Watson and tossed it again. "I was going to ask him," he said, "if he could pull apart that flare before I shot him."

"And you thought better of it?"

"I was afraid of the answer," he said as they walked along. "Now I'll ask you one." She turned toward him. "Do you like lobster?"

"I do."

"When you get the boat to Maine, I'll drive up and buy you dinner."

"That could be a while," Gloria said.

Jake shrugged. "That's the nature of sailboats."

"Or the nature of men afraid to fall in love." Her voice seemed to hang in the air.

Jake looked at her self-consciously. He felt as though some emotional sanctuary had just been breached.

"That's it, isn't it?" she asked. "There're a million William Rices in the world, and with them you don't even blink. But when someone tries to get close to you, you run like Watson chasing sticks." She stared at him, her eyes searching his handsome face. "What are you afraid of, Jake?"

"Do I have to be afraid of something?"

"Aren't we all?"

He didn't answer.

"All right," Gloria finally said. "When I get to Maine."

"When you get to Maine," he repeated and took her hand tenderly in his as they walked along in the still, warm night.